"Over the course of this novel, Reid stirs all of these elements into an inviting and easygoing story—one that feels like a version of Dan Brown's *The Da Vinci Code* (2003) with cozier chats and artisanal tea blends. . . . Reid adds liberal amounts of art history along the way, with figures such as Michelangelo, da Vinci, and especially painter and writer Giorgio Vasari feeling like full-fledged characters."

—Kirkus Reviews

". . . Reid deftly balances an enticing art history mystery with heady romance.

"Rose and Beatrice's Italy is a living museum complete with street artists as besotted with the Renaissance as the leads. Sleek charmer Vince continually repopulates da Vinci's *Last Supper* table, and the vigorous, unpolished Mike reconfigures classical and mythological iconography. While these rivals challenge societal norms with their confrontational murals, their world—as well as Rose and Beatrice's—feels removed from contemporary life, a Cinquecento fantasy of art for art's sake. But readers looking for a romantic escape to an Italy as full of glorious art as revitalizing as brilliant sunlight and abundant pasta will relish this tale."

—Booklife Reviews

"Who wouldn't want to escape to Florence and Rome at this time for a delightful story involving a secret linking two of the greatest Renaissance painters?"

—Rhys Bowen
New York Times and Kindle best-selling author of the Edgar award–nominated *The Venice Sketchbook*

"With a remarkable flair for recreating the sounds, textures, flavors, and colors of Rome, Kathleen Reid's latest novel is as engrossing as it is picturesque. Well written, well researched and, as with all her works, well worth a slow and luxurious reading."

—Greg Fields
Author of *Through the Waters and the Wild*, 2022 Independent Press Award Winner, Literary Fiction

"Through Rose and Beatrice, author Kathleen Reid tells two modern romantic stories while solving this Renaissance mystery, intertwining past and present in a timeless novel."

—Margo Weinstein
Author of *Jalan-Jalan*

Secrets in the Palazzo

By Kathleen Reid

ISBN 978-1-64663-676-1

Published by

◤ köehlerbooks ™

3705 Shore Drive
Virginia Beach, VA 23455
800—435—4811
www.koehlerbooks.com

Secrets in the Palazzo

in the

a novel

KATHLEEN REID

Live. Love. Leonardo.

♡ Kathleen Reid

VIRGINIA BEACH
CAPE CHARLES

Author's Note

My book *Secrets in the Palazzo* was inspired by the real-life artistic rivalry between Michelangelo and Leonardo da Vinci. In the early sixteenth century (1505), there was a painting contest between these two masters to decorate the walls of the Council of Five Hundred in the Palazzo Vecchio in Florence, Italy. Currently, a rendition of Leonardo's work exists in a painting by Peter Paul Reubens housed in the Louvre in Paris, France (see above). To this day, a mystery still surrounds Leonardo da Vinci's *Battle of Anghiari*, which has been called the *Lost Leonardo.*

Chapter 1

TWINKLING LIGHTS GLITTERED, surrounding the Duomo in an incandescent glow of Florence, which always inspired Rose with its majestic beauty. Terra cotta rooftops darkened as the sun began its descent into a slate-colored sky. She inhaled deeply, reveling in the spectacular view from her balcony. She was indeed grateful for the experience of living in a city that boasted some of the greatest art treasures in history. Her passion for the iconic Michelangelo, whom many consider one of the most gifted artists of the Renaissance, was fulfilled on a regular basis, as she was able to see his work that never failed to enthrall her. After all, who would ever tire of going to see the seventeen-foot-high *David* standing proudly in the Galleria dell' Accademia?

Each day radiated adventure as she marveled at the reality of living in the birthplace of the Renaissance. The whole experience was dreamlike. Rose still found it hard to process that she had recently quit her secure teaching job in Charlottesville, Virginia, to buy an apartment here, following her dream of becoming an artist. The relentless hours of hard work had paid off since she developed a foundation for this new career.

The success of her first gallery opening gave Rose an incredible feeling of accomplishment. The summer had practically flown by in the whirlwind of speaking engagements and interviews. Picking up a magazine, Rose scanned the contents, thumbing through to read yet another positive review of the exhibition. She wasn't sure which she liked better, the fact that she could translate most of the Italian commentary or the sudden influx of exciting opportunities.

The exhibit, aptly entitled Humanity, was being scouted by a major art dealer with offices in Rome, New York, and Palm Beach. Love and kindness had resonated from the works. Art enthusiasts embraced the nod to Michelangelo's *Creation of Adam*, which gave Rose great satisfaction. Her passion for the Renaissance was rewarded daily as she lived and painted in the city where the true geniuses of history had once resided. The magazine shot of Rose in a smart navy pants suit with her blond hair pulled up in a high ponytail felt surreal. The success transformed her view of herself as she navigated this new life as an artist.

Looking down at the exquisite antique ring on her finger, she also felt like the luckiest girl in the world to be engaged to Lyon. Michelangelo may have engendered her move abroad, but Lyon captured her heart. She recalled their first email exchange when she contacted him about buying a home in Florence. Who would have ever thought that their easy banter and eventual house hunt together would turn into such an amazing relationship? His adventurous spirit and unwavering support made her mundane life extraordinary. Lyon understood her passion for the great Michelangelo and respected her need for independence. Now that the exhibition had ended, it was time to focus on planning their wedding.

A brisk walk by the Santo Spirito church reminded her of the time Lyon brought her inside to see the wooden cross carved by a seventeen-year-old Michelangelo. Her awe and wonder were still palpable as she stood transfixed by the master's work in the octagonal sacristy on the west side of the church. Rose realized their connection was special at that moment.

She adored Lyon. Calculating that his office was nearby, she decided to take a chance and surprise him. They had both been unusually busy lately and needed to make more time for each other. Rose took the stairs and opened the door to the front lobby of his office, which boasted huge windows overlooking the street. Rose noticed a new mural of a butterfly across the way; street art was popping up everywhere in the city. Directly across the street, she looked down to admire an ornate wooden door capped by an arch. Lush terra cotta pots filled with tree plants framed either side of the entrance of an elegant townhouse. With the receptionist nowhere to be found, she peered through Lyon's glass office door, observing that he was on a call. She slipped into the chair across from his desk, careful not to interrupt.

Lyon seemed irritated with his caller as he marked up a contract in front of him. When he looked up to lock eyes with her, he smiled warmly, and then he made a mocking face into the phone, which nearly made her laugh aloud. Taking a cue from her visit, he promised to call his client back later.

"Now this is a surprise. Hello," he said, standing to greet her in European style with a kiss on each cheek. "You saved me from a painful contract negotiation. I should refuse to work with anyone in the legal profession."

"Hi, darling," she replied with an excited grin. She was wearing a new gray silk wrap dress and black heels for a change of pace, her blond hair cascading down her back just the way he liked it. "I thought I might be able to coax you away for lunch."

"Rose, I'm so sorry, but I can't make that happen. I have back-to-back appointments all day long. You always call first."

"Yes, I tried to leave you a message before I came over, but your mailbox is full. You work too hard, Lyon!"

"So do you," he said thoughtfully, gathering up the files he needed. "But I appreciate the offer."

"Where are you going?" she asked, inching closer to him.

"I'm showing a young American couple an apartment. They're getting married in December." He cleared his throat. "I think that's a wonderful month to tie the knot."

Rose blushed, painfully aware that he was weary of her inability to set a date for their wedding. "I agree. December would be ideal. In the meantime, why don't I come with you on your appointment? I think I could be helpful."

He thought for a moment, then wrapped his arms around her. "Well, that's an offer I can't refuse. Besides, Olivia might like having another American transplant along for the afternoon."

"Perfect," said Rose, delighted with the idea of meeting another young couple.

On the way, Lyon explained that he planned to show them several one-bedroom, one-bathroom apartments. They were getting married before the holidays and wanted to start their life together in the center of town.

"So, we're going to sit with American ex-pat Olivia and her fiancé, Antonio. Their budget is twenty-four hundred per month, and I've already made a list of potential properties that could work."

The outdoor café was moderately crowded as Rose watched Lyon scan the stylish seating area and find them a table overlooking the street corner. Olivia and Antonio arrived holding hands, their mutual adoration evident on their faces. Their excitement was palpable as they ordered up a round of coffee. They welcomed Rose's input, and the conversation naturally turned to the pros and cons of various neighborhoods. Rose was delighted to join the hunt.

"We want to be where the action is," Antonio said, taking a steaming cappuccino from the waitress.

"Agreed," said Olivia. "We love all the beautiful churches, shops, and restaurants in the Santo Spirito neighborhood."

"I know," replied Lyon. "But it comes at a price."

"I understand," said Antonio. "We might like to see some things under budget and perhaps a little bit over our price range."

"Fair enough. What are your priorities for an apartment?"

"I want an updated kitchen and washer/dryer but a place that still has a Florentine feel to it," Olivia said.

Antonio added, "Location and proximity to my job are extremely important to me."

Lyon went through his list and selected three properties that could work for them and pointed out that all were within walking distance. As they made their way to the first option, he engaged in polite conversation.

"So, when is the wedding?"

"The first Saturday in December," said Olivia. "I can't wait. My family is coming over from Atlanta."

Rose felt a sharp pain in her gut at this news, realizing how self-absorbed she had been these past few months. It was on the tip of her tongue to tell Olivia that she wanted her wedding the same day, but she refrained.

Lyon offered, "We need to find you the perfect place to live and enjoy our beautiful city."

"Olivia needs to work on her Italian," Antonio mused. "It will make the transition much easier."

"Absolutely," said Lyon, entering the code to get them into the first building.

"I understand completely! I've been taking lessons, which makes a big difference," said Rose. Olivia gave her a knowing grin and whispered that she needed her teacher's name.

The lobby was simple with a couple of chairs and a nondescript tan tiled floor. Once inside the space, Rose watched as Olivia took in the older appliances, blue-and-white-striped wallpaper, and dim lighting.

"It needs a little updating, but keep in mind that it's under budget and extremely well located," said Lyon.

They perused the old bathroom with chipping tiles and an old shower curtain.

"What is the price?" asked Antonio.

"This unit goes for two thousand fifty per month."

Olivia shook her head. "I'd like to see something that has more charm and better appliances for that price. This is really small."

"Look over there, Liv," said Antonio. "That geometric wallpaper looks like we're living in the 1960s."

"That was probably the last time this place was renovated," Olivia said.

"Location, location, location," said Lyon, telling them to keep an open mind because they would have the money to freshen things up.

Rose observed Lyon was always professional, not pushy. His genuine desire to educate his clients by showing them a range of options made him successful.

The second apartment was across town, and they walked thirty minutes to get there. The outside was painted a fresh golden hue and the black shutters were pristine.

"This is really nice," exclaimed Antonio. "But it's so far away from my job."

"I understand," said Lyon. "Take a look around you. This is a great neighborhood and a well-maintained building."

"Good point," said Olivia. "But I agree with Antonio. It's a little far from where we want to be." The second apartment had much more space with an open living room floorplan, built-in bookcases, and some amenities.

"This is a nice room," said Antonio.

Lyon pointed out the beams on the ceiling, classic moldings, and general good condition of the property. "It's been very well maintained. You really wouldn't have to do much but get married and move in." He explained that the apartment was over budget by two hundred dollars because of the extra space and overall condition of the building.

Olivia turned to Lyon. "Have you lived here long?"

"Ten years and counting," said Lyon. "I wouldn't want to live in any other city."

"Where do you live?" asked Antonio.

"My apartment is in the Santo Spirito neighborhood."

"Right where the action is," said Antonio. "Is there anything else in our price range that could work?"

Rose checked her watch. It was almost six, but Lyon decided that he would take time to show them one more listing. She could feel their angst as they shared bits and pieces of their wedding plans and how they had to put several pieces of furniture in storage.

"It's a big change. Moving here from America."

"I understand completely," said Rose. "But it was the best decision of my life. I absolutely love living here."

"When are you getting married?" asked Olivia.

"We haven't set a date yet. Both of us are crazy busy. A move abroad and a wedding are stressful."

"And an Italian mother-in-law," said Olivia, rolling her eyes. "She doesn't like my cooking."

"That's because she wants to prepare all of the meals," Antonio said.

Rose was reminded of how well she and Faith, Lyon's mother, got along. Faith was an accomplished artist, and they had worked together to create the paintings for the gallery opening. The experience had been amazing. Quickly focusing upon the task at hand, Rose listened as Lyon discussed the next apartment, which was closer to town.

"It's got a lot of the features that I think you'll enjoy."

They walked back toward the Duomo so that Lyon could show them option three, which was right in their price range. They walked in the building and spied the staircase. Lyon said nothing but led them up the stairs.

"How many flights?" asked Olivia, panting harder.

"Six," he replied.

"That's a lot of stairs," remarked Antonio.

"It will be worth it," said Lyon, who went ahead to open the unit for them.

The interior of the apartment was clearly Florentine, with a vaulted, exposed dark wood ceiling and a burnt-orange tiled floor. Olivia walked immediately to the kitchen where she admired the blue-patterned tile work above the sink and stovetop.

"Look at all of these new appliances," she said, reverently running her hand over the oven. Lyon opened a closet to show her a modern stacked washer and dryer. He looked over to see Antonio admiring the view of the street below. "I told you it would be worth it."

"Liv, do you think you can carry groceries up six flights every time we go to the store?"

She rolled her eyes at him, then checked out the large main suite, with its updated bathroom, boasting a gray-and-white-tiled shower with a modern glass door. "This is really nice."

"How much?" asked Antonio.

"Right on budget at twenty-two hundred per month."

Rose met Lyon's knowing stare, noting that this would be the apartment they chose. "Most of the furnishings will stay, but there is room to discuss this issue with the owner."

"That's ideal for us to not have to buy too much when we start our life together," said Olivia. "But those stairs!"

"We can eat more pasta," joked Antonio.

After some banter about the delights of his mother's cooking, Tony and Liv agreed to meet the following morning to sign a year-long contract.

On their way home, Lyon's mother called and invited them to dinner the next evening.

"Are you free?" he asked casually.

Rose checked her calendar, noting a conflict at seven, which she decided not to mention. "Yes," she said earnestly. "I'd love to go."

"My mother wants to know why we haven't set a date yet. Perhaps you can shed some light on the subject."

Rose felt embarrassed. Lyon came from a very close-knit family; his parents, Faith and Joseph, planned to have the wedding at their stunning villa with the most spectacular view of the countryside. His sister, Katherine, volunteered to use her modern calligraphy on the invitations. Joseph, a vintner, was working on a special white wine for the celebration with help from his brother, Peter, who was probably doing more tasting than helping. Nevertheless, Rose realized that she had done next to nothing thus far.

"I've gotta go finish up some paperwork at the office," said Lyon.

"Are you sure? I'd love to see you later."

Rose sensed his displeasure.

"Sorry, it doesn't work. I'll confirm tomorrow."

He gave her an impersonal kiss on both cheeks before departing.

Rose felt a knot forming in her stomach. What was holding her back?

Chapter 2

THE SUN DIPPED SLOWLY into the skyline as Rose stared out at the vista of amber rooftops from her balcony. It was magical, as always, and she felt that same sense of gratitude and wonder that accompanied her move to Florence. She would never tire of seeing the octagonal dome of the Cathedral of Santa Maria del Fiore in the distance. It was a crisp sixty-five degrees, and the cool air smelled like fresh bread from the balcony below and a hint of musky leather. Leaning over the balcony, Rose soaked in the scenery.

They still hadn't figured out their living situation after the wedding, but Rose assumed it would come in time. She didn't want to leave her new apartment, a symbol of her independence, but Lyon thought they should buy something bigger to entertain and accommodate a future family.

Perhaps she was extremely selfish, basking in all the praise. Rose thrived professionally, although pulled in a hundred different directions, and found all the attention validating. The voice of her disapproving mother, Doris, had quieted in her mind, which was a welcome novelty. Doris had always agitated and intimidated her, but at long last Rose was overcoming her insecurities. She had always been hard on herself, never quite feeling good enough for her mother's lofty expectations. Looking heavenward, she embraced her independence. She was, at long last, finally experiencing a new level of confidence and sense of optimism.

It was exciting talking with the press, giving guest lectures and garnering support for the project. Her public appearances were well received, and she really enjoyed meeting people. Lyon, on the other hand, was more of an introvert who guarded his privacy. She paused to consider Lyon's curt departure last night, and knew that he was out of patience with all of her requests to delay the wedding. Rose promised herself to make it up to him. She was fully aware that her relationship needed her undivided attention, and it was her intention to fix things.

Rose checked her watch and realized that she needed to freshen up and dress for dinner. She didn't want to be late. The hot water was soothing. Rose brushed her long blond hair. She chose white pants paired with a black silk blouse as the perfect combination to herald the fall. Anticipation hung in the air as well as a sense of urgency. Grabbing her caramel leather bag, a gift from her future mother-in-law, Rose raced out the door to meet everyone at Fuor D'Acqua.

She spotted a group of American tourists on one corner and waved to her friend Alessandro, who worked around the corner at the outdoor café. At that moment, Rose really felt like a *local*, which warmed her heart. Gazing down at her gorgeous engagement ring, she realized what a fool she had been to put off their wedding. As she rounded the corner to the restaurant, she caught sight of Lyon, who was on his cell phone outside the restaurant.

Before she could catch his attention, a woman stopped her and said, "You're Rose Maning!"

"Oh, yes," she replied, embarrassed by the attention.

"I just read an article on your fantastic exhibition. Congratulations!"

"Thank you so much," replied Rose as the woman was joined by two of her friends who all declared that she was a rising star.

"You're so beautiful," another woman exclaimed. "And I love your chic blouse. Did you buy it here?"

Rose looked over at Lyon, who ended a cell phone call with a client and stuffed his hands in his pockets.

"Thank you so much but I need to go," said Rose.

Rose broke away from the group to embrace Lyon. "I'm so sorry," she exclaimed.

"Why apologize? You love being the center of attention."

His words stung, and Rose bit her lip in indignation. She said nothing but swung forward on her way to the restaurant, reining in her hurt feelings. She had been caught in a whirlwind after the night of the gallery opening, and Lyon had been extremely patient with her crazy schedule. Then, she stopped short and turned around, saying firmly, "You're right."

"What did you just say?"

"I agree with you. It's been all about me, and you've been incredibly patient. I am so sorry."

"Go on," he said, facing her with a grin.

"I don't know what happened after the show. I just got so excited by all the press attention. It was so, so . . ."—she paused to catch her breath and went on—"validating for me personally and as an artist. I just feel so confident and empowered. And I haven't heard the negative voice of my mother in my head telling me that my art is a waste of time!"

Lyon took her hand and pulled her in closer to him. "I'm proud of you and I've tried to give you your space. You know I didn't protest when you asked to wait until after the opening to plan our wedding."

"I know, I know. You're the best person in the world, and I love you so much!"

He leaned down and kissed her passionately. Rose felt that same thrill of excitement run up her spine. A loud cough interrupted their embrace, and they were greeted by Lyon's parents at the restaurant. She was always awed by how easy and natural it was to be with them—a far cry from her parents in Charlottesville.

"*Ciao*, Rose," said Joseph enfolding her in great big hug.

"*Ciao*," she replied. Faith kissed her on both cheeks, cupping her chin like she was already their daughter. Rose adored everything about them.

They went inside, and a huge flower arrangement of white roses, white lilies, and orange ranunculus immediately caught her eye. She had a sudden vision of her bridal bouquet and locked eyes with Faith, who whispered in her ear.

"Those roses are so large and beautiful," Faith said with a smile. "Maybe I'll paint a still life this week and we can use it as inspiration for the wedding."

"What a novel idea! I know your painting will rival the real thing."

"Such flattery, my dear. I can't wait to hear more about the lecture you gave the other day on the exhibition."

"Please no," said Rose. "Lyon needs a break from all of the art talk."

"I understand."

The waiter appeared, and they ordered a Bisol Cartizze Prosecco Superiore for the table. The pop of the cork made everyone dining around them clap, sharing in the excitement. When their glasses were full, Joseph toasted to their future filled with health and happiness. "*Alla salute e alla felicità*," he exclaimed.

"And a wedding this Christmas, I hope!" added Faith.

Rose chimed in. "I was thinking the first weekend in December before the holiday rush." She felt embarrassed for throwing out a date without consulting Lyon. She quickly added, "Lyon and I want to make something work soon!"

"I'll drink to that," said Joseph happily before taking a sip of his wine. "I'm creating a new sauvignon blanc for the big day. You won't be disappointed."

"How lovely." Filled with joy, Rose exclaimed. "I can't wait to marry Lyon!"

"Absolutely, my dear. We already think of you as our daughter," said Joseph.

Rose peered at Lyon, who seemed detached. She felt the stirrings of anxiety as she watched him check his phone. Running his hand through his dark hair, he looked down and said, "Excuse me, everyone. I need to take this call."

She wondered what was so important and noticed that Faith

started speaking very quickly about how much she liked the color of the linens in the restaurant.

"Is everything alright?" asked Rose, wondering at her sudden nervousness.

"Well," said Faith in a hushed tone. "You don't know? Lyon's in the middle of a major deal. I think he's about to sell a ten-thousand-square-foot building to a famous American designer."

"What?" asked Rose, caught completely off guard. "Uh, that's great."

"Oh," exclaimed Faith. "He's been so busy making it happen."

"Yes, we've both had crazy schedules." Rose was embarrassed that she had no idea; she did a mental inventory of her events in the last week, recalling two lunch dates with an art dealer and numerous trips to the gallery.

Why hasn't he mentioned it? Rose realized that they had been leading separate lives recently, and it hurt. She felt anxious and told herself not to worry.

Chapter 3

BEATRICE VON DER LAYMAN was a complete workaholic, rarely taking time off from her conservator duties at the Vatican laboratory in Rome. Her friendship with Rose, however, was an exception, perhaps because they shared a similar passion for art history. It all started after Rose discovered three drawings in the wall of her apartment during renovations. Although they were damaged and moldy, Beatrice's countless hours and hard work had revealed three images: a baby, a nobleman, and a drawing that showed clasped hands with a background that mirrored Michelangelo's *The Creation of Adam* panel in the Sistine Chapel. No one knew these drawings existed because Beatrice's mentor, Cardinal Baglioni, purchased the images from Rose to safeguard them.

Rose's ex-fiancé, Ben, had wanted to sell the precious drawings to the highest bidder in New York. In fact, he tried to steal them from her, which led to the demise of their relationship. *Good riddance*, thought Beatrice, as she recalled how Rose had stayed at her apartment in Rome during their messy breakup. The silver lining of her broken engagement to that deceitful American businessman was Rose's close friendship to Beatrice. Afterwards, Rose fell in love with Lyon, whom Beatrice admired. Their relationship seemed like something out of a fairy tale, inflaming her longing for a soul mate of her own.

Meanwhile, Beatrice was consumed with solving the mystery of the drawings. Who had placed the drawings in the wall? And, most importantly, why. The second drawing was a portrait of a well-dressed nobleman, which could very well be noted architect and painter Georgio Vasari. Vasari was a great admirer of both Michelangelo and Leonardo da Vinci. He was also the one who documented their accomplishments for future generations in his book, *Lives of the Most Excellent Painters, Sculptors and Architects*, published in 1550. Although a painter and architect, his legacy would endure as an author; Vasari's firsthand biographies in *Lives* became the most influential book about art history ever written. It was valued by almost everyone who wrote about art history for over three centuries.

Beatrice kept a copy of *Lives* on her bedside table. On Rose's second drawing, Beatrice observed the beginnings of the curved letters *CERC* and had spent the last few months working to uncover its meaning. She knew that the words *Cerca Trova*—"seek and you shall find"—were currently emblazoned on the wall of a Giorgio Vasari painting in the Palazzo Vecchio. She believed that if Rose's ancient drawing used the same words, then it could, in fact, be a treasure map.

Beatrice suspected that Vasari's likeness would provide further proof that a brilliant Leonardo da Vinci painting still existed. Beatrice scratched her head as she pondered how best to explain her theory. It was, in fact, Vasari who was commissioned to paint over the work of Leonardo a few years after he completed the *Battle of Anghiari* as well as Michelangelo's half-finished *Battle of Cascina* in 1555. Vasari's commission to redecorate the Hall of the Five Hundred was a project that spanned seventeen years in which he and his assistants painted six historical battles. Many consider it his best work. Nevertheless, Vasari was a huge admirer of both men, especially Leonardo; he would never willingly destroy the work of a master in favor of his own. Was it Vasari or one of his family members who had placed these drawings in the wall for future generations to find?

When Beatrice saw *CERC* on Rose's drawing, she connected the dots, convinced that she possessed the ancient document that could substantiate her theory. After weeks of hard work, Beatrice studied the fragile paper that revealed the final letters on Rose's drawing, which said the same thing. Beatrice gasped, wondering at fate.

"Oh my God!" she said aloud. "That's it!"

If this was the missing clue to a lost Leonardo, it would be monumental for the art world. The phrase was there in black and white. Unable to contain her excitement, Beatrice called Rose.

"I want you to come to Rome immediately and meet with Cardinal Baglioni and me!"

"Really? What did you find?"

"Let's just say we have a new theory that is very, very interesting."

"Can I bring Lyon?"

"Absolutely! Can you be at the Vatican first thing Monday morning? The cardinal has said it would work for him."

"I'll do everything in my power to make that happen."

"I know you're incredibly busy, but I promise that you won't be disappointed!"

"Now, that's exciting!"

"Try explosive."

"What? Beatrice, you can't say something like that and make me wait all weekend to find out."

Silence.

"You've got to give me a hint!"

"Okay, okay," she said with her voice rising a notch. "Your discovery didn't only include Michelangelo."

"What are you talking about?" Rose asked excitedly.

"I think Leonardo da Vinci was involved too."

"Amazing! This is unbelievable!"

"See you Monday morning at nine sharp!"

"I can't wait."

Not long after she hung up with Rose, her cell rang. It was her mother, but she didn't answer, fearing the same old circular conversation. It usually started with her mother asking her what she was doing this weekend for fun. Silence would ensue. And then Elsa would give her another lecture on work–life balance. Maybe she would throw in something about the need for family time.

Beatrice decided to do something novel—leave work early. Although she was only twenty-nine, the last few months made her feel like she was middle aged. Always the last one in the lab, having become obsessed by the storied feud between the great Michelangelo and Leonardo da Vinci, which fueled endless ruminations. Her analytical mind needed a break, and fortunately it was Friday night. A vision of dinner and drinks among friends energized her, and hopefully she wasn't too late to find them. She decided to give it a try and sent a few texts. With renewed optimism, she headed to the restroom to freshen up.

Looking at herself, Beatrice tried to calm her riotous long dark hair, placing some strands behind her ears. Shadows had formed under her expressive blue eyes, and she deftly took out some concealer and applied it. The face that stared back at her had depth, she concluded, proud that she had at long last embraced her appearance. A prominent nose made her look distinctive. Having worked alongside the historical definition of feminine beauty, she decided that classic pretty was overrated. She would accept her curves and wildly unpredictable hair. Her self-inflicted sarcasm made her smile, revealing a set of dimples. She received a return text from her friend Chelsea, who said a group was meeting for drinks at an undecided location. Once they figured it out, she would be back in touch.

It was an old wound and one she tried to keep at bay. Her friendships felt fleeting at times, and she didn't like feeling like the add-on in a group. A rush of insecurity poured forth as she recalled that growing up, she always felt different and apart from the mainstream students. Her quiet intensity served her well professionally but had made her the butt of jokes in school. Kids labeled her "Busy Bee" as a teenager because she was a favorite of all the teachers. Their taunts were part of the fabric of her being, micro cuts that festered. The names changed in high school to things like "Spelling Bee," "Loser Bee" and that morphed into the moniker "Home Alone," which she detested.

Recalling those awkward teenage years, the thought of physical education classes made her break out in goosebumps. If anything, Beatrice was uncoordinated, and no one wanted her on their team. She was always standing alone, praying to become hot wax and melt into the floor to disappear. One time, they had a tennis tournament, and the two captains just pretended that she wasn't there. Teams were picked, and the other girls began playing. Beatrice quietly found a spot on the edge of the court and put her face in a book until the coach noticed that she had not had a turn. He marched her to a team where she would have to play. *Oh, Beatrice,* she reminded herself, *you are enough!* That's what her mother told her daily, and it mitigated past hurts. *The past is over, and I am enough,* she reminded herself confidently, reassuming a smile.

With a spring in her step, Beatrice packed up her leather satchel, a prized possession from the cardinal one Christmas, and departed through the security exit. Beatrice said good night to two security guards, whose presence reminded her of the important work that her team did in restoring and cleaning paintings and sculptures. The September evening was crisp and clear, and she embraced the cooler temperature. Her scarf easily deposited in her satchel as she headed downtown, hoping Chelsea would text her their location. She could always slip into a restaurant and wait.

The Vatican was its own city-state with a radio station and post office. The sheer size of Vatican City always amazed her as she left the maze of buildings behind. Tourists came by the thousands to admire its imposing collection of eighty thousand works of art. They were never disappointed because the collections, architecture, and history were rich and layered. Beatrice longed to work on restoration for the Raphael Rooms that housed some of the most beautiful paintings she'd ever seen. Rose would argue that there was nothing in the world more iconic than Michelangelo's paintings on the ceiling of the Sistine Chapel. They would probably debate this topic forever.

Most people didn't know that Leonardo lived at the Vatican from

1514 to 1517. His apartments had one of the most beautiful views in Rome. Beatrice recalled the stories of how Leonardo, ever the scientist, would go exploring for shells and fossils at the nearby hill.

As she walked closer to the city center, the streets filled with college students as well as tourists from France, Germany, and London. Spying various families laughing together, a wave of homesickness assailed her. Beatrice decided it was time to plan a trip home to Switzerland to visit her parents.

Time together was long overdue. Had it really been almost two years since she had seen her childhood home? Her parents, mostly her mother, almost always came to visit her. Anyway, they all loved to ski, and she couldn't remember the last time she navigated down a mountain. Perhaps her mother was right; Beatrice was, in fact, way too passionate about her work. A break would help her recharge. Beatrice made a mental note to return Elsa's call the following morning and make plans. She smiled at the thought.

As she took in the elegant brownstones in the Prati neighborhood, Beatrice changed directions, wandering through several streets unknown to her. Lost in thought, she wondered how she was going to use her newly discovered art history information for the general good. Noted historian Giorgio Vasari had written about how Michelangelo and Leonardo da Vinci despised each other. Michelangelo had a reputation for solving complex problems. On the other hand, his elder, Leonardo, was a bit of a charmer and dreamer who often didn't complete his commissions. They were opposites, yet both geniuses and stars of the Italian Renaissance.

Beatrice observed a crowd forming by the side of a low building. A series of outdoor spotlights cast a bright beam on an ethereal figure rapidly coming to life on the dingy brick. Curiosity won out, and she joined the group to learn more. The lifelike profile of a beautiful woman with long, wavy, cascading red hair commanded attention. Inching forward, she studied the man who was creating such an eye-catching portrait, oblivious to the people watching him.

He wore a dark-green wool hat from which his jet-black hair peeked out in back. Even from a distance, she was drawn to his hands; they looked like they were covered in paint and chalk.

Beatrice was mesmerized by his rapid movements and the way he drew the lines and shapes so effortlessly. His strokes were methodical yet fluid as he transformed the graffiti-ridden partition into something fresh. At first, Beatrice was reminded of Botticelli's *The Birth of Venus,* which resided in the Uffizi in Florence. This painting depicted the ideal woman with red flowing hair, naked on a seashell. Beatrice looked closer, then changed her mind, laughing at her own initial hypothesis given this figure's abundance of clothing. The image looked as if she were from the Renaissance thanks to a jeweled crown and a ruffled collar.

Several people clapped, which seemed to irritate the artist, who looked up as if to warn them not to interfere with his creative process. Beatrice whispered to the fashionable woman with the auburn ponytail next to her. "Who is he?'

"You don't know?"

"I've never seen his work before."

The woman looked at her as if she had been living under a rock. "You should know Mike. Where have you been?"

Beatrice was taken aback by her condescending tone.

"Some of us work full-time," snapped Beatrice.

Reining in her irritation, the woman added, "His street murals and portraits pop up all over the world. He has a huge following, as you can see."

"Guess you learn something new every day," she replied. "Now I know." Beatrice quoted, "Blinding ignorance does mislead us. O! Wretched mortals open your eyes."

The woman gave her a blank stare.

"Da Vinci," said Beatrice with a wink.

"Touché," said the young woman, who nodded approval before moving on. Beatrice smoothed her own long brown hair, wondering why she felt so ridiculously self-conscious. It wasn't as if she knew anybody there.

Beatrice watched Mike draw, and with each movement felt the intensity of his craft. There was something about him that took her breath away. She remained still, captivated by his artistic prowess. She inched closer and planted herself in the front of the crowd. Mike's very presence commanded attention. He had removed his wool hat, revealing long dark hair, which fell nearly to his shoulders.

As throngs of people came and went, Beatrice couldn't stop watching him and the birth of a modern-day Venus on the side of the building beside a schoolyard. Finding herself alone, she pulled out her cell phone to take a picture and accidentally set off the flash. The next thing she knew, he loomed in front of her, emanating disapproval in torrents of Italian.

"No pictures yet!" he snapped.

"Why ever not?" she replied, surprised by his tone.

"Because I said so."

She bit back a sarcastic remark and they stared at each other.

She offered politely, "I'd like to take a picture."

"When I finish."

"When is that?"

"Probably another few days, *bellissima*."

"That's ridiculous," she said, so overjoyed by the compliment that shards of laughter spilled into the night. "I can't be the first person to try to take a picture of a work in progress."

"You're not," he said with an intense stare. Just as quickly, his mood shifted as he moved closer. Electricity flowed between them, catching Beatrice completely off guard. "*Yet*," he said softly.

His word seemed to hang in the air like the first breath of spring. He added, "But how else might I get you to stay around, bellissima?"

When he backed away, Beatrice felt a rush of cool night air on her face. Her heart flip-flopped. Pragmatic by nature, Beatrice was dumbfounded by the rush of emotion. It felt like the roar of a crowd after being silent for so long. Beatrice wondered what the smartest thing to do would be. Could she honestly stand here all night and stare at his mural? The answer was an unequivocal *yes*, but to be on the safe side, she texted her friend Chelsea and asked her to come see the lady on the building. After a brief chat, Chelsea declined: *Sorry to not make it but call me if you get stuck.*

A while later, Beatrice realized that she was standing alone on a darkened street with a stranger, who had jumped down from the scaffolding to turn off various lights. He sauntered up to her and said, "You look completely chilled, love, and I don't even know your name."

"Beatrice," she said, though her teeth chattered slightly.

"I'm Mike. How about a glass of wine to warm us both up?"

"Yes, I'd like that. Where?" She heard her own immediate acceptance, reveling in the moment. A little voice inside her head kept telling her to *be bold.*

"There's a café about two blocks from here. It's going to take me a few minutes to put everything away."

Beatrice knew it was crazy that she had stayed, and yet she felt so alive at this moment. She said casually, "I can meet you there. What do you do with all your supplies and equipment?"

"Leave them with a covering. So far, I've always been lucky, and seeing you in the crowd tonight, I'm convinced that I'm invincible."

Warmth spread through her being, wrapping itself close to her heart. Perhaps a warning bell should have gone off in her head, but she would've discarded it. After all, it was simply a glass of wine on a Friday night—better than going home to an empty, silent apartment.

Walking swiftly up the street two blocks, Beatrice spied the Greek café, a wall of ivy above the entrance door, and walked inside its classic confines. She was struck immediately by the polished, dark wood booths, the tinkling notes of a piano player, and the string of lights behind the mirrored bar area. A hostess walked over with menus, and Beatrice asked for the table by the window, a bundle of nerves. Would they have anything in common? Had she conjured him up in her own imagination?

Fifteen minutes, a piece of bread, and two glasses of water later, she spied him across the room. She felt his hawk-like stare when he caught sight of her. *There is something rare and special about him*, she concluded, admiring his large nose with the bump in the center as if it were once broken. He was unlike anyone she had ever met, she decided, feeling her heart hammering. Small in stature, Mike moved like a cat, weaving his way toward her effortlessly.

"Hi," she said. "You made it."

"Of course, why would I not?"

She looked away, hoping that he couldn't see her blush.

As soon as he sat, a waitress appeared to take their order. They each asked for a glass of Chianti, which she hoped would calm her jangled nerves. After the glasses were poured, they toasted to new beginnings, each taking a sip. Beatrice looked up to see his expressive brown eyes staring unblinking at her as if he could see straight through to her soul.

She cleared her throat and nervously put her napkin in her lap before meeting his gaze again.

"Your version of Lady Justice is incredible. I would even go as far as to say masterful."

"How did you know?"

"I'm a conservationist at the Vatican. It's my job to understand and preserve history."

"Aha!" he said with a wide grin that practically took her breath away. "I have a long way to go, but I am debating whether or not to portray her blindfolded. I drew the outline of the scales for her this afternoon."

"You must have her blindfolded!" said Beatrice, her voice rising a notch. "Lady Justice points to divine order, law, and custom, but the blindfold represents impartiality in any system. Justice should be applied without regard to wealth or power or any social status, for that matter."

The way he looked at her made her feel as if they were sitting alone in front of a roaring fire. She nearly laughed aloud at what she imagined next. The direction of her thoughts banished any cold from her body.

Their eyes locked and he chuckled softly. "You know, I was testing you."

"Oh," said Beatrice nervously. "Why would you do that?"

"Not everyone is impartial. It's why I do what I do."

"So, you're a political artist?"

"No, I wouldn't say that. I like to create beauty on the streets. But I also like to weave in a theme of social justice when I can. There's always unrest, political or otherwise."

"You mean, there's always a fire? That being said, I'm an art historian not a politician. So, where are you from?"

"I was born in Milan, but my father was American. He served in the US Army for over twenty years. My mother died when I was a boy. We hopped around from place to place all over the world. My father died two years ago, and I've been on the road since then."

"So, where do you call home?"

"I have no home, and I belong to no one country or affiliation."

Beatrice gulped, knowing full well that this should be her cue to disengage. He was fiery and artistic, oddly reminding her of the men who consumed her professional life—Raphael, Caravaggio, and the great Michelangelo. Michelangelo was known to be hot tempered and difficult at times. Often, he was so absorbed by his work that he didn't bathe and forgot to eat. Beatrice noted the paint under his fingernails and the streak of dirt on his jacket.

"You said you worked at the Vatican. What's that like?"

"I believe that history has the power to save us all. By caring for the works of the great masters, I hope to keep visitors connected to their roots and even religion."

"Do you have to be Catholic to work there?"

"Not necessarily, but I am, if that's what you're asking."

"Ah," he replied. "A woman of conviction."

"That's not how I see it." She took a sip of her drink. "Are you going to ask me if I believe in God next?"

"Well, do you?" he nudged with a wicked grin.

"Of course. Do you?" Beatrice wondered why his next answer made her hold her breath.

"I will answer that question in my own time. I do believe in fate, however."

She took his evasive answer for a no, but a tiny voice said it could be a *maybe*. She could work with that. "Are you a sinner or a saint?" she blurted.

Mike threw back his head and laughed. "I think we all have a bit of both in us. It's the choices we make."

The manager came over to tell them that the restaurant was closing in fifteen minutes. It was already two in the morning.

"May I walk you home?"

"Thank you but no. I can get a ride. I've got the app on my phone."

"I don't like technology. It's too distracting," he said, and then blurted, "You are so beautiful."

Her heart skipped a beat.

"Meet me here tomorrow night? Would you do that?"

"Yes," she said without hesitation.

Had she gone completely crazy?

***

The following morning, Beatrice headed to the local coffee shop with the faded red awning and ordered a double espresso. Taking a seat on the outdoor patio, she breathed in the smoky liquid, allowing the bitter taste to clear her mental cobwebs. Beatrice wondered about her meeting with Mike. He was dark and brooding, and any form of relationship with him could only lead to disappointment, her rational mind argued. And yet, she was more than intrigued. Should she go back today and follow a thrilling path that may break her heart?

To live without risk is to risk not living, Pope Pius XII had advised.

Why did that quote just pop in her head? She laughed at herself. The practical part of her offered that there were numerous tasks that she needed to get done. She made a full list that began with cleaning her nearly barren kitchen, hanging those pictures in her den, repainting the antique chest in her bedroom, organizing her collection of vinyl records, mostly Bob Dylan, just because, ordering some new linens, and, most importantly, making a trip to the market to pick up groceries since her cabinets were nearly bare.

To compound her anxiety, her desk at work beckoned as usual as it was piled high with projects. The cardinal had hinted that she may be assigned to help with restoring Leonardo da Vinci's *St. Jerome*, which was beyond exciting. The painting had quite a history, and she wanted to delve into it. Leonardo da Vinci's work had a way of captivating her, and she couldn't wait to tell Rose about her latest discovery on Monday morning.

Beatrice played mental gymnastics all day. *Should I meet Mike or not?* To turn down the noise in her mind, she attacked her to-do list and set upon organizing her apartment. Her main living area was anchored by a small fireplace where she hung her most prized possession, a traditional family portrait painted in the seventeenth century. It had been a gift from her grandmother, along with a set of antique blue-and-white plates that adorned the walls in her dining area. There were two caramel leather sofas that formed an *L* with a large throw draped over one side. Her mother had insisted on a plethora of patterned pillows in various shades of gray, which Beatrice thought looked quite smart.

At the nearby market, she selected some cheese, picking a creamy brie that could be heated. After loading up on her usual staples, she decided to add in some fresh bread, pears, and a bit of chocolate. Who knew what tonight would bring? She admonished herself for being frivolous, then decided her insane workload justified all of the extra groceries.

Indeed, she added a few bags of pasta to her cart. A simple meal of penne pasta and parmesan always worked in a pinch whenever she was starving after returning home from a twelve-hour day.

Her kitchen had been begging for attention, and she wiped, scrubbed, and organized everything until it shone. Buoyed by her own efforts, she even hung several pictures and placed some fresh flowers on the coffee table for good measure. Fortunately, her friend Chelsea phoned and asked her out to dinner, which Beatrice gratefully accepted.

***

Chelsea, always meticulously groomed, wore a dark pants suit that complemented her copper hair; she had a degree from Oxford and had been working for Sotheby's for the last seven years. They met years ago when the cardinal purchased a painting from the famous auction house for the Vatican Museum. Chelsea handled the sale and stayed involved during the restoration process. Their friendship blossomed as they talked about art history, legacy, and their latest debates about the true soul of a painting. And yet, outside the confines of work, Beatrice found her to be a breath of fresh air. Chelsea was bubbly and fun, always full of mischief.

After a warm embrace, they sat in the trendy restaurant with the red walls and sparkling marble floors.

"You're not going to believe this," announced Chelsea, "but I applied for a position in New York."

"What? Why?'

"There's an opening in management, and I'm ready for a change. I've got an interview next week."

"I wouldn't be a bit surprised if you got it, but I'd hate to see you go."

"There are planes," Chelsea replied, taking a sip of her drink. Deftly changing the subject, she asked, "So, who's the main man in your life these days?"

"Leonardo da Vinci," replied Beatrice. "How can anyone else be more intriguing? The cardinal has me lined up to work on his *St. Jerome in the Wilderness.*"

"Is that the painting where he is depicted beating his chest with a lion by his side?"

"Yes," said Beatrice. "And supposedly someone once cut the painting into five pieces. Cardinal Fesch, the uncle of Napoleon Bonaparte, originally discovered it. He found Saint Jerome's torso as a tabletop box at a shop and then found another panel at a shoemaker. Whatever happened, the painting was restored and sold to Pope Pius IX."

"Who was Saint Jerome?"

"He was considered a doctor of the Western Christian Church for translating the Gospel of Mark into Latin."

"How thrilling," said Chelsea in a monotone, taking a sip of her martini. "You need to get out more if you're enthralled by a penitent monk in the desert."

"It's a masterpiece, and you know it." Even to her own ears, she thought she sounded like a teenager.

"You're so *involved* with your work that you've lost sight of what's important in life. Darling, you're almost thirty years old and you've been chained to your desk ever since I met you. You need to live more!"

Without thinking, Beatrice shot back, "I met someone last night."

"Oh really," said Chelsea, with a Cheshire cat–like smile. "That's far more intriguing than the monk."

"His name is Mike. He's currently painting Lady Justice on the side of an old building a couple of blocks from here."

"He's a street artist?" Chelsea replied. "I must say that I am genuinely shocked for the first time since I've known you. I love it."

Warming to her story, Beatrice added, "Yes, he has a huge following." She didn't want to share that she had only just heard of him yesterday so as not to sound too utterly pathetic. "Anyway, I watched him work and he's so talented. We had a drink last night after he finished. That's all."

"Well, we'll have to go have a look after we finish up," offered

Chelsea. "I'm truly curious. You work with the masters all day long, so if you think he's talented, that's quite a huge endorsement. Sorry I missed last night. I really should have joined you."

"I was actually blown away by his talent. He's transforming the side of the building by creating such a beautiful mural." Beatrice paused. "He seems rather elusive, and says he belongs to no one or no place."

"Not exactly relationship material."

"That's why I've avoided going all day."

"Absolutely not. You must seize the moment." Chelsea glanced at her friend. "You've been in that lab day and night since we met."

Beatrice felt the hairs rise on the back of her neck. Her life sounded so mundane, or was she just imposing her own restlessness on her friend's words? "True. Let's go and watch him work. I'll decide what I want to do after that."

Their appetizers arrived; they settled into sharing *carciofi alla giudia* (friend artichokes) and fresh buffalo mozzarella. The sublime rosemary chicken and spinach matched the joy of connecting with her friend. Beatrice acknowledged that she was alone too much of the time; she promised herself to change things and nurture her existing relationships more. They wrapped up their meal, trading stories about landlords and the high cost of living in Rome. Beatrice announced that she was seriously thinking of heading home to Switzerland; Chelsea talked nonstop about her trip to New York.

"So, you are quite serious?" said Beatrice, dropping her fork, which clattered to the table.

"Absolutely. I want to move to the States," she announced. "I applied for the job, and if I don't get it, I'll try something else."

"I'm still so surprised." Beatrice knew she sounded a bit like a hurt child rather than a supportive friend, but she just couldn't help herself.

"I need a new adventure. In my mind, I'm not married and have no children, so it's the perfect time in my life to try something new."

"Alright then," said Beatrice, mustering up the emotion to say goodbye to her one close friend in Rome. "It sounds wonderful!"

"You'll come visit me?"

"Of course!"

A short time later, they wandered over to where Mike was painting. A crowd had formed as he brought his Lady Justice to life. He was intensely filling in her dress, which was a pure white. The color seemed to draw the eye directly to the scales of justice. Not long after they took their place among the crowd, Chelsea whispered, "This mural is thought provoking. Look over there at those swirls of black and gray, almost as if he has started another theme. What does it look like to you?"

"Seems like anger personified in those swirls of colors. Or it could be the back of someone's head."

"No, I think it looks like men in chains."

Just as they debated the new twist to the mural, three black Range Rovers blaring rap music pulled up. Caustic drumbeats combined with a symphonic background pierced through the night. Anticipation filled the crowd as the music added a new sense of drama. People seemed to freeze, waiting and watching what was about to unfold before them. Beatrice suppressed a shiver as she watched the scene, holding her breath. Mike seemed oblivious, immersed in his work, painting with ferocity a new swirl of black to contrast the lady's gown.

An impossibly tall, handsome Black man emerged from the car, dressed in a black leather jacket and stylish boots. He seemed almost regal as he waved to the crowd in a charismatic manner. Everyone began to cheer.

"Who's that?" whispered Chelsea. "He's dreamy."

"Not a clue," replied Beatrice.

The man walked up to the mural with two other men and stood stock still, almost in an insolent manner. He began pointing at the mural, slapping one of his friends on the arm. It wasn't until he was a couple of feet from Mike that Beatrice saw her artist friend pause and look at the other man coldly. The tension increased as the two men glared at each other.

In response, Mike jumped down from his post and started cursing at the newcomer to leave. The newcomer responded with gales of laughter. His very presence dwarfed Mike's form.

Moments later, they stood facing each other, and the crowd began to make noise.

"What's going on?" asked Beatrice. "They look like they're about to kill each other."

"I don't know," said Chelsea. "But I'd put my money on the man who just arrived."

"No way! I'm on Mike's side. He's clearly brilliant and that other guy is jealous."

Chelsea shook her head. She studied the scene and said, "Leather jacket radiates power and success."

"Mike is extremely gifted, which agitates his rivals," said Beatrice. A vision of the past struck her. Two of the greatest artists of all time hated each other. Both were the personification of true genius. Their competition was relentless, but it fueled each of them to aim higher and achieve the most important accolades of the Renaissance. Suddenly, it was as if their ghosts were here on a palazzo in Rome, Beatrice realized, and she felt the sizzling energy of hate and passion, genius and creativity.

"Who is he?" said Beatrice, feeling once again naïve.

"It's Vince," said a man in a black hoodie. "He's the man."

"Is he an artist?" Beatrice asked, looking over at Chelsea. Beatrice already knew the answer.

"He isn't just an artist. He's a visionary."

Beatrice felt the chill of the night air.

"This is surreal," muttered Chelsea. "I want to meet him."

Beatrice grabbed her arm. "I think we should back away."

"Not a chance," said Chelsea, maneuvering to the front of the crowd.

Chapter 4

ROSE VENTURED INTO her rented studio for the first time in months, wondering what on earth she was going to paint next. The tiny space boasted a functional window, easel, two shelves for her paints, and a dented sink that barely trickled water. She turned on the exposed overhead light, hung up her jacket, and sat in a creaky metal seat. Surveying the space, she nearly groaned at the room's austerity; it was all she could afford because she refused to accept money from Lyon.

Her last project was inspired by the great Michelangelo. She'd put a modern spin on *his* concept; the *Creation of Adam* depicted the hand of God touching fingers with Adam, which graced the ceiling of the Sistine Chapel. When she found the drawings in the wall, the hands were clasped. In her mind, this image represented the ultimate symbol of love and kindness in humanity. So, she and Lyon's mother created wall-size murals of people of all ages and races holding hands. Given the overwhelming response, Rose decided that the world craved positivity.

A new idea felt daunting, and yet she was determined to return to her craft. Several concepts floated through her mind. She wanted to capture joy and excitement in everyday events, thereby making the ordinary appear extraordinary.

Picking up her charcoal pencil, she recalled the park where she met Lyon. It was the very spot where she'd decided on the apartment she planned to buy in Florence. That moment was a pivotal point in her life, and the memory sparked her creativity. Parks represented outdoor space available to everyone to enjoy the beauty of nature. Rose considered the scene, contemplating it from various angles. As she recalled the day, she drew flowering azalea bushes with pinks and yellows from late summer. Her hands formed a rhythm as she conjured up the image in her mind's eye. Reality would be easier, she decided, recalling how Faith, her future mother-in-law, often took her easel outdoors to "experience the colors."

After several hours of laying the foundation of her portrait, Rose scanned the room for a few supplies—tote bag, a smaller palette of oils, a few charcoal pencils, and a light jacket since the weather was so mild. A hunger pang interrupted her focus. She decided to stop at the market for her favorite cheese-and-prosciutto sandwich to take to the park to work for a few more hours.

At last night's dinner, she talked to Faith about the guest list, and they both agreed that a hundred people would be perfect. It would keep the event big enough to include Lyon's massive family but small enough so that it remained intimate. They were scheduled to have lunch next week to nail down more of the details Rose wanted; she was so grateful to have found Faith, the kind of mother she had never known. Their relationship was so natural and relaxed. She didn't have to force it or try to be anything but herself, which was truly a blessing.

Her mother, Doris, was another story. Every interaction with her set Rose's nerves on edge. She was controlling and manipulative. *Thank goodness for a sense of humor,* Rose thought, as she darted back to her apartment to grab her charcoal eraser. When she arrived, a small box was wedged in her mailbox with the return address from the States. Rose hurried up the steps to pry open the plain rectangular cardboard box. It took a few minutes to free a long white box that looked very elegant. She opened the lid to reveal a pair of long, white leather gloves. Reaching into the tissue paper, she saw a note in her mother's handwriting: *These will be your Something Borrowed.* Rose stared at the white gloves in complete horror. *What was she thinking?*

Grabbing her cell phone, she tried to reach Lyon to tell him about the presumptuous gift. When no one answered, she phoned her best friend, Zoey, in Charlottesville, Virginia. Rose and Zoey would always share a special bond; they were not only childhood best friends, but they had also taught side by side at Bellfield for years. Rose had been a bridesmaid in Zoey's wedding, and it was Zoey who flew across the Atlantic with her when she made the monumental decision to live abroad. How she missed their easy camaraderie.

It was dinnertime, but Rose breathed a sigh of relief when she heard her friend's cheerful voice. After exchanging hellos, Rose said, "I just received a package from you-know-who," Rose cried, holding the dreaded icons of debutante balls past.

Zoey laughed aloud. "Doris has struck again, no doubt."

"This is ridiculous! I'm not wearing white leather gloves on my wedding day. That's so not me!"

"I'm not surprised. Can you tell her they got lost in the mail?"

"She has no idea who I am. Everything is an issue with her. She's still trying to control me from across the Atlantic. How about asking me if I might like to wear them rather than sending some note that says, 'These will be your Something Borrowed.' Isn't it supposed to be about me?" Rose railed on and finally stopped. "Sorry for the rant."

"I understand. Could you reframe it to mean that maybe she thinks she's being helpful?"

"Do you believe that?"

"Absolutely not, but it was worth a try!" She paused. "I think you tell her that they don't work and ask if she has something else like a pin from your grandmother. You know, is there something sentimental that could replace them?"

Still angry, Rose said, teary eyed, "You know what bugs me the most? She always sends these obnoxious messages of who she wants me to be. She wanted some debutante daughter who would have a country club wedding. This is so passive aggressive!"

"Calm down, Rose. You don't have to always let her upset you."

"Are you saying I'm wrong?"

"Hey, I'm on your side. She's not going to change, and you know that. And be prepared for some mischief on your wedding day."

Rose groaned. "She'll probably wear a white sequined evening gown."

"Probably," said Zoey with a knowing laugh, "but you, my dear friend, will be radiant! So, when's the big day?"

"Actually, that's why I was checking in. We've decided upon the first Saturday in December. I just saw this beautiful navy dress in a shop window for my matron of honor. I'll text you a picture"

"Awww. You have such great taste. I'm sure I'll love it."

"You're going to be as gorgeous as always!"

"Well," said Zoey, "you might need to get me a size or two up. I have some news." Her words hung in the air.

"Is everything okay?"

"Never been better, except, of course, the sudden throwing up before class."

"What?" Rose shrieked.

"Yes! I'm eight weeks."

Joyful tears fell. "Oh wow! What a day brightener! I'm so happy for you guys!"

"Stan wanted me to wait until I saw you in person, but I just couldn't!"

"That is fantastic!" said Rose. "When are you due?"

"Early March. It'll be perfect. I can have the summer to be a mom and start back during the fall term."

"Smart! You always were the most organized person I've ever met."

"Hardly. I need to get going on our plane reservations. Stan and I can't wait!"

"Congratulations, Zoey. You're going to be the most amazing mother . . . ever!"

"Well, and you're going to be the most amazing godmother ever!"

"You've made my day! I can't wait to tell Lyon," said Rose. "And thanks to you, the glove incident is officially over." They both laughed.

Rose couldn't wait to share the good news with Lyon. She hung up, took the gloves, and threw them in the back of her closet. Then, finishing every bite of her delicious sandwich, she checked her watch and tried to call Lyon, who was not picking up his phone. She gathered her supplies to head to the park as she had planned, but not to complete the painting she began that morning. The early fall day beckoned her to go outside and try something out of her comfort zone; the Impressionist *en plain air* approach intimidated her.

On a whim, she decided to cart her supplies, a medium canvas, and a few small tubes of paint to the Giardini Bardini to capture its magnificent view. The daunting flight of stairs usually deterred her from visiting this gorgeous sanctuary, but the exciting news that her best friend was expecting propelled her forward, or upward, in this case. She got to the top a little breathless, but the view proved worth the extra effort. After scouring the landscape, Rose headed toward a corner area that had a bench where she planned to work.

No sooner had she put her supplies down than she looked over to see the back of Lyon, walking with who appeared to be his ex, Dominique. The woman wore a long, dark, perfectly tailored jacket complemented by red designer pants. Rose was sure her red fingernail polish coordinated perfectly with the outfit. Gold bangle bracelets gleamed on her wrists. Rose would recognize Lyon's gait and his camel suede jacket anywhere. Her mouth practically dropped open as she watched them having an animated conversation. Rose was so shocked that she had to sit to let air back in her lungs. *How many times had Lyon reunited with Dominique these last few months? Are they seeing each other? Of course not! I trust Lyon completely,* she told herself.

There was nothing that would have put her here in this exact spot except fate. Rose knew she had to trust her own instincts about the man she was supposed to marry in a few months. There had to be a logical explanation, but, more importantly, when was he going to tell her that he had been meeting with his very manipulative ex?

A text from Beatrice caught her eye:

If you have time this weekend, do some homework on Michelangelo's Battle of Cascina (1364) and Leonardo da Vinci's Battle of Anghiari (1440). They were painted for the Hall of the Five Hundred. They were two very important battles that symbolized the Florentine Republic and ultimately freedom . . .

Rose eagerly responded, *Actually, I can swing by there this afternoon. I'll head over and take a look.*

Perfect! Always good to have a frame of reference.

See you Monday. Anything else?

No! Looking forward to it! xx

The rational part of Rose thought she should flag Lyon down and say hello. Pondering her options, she considered catching up with them, but decided that it was all too awkward. She didn't want to look like she was jealous, which of course wasn't the case. *Is it?* She bit her lower lip. *I'm off to the Hall of the Five Hundred. What a perfect distraction right now!* Part of her wanted to run down Lyon and tell him how hurt and angry she felt. There was no way he would have known that she'd changed her plans and taken herself to the park. She was looking for inspiration—not agitation. The irony of it all struck her.

Apparently, Beatrice wanted her to understand Renaissance history before their meeting. What had she uncovered? Trying to recall the story, Rose knew that there was a contest where the two rivals, Michelangelo and Leonardo da Vinci, were pitted against each other. She needed to piece together the details of what happened and how it related to the drawings she found. There was so much more to know about this ancient rivalry and how uncovering the past could affect modern-day Florence. The mystery was thrilling, and yet it would not be without consequences of some sort, either political or social. With her passion for art history ignited, Rose wondered how this age-old feud had played out.

A walk to the Palazzo Vecchio would hopefully clear her head. She bought a ticket to study the largest and most important room built in the fifteenth century. Originally constructed in 1494, it was commissioned by Fra Girolamo Savonarola, who had gained power over the Medici dynasty to establish a Florentine Republic from 1494 to 1498. His goal was to establish a more democratic government for the city of Florence, which was why he created the Council of Five Hundred or Great Council. The Great Council would control government decisions rather than one ruling family being in charge.

Rose perused the plethora of brochures in front of her, trying to assimilate hundreds of years of history into a few short summaries. The ambiguity of the moment amused her as she sorted through the vast array of information displayed on a side table. This movement caused her to drop a couple of the pamphlets, scattering them perilously on the floor. With one fluid motion, a distinguished older man swooped in to retrieve them for her. When he stood back up to offer his assistance, she looked at his intelligent eyes behind a pair of tortoise-framed glasses.

"I'm so sorry," she offered. "Thank you for getting my piles of information under control."

"Happy to help. I'm Dr. Edwin Saunders from Boston. It looks like you're trying to take a crash course in Florentine history. By the way, I'm very familiar with this hall."

"Nice to meet you. I'm Rose Maning." She held out her hand. "You're very perceptive. I should admit that I'm a former schoolteacher. I wish I knew more of the history here." She perused his tweed jacket before placing the stack of pamphlets in her satchel.

"Your timing couldn't be better!" he said with a knowing grin. "I happen to be writing a book on the rise and fall of the Medici family. The government functions in this hall also happen to be part of my research."

"This must be my lucky day," said Rose as she walked beside him into the stunning chamber. "You don't happen to know about the original paintings, the one commissioned to Leonardo da Vinci?"

"You mean the greatest artistic competition of all time with he and his younger nemesis, Michelangelo? As a matter of fact, I do."

"I'd appreciate any information you'd be willing to share. I'm fascinated by their rivalry."

Heading inside the chamber, Professor Saunders began to point out and explain the detailed architecture. "After the hall was built, Piero Soderini came to power, and he wanted to decorate this hall with paintings from two the greatest artists of all time—Michelangelo and Leonardo da Vinci. They were supposed to do battle scenes glorifying the Florentine Republic. Leonardo would sketch out the Battle of Anghiari, while Michelangelo would focus on another part of the wall for the Battle of Cascina." He paused. "There is much speculation on this so-called competition. That Soderini had an ulterior motive when he set these two Renaissance giants to work on the same wall. It was an explosive concept, one that didn't end well.

"Leonardo was commissioned in 1503, and accounts point to the intensity of his original drawings, which captured the raw emotion of battle." He paused.

"Leonardo's painting was considered one of the greatest depictions of war ever made. It was a fifty-four-foot by twenty-one-foot rendering of the June 1440 attack on Florentine papal troops at Anghiari by Milan commander Niccolo Piccinino at various points. The most copied scene shows the intense engagement of horses and soldiers. Let me be clear that a lost Leonardo then is like a lost Leonardo now—a national and historic treasure!"

"Or a lost patriotic masterpiece," said Rose, pondering the mystery. "Then what happened?"

"Let me explain the surrounding events. In 1504, Soderini commissioned Michelangelo to do a painting of the Battle of Cascina. A young prodigy, his sculpture of the *David* had established him as an international sensation. The young Michelangelo worked furiously on his battle drawings—many of which have been copied today. Ultimately, Michelangelo was called away to Rome to work on Pope Julius II's tomb, so only a portion of the fresco was completed.

Alas, it is believed that the two unfinished battle scenes decorated the Florentine state hall for years, influencing many artists.

"Around 1555, Georgio Vasari, a noted scholar, architect and painter was hired to redesign the Hall of the Five Hundred. Take a look around you. These walls are a bit vapid in my humble opinion."

"So, has anyone tried to find the Leonardo?"

"Well, there are rumors, of course. They've been circulating for about five hundred years."

"Do you have a card, Professor?"

"Of course."

Rose looked into his intelligent blue eyes, wondering why this mystery was still unsolved. "Why hasn't anyone tried to look behind the wall?"

"They have. More than once, but it's all very political and controversial." He studied her for a moment, suddenly looking at her hand. Rose wasn't wearing her engagement ring, realizing that she'd taken it earlier off to paint. "I'd welcome a chance to talk further, maybe over dinner?"

Rose realized that she had taken up enough of his valuable time, and she wasn't quite sure how to interpret the dinner invitation. Besides, the hall was closing, and she needed to get back home. "Thank you, Professor, you've been so kind. I appreciate your insights, but I need to get home."

"Thank you, my dear. I wish all of my students felt that way," he said with a wry grin. "If you email me, I can most certainly give you more references and information."

"I'd appreciate that."

Rose secured his business card in her wallet. Before departing, she remembered that there was a lesser-known Michelangelo sculpture, the *Genius of Victory*, located at the southern end of the Salone dei Cinquecento (Room of the Five Hundred), and she decided to take a quick peek. Rose didn't know the exact date the sculpture was created, but she knew it may have been intended for the tomb of

Pope Julius II. The head of the winner was decorated with oak leaves, which served as an allegory of victory. The battle was personified by the beautiful figure of a young man with a leg thrown over a bearded older warrior who had been defeated. How Rose loved seeing the work of the great Michelangelo up close.

A security guard politely asked her to leave so they could lock up. Rose reluctantly headed outside and checked her phone, noting several missed calls from Lyon. Rose wondered if he had seen her as well. As soon as she stepped back into the street, Rose walked briskly for ten blocks, resisting the urge to call a cab. It wasn't long before she let herself back in her apartment where Lyon was waiting for her, lounging on the sofa.

"Hi," she said cheerfully. "What are you doing here?" she asked, putting her satchel on the kitchen table. He was hard to resist with his dark hair and chiseled cheek bones. Lyon emanated strength and confidence, which challenged her in a good way.

"Looking for you," he replied calmly.

"Really?" she said cautiously. "I called you several times today."

"Rose, we have to talk."

"About what?"

"You were supposed to be here an hour ago and—" He paused for a moment, then exclaimed, "Surprise! I've got two tickets to see Andrea Bocelli tonight. Can you get going please?"

"You're kidding me!" Rose shrieked in excitement. "How did you land them?"

"I have my secrets," he replied, standing up to embrace her.

"Wait, what? How?"

"You're on a need-to-know basis. Haven't you told me a thousand times that you would love to see him in concert?"

"Yes, but probably closer to a million times. I'm so excited!" She jumped into his arms and kissed him passionately. "This is a dream come true!"

"You can thank me later."

Rose dashed into her bedroom, peeling off her jeans and old painting sweatshirt. She had always dreamed of seeing Bocelli in concert. His voice was like music from the heavens. Digging through her closet, she found a simple yet elegant black dress that she had put away for the right occasion. Looking at the black leather bodice, she refused to think about the outrageous price tag or the snobby saleswoman in the pricey boutique. A pair of black high heels complemented the dress. Putting her hair in an elegant chignon, she took a selfie and typed *#datenight #andreaboccelli*

Lyon had changed into a dark suit, which contrasted well with his olive skin. He looked impossibly handsome, and Rose's heart skipped a beat when their eyes met. The night sky was a cascade of stars, and the cool air held the secret promise of her dreams. A driver was waiting for them at the bottom of the stairs, and they climbed into the back of the black Mercedes.

"You think of everything!" exclaimed Rose as the driver held the door for them. "What a surprise. I think I'm the luckiest person in all of Florence."

"Absolutely not. I don't know what I did to deserve you. You look beautiful, my love."

"Oh, Lyon," she said. "I'm so sorry for everything these past few months. I've been so selfish. You are my everything."

His smile melted her heart. "I can't wait to make you my wife."

Just as he leaned over to kiss her, Rose sat up abruptly. "I have news!"

He looked at her with a sardonic grin. "This must be good."

"I called Zoey this afternoon. They're expecting a baby! I'm so happy for them. You know how much I want children."

Silence.

"You've not mentioned this before?"

"Absolutely, I've always wanted three or four children."

"What?" cried Lyon. "That's an army! We shall see, but practice makes perfect."

Rose blushed as she looked over at the driver listening to them. "I'm not making that decision right now," she said. "I forgot to ask, where is the concert?"

"The Palazzo Vecchio."

"So that was what they were doing. I was just there this afternoon."

"Why?'

"Beatrice wanted me to do some research for her. Where are we?"

"Picking up some of the best pizza in Florence." He winked as he got out of the car only to return a few minutes later with a warm cardboard box.

"You know how much I love pizza." Her mouth watered when Lyon opened the box and handed her a napkin and a hot slice of a thin-crust margherita pizza. "I really think pizza is the way to my heart."

"I know so," said Lyon, taking a bite of a mouthwatering slice.

Shortly thereafter, a huge crowd teeming with well-dressed men and women overloaded the front of the evening's concert hall. Lyon instructed the driver to drop them off at a side door. He took her hand, guiding her inside where they made their way through the crowds to the front rows.

As her questioning look, he acknowledged, "My parents are strong supporters of the arts."

"Where are we going?" she asked incredulously. "We're this close? These tickets must have cost a fortune."

"Rose, darling," he said. "Relax. It was a gift."

"Are you serious? This is so incredible." Rose felt a lump in her throat.

They sat together, held hands, and Rose was completely transported in time and place. She wondered about the lost Leonardo da Vinci masterpiece in proximity. Could somewhere in this building be a secret that had been buried for five hundred years? It was dreamlike, and yet, she wondered what it be like to find it. Lyon whispered something in her ear, bringing her back to the present.

The excitement in the concert hall was electric as they waited in anticipation for the legendary singer to appear. Soon thereafter, a hush fell over the audience. She looked up at the stage as the men walked on to deafening applause. Two handsome men in tuxedos, one younger and one older, took their seats at a set of Steinway pianos that faced each other.

Lyon whispered, "There's Andrea on the left, and that's his son, Matteo, on the right."

Once the lights dimmed, the first notes of the song "Fall on Me" were stunning in their perfection. The love on Andrea's face the moment his son began singing was the most beautiful thing Rose had ever witnessed. Tears formed; this moment was beyond her wildest dreams. She was sitting with the man she loved, watching a once-in-a-lifetime performance by one of the greatest artists of his day. Each note filled the room with its beauteous melody. Andrea and Matteo's voices joined together in a song that one would expect only to hear from the heavens above.

Rose was transfixed by the music and the beauty of the night. And when they sang "Ode to Joy," Lyon put his arm around her and whispered, "I love you." Something magical happened in that moment; she felt free of her fears and doubts, knowing that she was with her one true love. With a newfound clarity, Rose envisioned her wedding day, and her whole being radiated with gratitude and love.

It was fear that had kept her from deciding on a wedding date. A part of her had held back in her love for Lyon simply because she didn't want to feel vulnerable. The one person she had loved the most in the world had died—her beloved father—and Rose subconsciously refused to ever feel that kind of pain again. Yet, she was ready to move beyond her emotions and embrace a new beginning with Lyon. In that singular moment of understanding, the world became filled with infinite possibilities as the sublime pleasure of the music washed over her.

As they headed home bathed in the magic of the night, Rose

said, "What do you think if we stop by your parents' house for a few hours tomorrow? Maybe your mother and I could work on more of the details."

"She would love to see you," he paused. "If I know my mother, she'll have lots of great ideas."

"She's amazing. We work so well together, and I want her opinion on the readings for the ceremony and my bridal bouquet. I know we talked about a civil ceremony, but I want something more faith based."

He looked askance at her. "Really?"

"Yes," she said firmly.

"I thought we weren't going to have a religious ceremony."

"I've changed my mind. I want our marriage blessed by clergy. What if we ask the cardinal what to do?"

"My parents went to the Church of England," Lyon said.

"Mine were Roman Catholic. Maybe we can represent both denominations."

"That's a tall order," said Lyon, reaching for her.

"I think it's important. I want to be married in the eyes of God."

"You realize that will change things," said Lyon, taking her hand. "I have to admit that I wasn't all that interested in all of the religious requirements, but I do see your point."

"Thank you. Will you consider it? I want our marriage blessed. The cardinal could help us find someone in Florence, I would think."

"Yes, but I'm curious about what made you change your mind?"

"I left the church after my father died. I didn't believe in anything, and I certainly didn't trust a God who would take away the man I loved most." She exhaled. "When I think about marriage and children, I realize that I want to start our life together out right."

"Well," said Lyon, taking her hand. "You will make my parents very happy. My mother wasn't too thrilled with just a civil ceremony, but she loves you, so she accepted our decision." He added, "I like the idea of representing both denominations, Catholic and Episcopalian."

"See, we make a great team," said Rose, giving him a kiss on the cheek.

His cell phone buzzed. He looked at the incoming text and glanced over at Rose. "You're not going to believe this, but my brother, Peter, wants to crash at my place tonight."

"Nothing like short notice," she quipped. Rose was disappointed. It has been such a romantic evening, and things felt so much better between them.

"He claims my mailbox is full, so it's all my fault." He looked over at her. "Darling, I can meet him in the morning."

"No," said Rose. "Go ahead and see your brother. Family is family."

"You can dream about me," said Lyon as he nuzzled her ear.

"Or I can dream about Andrea Bocelli," said Rose with a wicked grin.

"I'm confident,"

"You should be," said Rose. "I'm still counting on December 5th and forever."

"So am I," said Lyon, kissing her good night.

Chapter 5

THE NEXT MORNING was clear and bright as Rose waited outside her apartment for Lyon to pick her up. She liked it when the streets weren't crowded with tourists, and she could admire the Florentine columns, pilasters, and semi-arches. This city had a way of making her feel like she was navigating through time. Florence had given birth to the Renaissance, which regularly ignited her passion for art history.

The thought of Lyon evoked a smile. Spotting his sportscar, Rose reveled in finding such a loving and supportive life partner.

"Good morning," said Lyon as he popped out of the car to grab her bag. "You're looking in high spirits today."

Rose kissed him soundly. "I'm still basking in the afterglow of the Bocelli concert. It was such an amazing experience. Thank you again for everything. You always keep me guessing."

"That's a good thing, I hope."

"Absolutely! I got you a coffee for the trip. It was the least I could do." She pulled out a list from her purse. "We have a few things to go over on this ride." He rolled his eyes and she punched him playfully. "Seriously, I want you to be part of the planning. It's our wedding, not just my day."

"I'm going to love everything you and my mother pick. I'm not worried."

"You have no opinions on all of this stuff?"

"I didn't say that," he replied with a chuckle. "I already made several inquiries into the band, and I think it would be great to go and see them live next week."

"Perfect! What do you want on the menu?"

"I'd like roast beef and potatoes."

"How about a fish option?'

"Lobster," said Lyon.

Rose made a notation on her pad.

"I also want a pasta bar with a chef to keep the food hot. And make sure to have red sauce and parmesan."

"Okay," she said.

"And my grandmother's secret clam sauce recipe."

"I will talk with your mother about that."

"I've already asked Peter to be my best man, and that leaves my childhood friends, Hank and Roberto."

"Check," she replied. "And you've all been fitted for tuxedos. I found the dresses for Zoey as the matron of honor along with my friend Page from Charlottesville. Your sister is excited about being a bridesmaid. She's been very helpful in securing the heels, which I'm sure you find scintillating. Anyway, I'm thinking of asking Beatrice to be in the wedding party."

"That's a great idea!" said Lyon.

"She was so helpful to me when I was having a hard time," said Rose. Rose didn't bring up her ex, Ben Pierce, whom she almost married. Even the thought of him left a sour note in her mind. Hard to believe that she ended their relationship, became engaged to Ben, and then was smart enough to realize her mistake. The fact that Lyon forgave her was a miracle!

"Oh look," he exclaimed. "We made it here in record time."

"Of course," said Rose with a knowing laugh. "You're lucky you didn't get a ticket." She got out of the car ready to make decisions.

Rose would never forget the first time Lyon brought her to his parents' Tuscan villa. It was a bit overwhelming. She could still remember what it felt like to drive up to a guarded gatehouse. The massive gates opened to a well-lit driveway with gorgeous cypress trees winding along a moonlit path. The grand estate looked like something out of a movie with its circular driveway and cascading fountain.

They headed inside and found his parents in their sunroom. Faith was poring over lists, and Joseph was reading the paper. The greetings were warm and friendly.

"Oh, darlings, you're just in time," said Faith, jumping up to give each of them a welcoming hug. "I've finalized the guest list and want to go over the floral arrangements."

"Lovely," said Rose as she sat down on the sofa beside her. "I'm more than ready."

"That's my girl, and my cue to depart," said Lyon. "Mother, any idea where I put my tennis racket? Peter thinks he can still beat me."

"Check the center closet in the front hallway," said Faith as she turned her complete attention back to Rose. "Lyon, you're welcome to join in the planning."

"Peter should be down here any minute. I'll have Rose go over everything with me in the car on the way to Rome," said Lyon, ducking out of the room. "I could use some fresh air."

It was always a pleasure to be with Faith. They made a great team that was both efficient and creative. Rose admired her artistic prowess as she held up several drawings of floral arrangements.

"I don't know many people who could capture the beauty of flowers on canvas the way you do!"

"Thank you, dear. This is such fun and a wonderful way to play with color on canvas. Which one do you like best?"

"They're all beautiful, but I do like the white hydrangea and white roses combination."

"You could do an all-white theme."

"But it would be December."

"How about adding in silver bells . . . excuse the pun." She laughed. "I couldn't help it."

"Oh, that's such a great idea."

They went on to discuss the linens and centerpieces for each table. After an hour, Faith stopped them and said, "My dear, I haven't even offered you a cup of coffee."

"Actually, I'd love to freshen up."

"Absolutely. Let's take a break."

Rose stretched and headed out to the hallway and powder room. The sound of Lyon's voice made her halt in her tracks. Some instinct made her tiptoe over to an open door where she spied Lyon talking with his brother, Peter. She paused for a moment, not wanting to interrupt.

"Well, we've got a wedding coming up. Only the finest for the youngest son, of course! Seriously, Mom and Dad love Rose and can't wait to welcome her into the family. We're all excited. She's very special," said Peter, who was a taller, lighter-haired version of his younger brother. He paused and added, "Have you told her yet?"

"No," said Lyon, slumping down into his brown leather chair. "It never seems like the right time."

Rose gasped and stood rooted to the spot.

"I believe you owe her the truth before you get married," said Peter, staring at his brother intently. "When's the big day, by the way?"

"Right now, it's December 5, but Rose just told me she no longer wants a church wedding. She wants the marriage blessed."

"Aha!" said Peter. "She's perfect for you. She loves you, Lyon. And you don't want this to be an issue when the time comes—"

"I know, I know," snapped Lyon.

"Come on, I can't wait to beat you at tennis!" He added, "Rose needs to know that her Prince Charming has an inconsistent backhand!"

"I've got no intention of losing to you," said Lyon. "But I have no idea where my racket is."

Peter snickered. "This was worth the trip home!"

Backing away from the door in a panic, Rose bolted into the powder room, trying to stem her fear and insecurity. *What does Lyon need to tell me? Does it have something to do with Dominique? Did he cheat?* Her mind raced as she jumped to several different conclusions. Her hands shook as she took a hand towel and wiped her face. The serene white-flowered wallpaper was lost on her as she stared at her reflection. *Calm down*, she told herself. *I shouldn't have listened outside the door.*

She waited several minutes until she heard Faith calling her name. Taking a deep breath, Rose willed herself to present a normal demeanor and finish her meeting with Faith. It was probably something ridiculous, Rose decided, because she trusted Lyon completely.

They sailed through numerous other decisions until Faith exclaimed, "I think we have a Grand Slam tournament going on outside. Shall we go look?"

"Absolutely," replied Rose. "I can't remember the last time I saw Lyon play tennis. He works too hard. This is good for him."

"Not if he loses," said Faith with a wink.

Peter and Lyon's sweat-stained shirts gave away the entire story.

"Lyon!" cried Peter. "I haven't got all day. Are you so afraid of losing that you can't hit the ball?"

Lyon whacked the ball over the net, hard into the left-side corner.

Peter swung and missed. "Good shot," said Peter as he wound up to serve. He sent a powerful shot into the corner of the box. Lyon returned the ball by hitting it into the net.

Each point was long and hard as the game progressed. They were very evenly matched. As they played, their comments ranged from the ridiculous to more serious gibes.

"Look at what we have here," called Joseph. "It's almost like watching Nadal and Federer."

"Almost," called Lyon, wiping his sweaty brow.

Joseph's entrance signaled the need for a break. As was his usual custom, he came bearing a bottle of wine. Lyon and Peter looked at each other and laughed.

"I think some ice water might be a better option," said Peter, wiping his forehead.

"That's your mother's department," said Joseph. "A vintner is always on the job."

Lyon rolled his eyes and checked his watch. "We've been playing two hours. I think I'm done. I've got to shower."

"Great idea!" announced Rose, backing away from his sweaty embrace.

Joseph raised one eyebrow at Faith. "You both haven't stopped talking since you arrived! The whole event should be planned by now."

Faith winked at Rose in solidarity.

"And to think I missed the whole conversation," joked Lyon, grabbing a towel.

Faith poured them all some ice water, then ordered them to clean up.

"My boys need showers before lunch," said Faith. "Dare I ask who won?"

Lyon smirked. Peter said nothing. Everyone laughed.

Chapter 6

THE NIGHT WAS PLEASANTLY CRISP, calling Beatrice to sit under the stars in the restaurant's white tent with contrasting clear side panels. Candles and tiny flowering plants decorated the white linen tabletops. The outdoor space was full of animated guests enjoying wine and such traditional Italian fare as fettucine alfredo. A familiar melody of 1980s American music serenaded them from a nearby street band. Several tall space heaters made the outdoor room very inviting. As the waiter cleared the nearby table, the glasses and silverware clattered into a bin, which was almost her undoing. Already on edge at the thought of seeing Mike again, she hoped he would keep to their plan of meeting at the restaurant. There were a thousand reasons why this was a ludicrous idea, and yet here she was, taking a chance. Thanks to Chelsea's encouragement via text messages, she maintained her courage and waited for him to appear.

"Can I get you another drink?" the waiter asked. Beatrice declined and instead ordered a cup of coffee. It was after eleven o'clock, and she was going to give it another fifteen minutes.

Chelsea had bolted to a local nightclub with a larger group of friends. Her instant adoration of Vince was amusing, and if Beatrice knew her friend, she would hunt him down and find him tonight. Another half hour passed, and Beatrice wondered if she should give up and go home. After all, Mike could have forgotten about their encounter. *He has a legion of followers,* she thought. Sensing the angst of her waiter, she broke down and ordered a cheese platter and another glass of wine. If Mike didn't show up after she finished, then she would leave.

Not long after, Mike walked in, and she felt a surge of excitement. It was as if she were suspended in time the moment that Mike spotted her at their table. *He's looking for me,* she concluded, looking down at her new pleather black pants Chelsea had insisted she purchase. He made his way to the table but radiated anger. Beatrice's exultation transformed into anxiety when she observed the fury in his eyes. Never had she encountered such raw emotion. Mike was like a powder keg as he propelled himself into the seat across from her.

"Did you see what happened tonight?" he asked, removing his green skull cap before sitting down.

"I did," she replied calmly. "Who was that man?"

He ranted on about his rival, Vince, and how much he hated him. Mike despised the ground he walked on and hoped he would disappear. "He laughed at my work. He is a complete fool. How dare he show up and try to make fun of my mural."

The waiter arrived to take his order. He asked for red wine as he drummed his fingers on the table. "Forgive me," he offered, realizing that she had no background information on this argument. "You need to know that Vince is a street artist known for his creative drawings on social justice. He creates tables. You know, like a copycat of Leonardo's painting of the Last Supper. Vince uses this medium to ask social and cultural questions," he said with a frown.

"I think I know who you're talking about. His work isn't in your league," exclaimed Beatrice.

Her comment made Mike laugh aloud. "I knew I liked you," he said, raising his glass to toast her.

"What about these tables? I don't understand."

"I've seen him create street murals about who is invited to sit at the table. His drawings include a government table filled with all women, which made him famous. I think it was just a cheap trick to get attention."

"Seriously, you're so talented, Mike. You have nothing to worry about."

"Ahh, Beatrice, you calmed the beast in me," he joked. "Thank you, bellissima, for waiting for me. I ran late tonight."

Beatrice remained mesmerized by Mike's charisma, despite the torn clothing and unruly hair. "Forgive my ignorance, Mike, but how do you get permission to do art in public spaces?"

"I know people," he said with a wave of his hand.

"I thought you said you aren't a political artist."

"I didn't say one way or the other."

"The plot thickens," said Beatrice. "I noticed that you're creating something to the left of the mural. Are you willing to share your vision?"

Warming to his topic, Mike detailed how he wanted to juxtapose the just or Lady Justice with the forgotten members of society. His vision was brilliant in its simplicity, but he was earnest in his desire to educate people through his work.

"Look around you, Beatrice. We live in this beautiful city, and yet, there are too many homeless people. There is poverty. There is social injustice. It's an age-old problem that the rich get richer. I want my work to make people think. I want them to love the unlovable."

"You said you weren't at all religious and you had no allegiance to anyone?"

"That's correct."

"Well," she said, clearing her throat, "that is precisely what the teachings of Jesus ask us to do."

"Are you telling me that my concept is not original?" he asked, skirting the comment.

"I'm telling you that your work emanates meaning and a concern for others. That's all."

"Don't tell anyone that," he quipped. "It would ruin my reputation."

Beatrice couldn't help the pull of attraction. She wanted to dive into those intense eyes and know everything about him. It was strange, this connection and this feeling like she understood him in a way that others couldn't. At least, that was what she kept telling herself to rationalize the intensity of her emotions. She looked over as he carefully helped himself to a slice of cheese, sliding it onto a piece of warm bread. He was capable of good manners, she concluded, despite the unruly image he presented to everyone.

"When did you know you could draw?"

"I used to create cartoon characters and things on napkins when I was little. My father was in the military. He strongly disapproved of my drawings. It was always contentious." He seemed far away as he recounted his childhood. He added, "So, how do you say . . . I was *self-taught* until I went to college in the US where I received my first formal training. I'm not sure if they knew what to think of me when I attended studio classes."

"I'm sure they thought you were brilliant."

"Yes," he laughed. "They recognized that I had some God-given talent, but it was raw, and they tried to tame me."

"What happened?"

"I got kicked out of classes more times than I could count," he laughed, "but I did manage to graduate. And you? You said, you are a *conservationist.* You went to school for that, no doubt."

"Yes, I did a graduate program in New York to get my doctorate. Then I came to Rome and found a job. It's thrilling work. I consider it an honor to restore the paintings of the great masters. Have you ever worked on canvas?"

"No. I will not succumb to the whims of others who sacrifice creativity for money!" He slapped his hand down on the countertop, nearly breaking his wineglass.

Beatrice felt a bit uneasy, like she had asked the wrong question at the wrong time. She wanted to take the question back, and she wondered how she could be so stupid as to offend him. Her words came out too quickly. "I'm so sorry. I didn't mean to bring up something that upsets you."

"No, no. It's not you, bellissima. It's the concept, that's all. It's just that I've seen too many fellow artists sell out, and I don't want to be forced to do that. I like my life. It's always different and completely uncomplicated. I'm free to do what I want to do and not be encumbered by anything or anyone."

Another flag, thought Beatrice, ignoring the warning lights in her head. The waiter came over to take the check, which Beatrice would have happily paid, but Mike insisted that he take care of it.

"What about tomorrow night? Same time?" he asked.

"I've got an early-morning meeting on Monday. It would have to be—"

"No problem," he said. "We don't have to—"

Beatrice felt an almost physical pain run through her. "I'll make it work," she said, thinking that she had truly lost her mind.

***

Beatrice tossed and turned that night in a mix of anxiety and excitement. Something about Mike fascinated her. Perhaps having a private audience with a street artist of his stature made her feel important. After all, he had picked her to talk to about his work and share his life story. *He must feel the connection too,* she concluded.

Her mind whirled like a thoroughbred on a racetrack. She desperately needed a distraction from obsessing over Mike, so she headed to the Vatican to work in the lab even though it was only five in the morning. Cardinal Baglioni would want her to be completely prepared for their meeting tomorrow with Rose, and she decided to work on her presentation.

There was so much information to convey to the cardinal, Rose, and Lyon! The words *Cerca Trova* swam in her mind, as they substantiated the findings of Dr. Saunders. Could one singular phrase in two places reveal the hiding place of a lost Leonardo? After all, it was fate that Rose found the drawings in the wall of her apartment. She had proven to the cardinal that they were authentic and placed there hundreds of years ago. *There must be a link,* Beatrice concluded, as she made notes for her presentation.

She pondered the story of the lost Leonardo because she wanted to be as precise as possible about his feud with Michelangelo. Many called the lost pictures that decorated the council hall a moment of truth that declared the unofficial end of the Renaissance. Beatrice found the concept sad but ultimately forthright.

How could a conservator like Beatrice put what really happened in context for tomorrow's explosive meeting?

The contest between these two masters represented more than just an artistic rivalry. Each was determined to prove that he was the greatest artist of all time. Leonardo da Vinci was in his fifties, having just completed the famed *Mona Lisa*. He was a legend, and painting the Battle of Anghiari would cement his status, showing that Florence was an international power. On the other side, at just twenty-nine years old, Michelangelo was considered a prodigy of growing fame. He had already completed the *Pietà*, which was revered in St. Peter's in Rome, Italy.

The assignment was clear—to create the greatest masterpiece ever made to glorify battle.

No one really knew what happened. Rumors had swirled for five hundred years. The historical facts all pointed to a distinct possibility that a lost Leonardo was hidden behind the wall, covered by another Renaissance painting. Beatrice was determined to find out whether this myth was true.

Beatrice paced the room, imagining Leonardo's soft and shadowy figures in heated contention. This painting would have been massive in scale, and his vision would ignite the fires of freedom and valor in men and women. A painting by Reubens taken from an earlier copy of Leonardo's brought the loss into perspective and could be viewed at the Louvre.

After hours of refining her thoughts, Beatrice leaned back in her chair and stretched. A text message from Chelsea caught her eye. Scanning its contents, Beatrice noted that Chelsea found Vince last night and wanted to see him again. *I'm not sure he feels the same way about me,* she added with several sad emojis.

It occurred to Beatrice that she didn't have any way of communicating with Mike. *Maybe he doesn't have a cell phone,* she thought. It would be just her luck that he was a true artist who didn't believe in technology. She realized that he could disappear just as easily as he appeared, which made her heart hurt.

There was no question in her mind that he was a genius who adhered to none of the norms of society; there was a high price to pay to pursue his art, which didn't bother him. Could she handle the potential chaos that he might bring into her life?

Chapter 7

THEY CHECKED IN TO THE HOTEL SPLENDIDE in Rome as "Mr. and Mrs.," which was sublime for Rose, who held Lyon's hand tightly as they headed to their suite. The concierge told them about the rooftop café that offered a spectacular view of the city. As they made their way through the lobby, she admired the stunning chandeliers, traditional stone fireplace, gold sofas, and landscape art on the walls. Her heart was full at the thought of having Lyon all to herself for the next twenty-four hours. As if sensing her thoughts, he leaned down and kissed her forehead tenderly. The promise of a romantic evening hung in the air as they savored being together.

The bellman interrupted their moment with his request to place their bags on his luggage cart. Rose went on ahead, and they took the elevator up to the twelfth-floor suite.

"This is gorgeous," said Rose, admiring the plush blue sofa with the coordinating damask-patterned armchairs. A welcome tray of fresh fruit and nuts were perched on a white marble coffee table. Rose put down her handbag to admire the view, observing white tents in the marketplace and a hooded statue. As she wondered what the tents held inside, a knock on the door interrupted her reverie.

The bellman took her hanging bag and put it away in the closet. Just as Lyon was giving him a tip, Rose asked, "What is that hooded statue in the center of the square?"

"Oh, yes, madame, that's Giordano Bruno. He was a philosopher, mathematician and scientist who was burned at the stake on that very spot."

"That's not very uplifting," said Rose, shaking off the ominous sign.

"No, but it is there because it acts as a landmark to free thought and science."

"Well, that's better," said Rose, reaching for the orange nested in the fruit tray on the table. Just as she was about to settle into a cozy armchair, Lyon cleared his throat.

"How about a walk to the Spanish Steps?"

"Okay," said Rose, wondering why they weren't going to wander around downstairs. "It'll be good to stretch our legs after the ride. Besides, I'd love to see some of those beautiful shops." She winked. "Who can resist Armani, Prada, or Gucci all located within blocks of each other?"

"That's exactly what I had in mind," he said wryly.

"Is everything alright?" asked Rose, thinking about his earlier conversation with Peter.

"Absolutely," he replied, grabbing the room key and his sunglasses. "I'd rather walk and talk. I just remembered that we could take a stroll through the Borghese gardens."

"Lovely," she replied, trying to hide her anxiety. She tried to remain calm but knew something was wrong; her stomach felt invaded by an army of butterflies.

While Florence captured her heart, Rome delighted Rose with its rich history. Beatrice had been an integral part of sharing stories with her about the ancient Romans, which brought everything to life. She once compared Rome to a lasagna with its layers upon layers of complicated history spanning nearly ten thousand years.

As they made their way through the busy streets to the Spanish Steps, Rose admired the fountain at the bottom, filled with people young and old enjoying its centuries-old beauty. Rose eyed a group of American teenagers with a guide. It brought back a rush of memories of her students and how much she missed them; her former job as a teacher seemed like a lifetime ago. The conversation seemed mundane as she and Lyon discussed the mild temperatures, the freshly cleaned streets, and the store window with the blue-and-yellow-patterned ceramic plates.

They broke apart as they made their way up to the top, weaving in and out to avoid the plethora of tourists. Rose looked down at the throngs of people, observing an elderly couple helping each other along. They were well dressed and clearly in sync with each other. Rose wanted to someday know the value of a lifetime together. As if he were a mind reader, Lyon reached for her so that they clasped hands again.

The Villa Borghese park on Pincio Hill, with its green meadows, fountains, and ancient statues, had been part of an estate. The gardens were converted to English style in the seventeenth century, then became a public park in 1903. It was an ideal place to escape city life. Expansive gardens lined with ancient monuments always inspired Rose to think about the people who came before them.

Lyon explained, "The Galleria Borghese has one of the largest art collections in the world and was once owned by Cardinal Scipione Borghese. And these grounds have become one of the most beautiful public parks in Rome. It's my favorite place to visit whenever I'm here."

"This is breathtaking. Look at all this green space." She pointed to an ancient Roman statue. "And the history is so alive here." She looked over at him, but his somber expression caught her off guard.

"Lyon, you look so serious all of the sudden. What's going on?"

"Rose, I'm afraid I haven't been completely honest with you, and—"

"Wait. What?" She couldn't contain the rush of anxiety that flooded to the surface. "What do you mean you haven't been honest?" The sound of her own voice seemed unfamiliar. Rose thought she might be physically ill. She paused and willed herself to be patient and let him speak.

"This is not easy for me." He paused.

"Go on," said Rose.

"You know how I feel about you. That will never change, and you've made me a better man. Before I met you, I was reckless and arrogant in my endeavors. I know it was a long time ago, but you need to know something about me."

They took a seat on a nearby bench.

"I was in a motorcycle accident in college. I was very lucky, but, well, I may have sustained some permanent damage." Lyon ran his hand through his hair, a nervous gesture that was completely out of character.

"You were in an accident? I'm so sorry. Why didn't you tell me?"

"I haven't ever really talked about it all these years. I don't know why. Maybe I was embarrassed, but Peter told me to get it out in the open." He paused. "Among other reasons, he encouraged me to talk about the incident."

"So, what did he want you to tell me?"

He took a deep breath and cleared his throat. "Rose, I'm not sure I can father children."

His words reverberated. In that moment, she felt plunged into a dark underground cave with no way out. Rose tried to quell the pain in her gut. "What?" She paused to catch her breath. "I'm not sure I'm understanding you correctly."

"I had to have surgery because I sustained serious injuries to my pelvis."

"I don't know what to say. I'm just so shocked right now." She covered her face with her hands. It felt like her dreams of a family had been smashed. Time seemed to stand still as she processed the enormity of his confession. Images of babies filled her head as she couldn't fathom not having children. He reached for her, but she pushed his hand away, feeling too upset to accept his comfort. The secret shattered something inside her. As much as she wanted to reassure him, her feelings wouldn't let her brush off the news. Pulling herself together, Rose exhaled. "That's a huge issue to have kept from me." Several tears welled. "Are you sure?"

"The doctors report was inconclusive."

"The accident was almost fifteen years ago. Have you gotten checked since then?"

"No."

"I'm really having trouble processing this just three months before our wedding." She tried to calm her pounding heart. "Don't you think we should have discussed this before we got engaged?"

"That's exactly what I was afraid you'd say."

"How else am I supposed to react? You kept a major secret from me and led me to believe that you wanted a family."

"I do want a family. You know that."

"We've discussed having children, and not once did you give any indication that there could be a problem." After a pause she added, "So essentially, you've lied to me throughout our entire relationship!"

"What's that supposed to mean?" He stared at her, upset by her accusations. "It wasn't like that at all. I'm not sure that I gave it enough serious consideration. I swear that's the truth and, in hindsight, very thoughtless of me. After the accident happened, I blocked it all from my mind and refused to deal with the consequences. Look, I just told you something very personal about my life. Where's the love and support about working through this together?"

"I WANT TO KNOW," she shouted, "IF YOU TOLD YOUR EX ABOUT THIS."

An older man in a green jacket slowed his pace to gape at them, but Lyon waved him away. "It wasn't necessary. She is married, so the issue of a family was not part of our relationship. Now that I think about it, I probably stayed with her so I didn't have to confront my own fears."

"You should have trusted my feelings for you," said Rose, wiping another round of tears from her cheeks. "When was the last time you saw Dominique?"

"A few weeks ago. We talked about a real estate issue."

"You just lied to me again, Lyon. I saw you walking in the park with her on Saturday afternoon."

Silence.

"Rose, I didn't mean to . . . you know how I feel about you, about us." His eyes became moist.

"I don't trust you anymore, Lyon. The way I see it, every time we discussed children and you didn't tell me the truth, it was all a lie." She took a deep breath. "There were a hundred different ways we could have worked together to address this issue, but you chose not to confide in me, and I resent it."

"I'm sorry," he said quietly.

"I'm so angry that I don't really want to be near you right now. I should go walk before I say something I'll regret."

Their eyes met and Rose dug in. The hurt in his eyes was almost her undoing, but she couldn't let this go. He had just bald-face lied to her, and these issues threatened their future.

"Where are you going?"

"I don't know, but I need time."

"How much time?"

"I can't answer that right now." Seeing his pained expression, Rose lowered her voice. "I'm hurt, angry, and disappointed. I think you should head back to Florence tonight. I will do the meeting tomorrow morning and get home on my own time."

"Come on, Rose," he said angrily. "You can't do this to us! Do you have any idea how hard it was for me to tell you the truth?"

"You act like it's a simple matter. It's not! You should have known better. This is a big issue, and it's going to take time to work through it. We can't just snap our fingers and come up with a solution."

"What are you talking about?"

"We need to see doctors and get you checked again. We need to figure out a backup plan. Do we adopt children? Do we pick a donor? How is this all going to work? I am very clear that I want children. I mean, haven't you considered any of these possibilities?"

"All I know is that I love you and want to marry you and we will work the rest of it out."

"It's not that simple, Lyon! Am I going to assume you're going to find Dominque every time we have a fight?"

"That's not fair. She wanted to talk to me about business. That's all."

"Then why didn't you tell me?"

"I don't know," he replied.

"Bad answer," she exclaimed. "Now, I'm going for a walk."

"Fine," he snapped. "I'll be gone from the hotel when you get back."

"Fine," she shot back.

"Thanks for being so understanding," he said, walking away.

"You have only yourself to blame on that end." She spun around and walked in the other direction. She was so upset she could barely see straight. How could he keep such a major issue from her?

Rose wandered the streets of Rome, stewing and hurt. He should have told her sooner, but even if he had, the outcome might be the same. The real question she had to ask herself was did she love him enough to come to terms with not having a child of their own? Her eyes blurred with tears again. *It's not fair,* she thought. And she couldn't stand the thought of Dominique near him. Rage bubbled over, but she willed herself to calm down. Where were her parents when she needed them? Her father was in Heaven, and this was not something she could discuss with her mother. Her brother, Jack, came to mind, but he was an ocean away.

In search of comfort, she dialed Beatrice. Rose refused to dump her problems on her friend, again, so she did her best to sound normal. It was such a relief when she picked up.

"Hi. I'm here," said Rose, wiping her eyes.

"Fantastic. I've been in the lab most of today and can't wait for our meeting tomorrow!"

"Can you give me a hint?"

"How about we wait until tomorrow when the cardinal can hear it too? He's been after me to give him some clues and I've refused." She paused. "Is Lyon with you?"

"Actually no." Rose thought quickly. "He had a work commitment, so I'm not sure if he can make it. Right now, it's just me."

"Well then, how about we grab something to eat? I'm starving."

"That would be wonderful. When and where?"

"Let's say seven, and I want you to stop by and watch this street artist with me. I'm captivated by his work. We can meet out front of Clementina, and I'll walk with you to see him."

"Perfect," said Rose, as she checked her phone and wondered whether Lyon had left.

For the first time in a long time, an image of her ex, Ben Pierce, came to mind as Rose walked. He had a beautiful little girl named Emily, whom Rose adored. They always had chemistry. Rose had nearly married him a year ago. What if he had been trying to use his business prowess to help guide her and not harm her? They had been great together until she found those drawings.

Rose couldn't help the onslaught of memories of what broke them apart. The hidden drawings were special, and something that could have only been created by a master of the Renaissance. Ben immediately grasped that the images were a money-making option. That they could be sold to the highest bidder for a fortune. Rose felt it was her duty to protect those images from the past and return them to their rightful place in the Vatican. Their difference of opinion drove a wedge between them. When Ben took matters into his own hands, Rose felt she could no long trust him. That being said, he was a highly successful businessman. Maybe she could have made more money to use for philanthropic purposes. A small voice inside her mind told her she was irrational considering Ben as a viable alternative to Lyon.

***

Thanks to the GPS on her cell phone, she found Clementina in the Prati neighborhood easily. Once inside, the hanging wooden love seat caught her eye. A couple held hands. They leaned into each other, laughing, and swaying gently in the window. Rose willed herself to be happy for them.

When she saw Beatrice, the first thing Rose noticed was that her friend seemed to sparkle from within. She had never seen her so radiant. Despite her anguish, Rose was happy for her and thrilled to have this one-on-one time with her close friend. With discipline born of self-preservation, she pushed aside her own awkward circumstances to connect. They embraced heartily and exchanged pleasantries. In a moment of weakness, Rose looked down at her phone, noticing that Lyon had not tried to call. Why would he? They were on two separate planes right now. Girl time was just what she needed.

Rose's stomach was in knots, but she managed to share a white cheese pizza with buffalo mozzarella and tomatoes without Beatrice noticing anything was amiss. She picked at the savory chickpea salad, pretending to enjoy it. The wine tasted bittersweet as this was not the evening that she had planned. Tears threatened, but she pushed them back. It was on the tip of her tongue to ask her to be in the wedding, but she refrained. Things with Lyon were too problematic, and she would have enough of a mess to unravel if they called off the wedding. The thought triggered another wave of anxiety.

"Hey," said Beatrice. "I'm so glad that you're here. It's been ages since we spent time together."

"I feel the same way. I'm glad this worked out and you were free."

"Did you take the train?"

Rose didn't want to admit that Lyon had driven her and they were fighting, so she merely nodded.

They made their way outside and took a leisurely stroll to see the street art that Beatrice had described as "magnificent" and "breathtaking." Rose thought such a description truly striking, and she was beyond curious. There was clearly something more to this story, and it was a relief to have something else to command her attention. The night had brought on a slight chill, and Rose tried not to think that she was supposed to be sharing a romantic evening with Lyon. He had planned everything, and a surge of disappointment bolted through her.

A short time later, they walked along Via Cardinal Agliardi. A crowd was forming as spotlights illuminated the face of an ethereal woman who seemed to come alive before their very eyes. Rose cocked her head to one side, recognizing Lady Justice rising into the night.

The raw power of the mural struck, and Rose realized that she was standing in front of something special. Too many heads blocked the artwork, so she and Beatrice elbowed their way through the crowd.

"What do you think?" asked Beatrice.

"He's extremely talented. The mural has a way of drawing you in," said Rose as she studied the left corner filled with black and gray swirls.

"His name is Mike, and we met on Friday night. I'm in love," she blurted, then quickly corrected herself. "I meant, I'm in love with his work."

Rose studied her friend. "Have you met him?"

"I was waiting to tell you. We met for a glass of wine after he finished these past two nights. I've never talked with anyone like him. He's so incredibly passionate about life and his art. It's like being in the presence of a force of nature."

Rose said, "That's exciting! Where's he from?"

"He has an American father and an Italian mother but says he belongs to no one affiliation. He likes to travel to various places and create these inspirational murals."

"Why Rome?"

"Why not Rome? So many master artisans have lived and painted here."

They were rooted to the spot as if something magical were occurring. Rose observed Beatrice's look of adoration while she watched him. She looked over at the mural again, sensing its power to make people feel his message. The scales were slightly tipped one way, and the left corner images emanated anger and hate. At that moment, her own anger at Lyon returned, but she willed herself to drop it.

Mike took a break to drink from a thermos. His eyes scanned the crowd and landed on Beatrice. Her face lit up as she saw him. Rose wanted to meet the man who had ignited this kind of response from the usually introverted and analytical Beatrice. Mike made his way over, and Beatrice introduced them. He smiled politely at Rose and took off his skull cap, revealing his dark hair.

"Hello," said Rose. "Your work is so powerful. I feel like the lady is going to take flight and reign over the entire city."

"You flatter me too much," said Mike, looking at his feet in embarrassment. Rose found his response endearing.

"Rose is an artist too," announced Beatrice.

"Oh no!" said Rose, cheeks warming. "Not at your level. This work is in another league."

"You are too kind. Perhaps we can all have a cup of coffee later."

"That would be wonderful," said Beatrice, grinning widely.

When he departed to climb back up on the scaffolding, Beatrice turned to Rose.

"Can you stay for a while longer? If not, I completely understand."

Rose felt torn between pretending nothing was wrong and checking in with Lyon. They had never had such an explosive parting. "I'll stay and watch for another hour, but it's getting kind of late, so I think I'll let the two of you meet later."

"Sure," Beatrice said.

Rose watched Mike begin work on the lower right-hand corner of the mural. It was dark and hard to see in places, but it was clear that he had a vision which was coming to life right before their eyes. His dexterity was remarkable, and Rose was, in all honesty, a little bit envious of his natural talent. She could have worked for months to try to get even one of those panels, and he was able to execute the image so easily to her discerning eye. She asked, "Did he go to school to learn?"

"He said he is self-taught but attended college in the States."

"Watching his process makes me wonder if I shouldn't go back to teaching," Rose offered dryly.

"I want to make sure the cardinal sees his work. There is something really compelling about his images."

"I agree."

An hour passed and then another. Rose shivered in the cold, but she could tell Beatrice was not going to leave. She looked again at the image Mike was creating, realizing that it was a group of children. Her heart sank, and a tear formed in her eye.

"Oh my!" said Beatrice. "You see it too."

Rose got ahold of herself and said, "Excuse me?"

"The children in the mural. They must represent hope for the future."

Rose felt a wave of sadness creep into her heart. "What a beautiful reference for the mural. I'm not sure I understand it completely yet."

"I'm not sure I do either," said Beatrice. "It looks to me like he is painting a balancing of the scales. He has portrayed a metaphorical image of hopelessness and anger on the left with the innocence of children on the right."

"You see how the scales are tipped one way, don't you?" said Rose, pointing to the left.

"No," said Beatrice. "You are wrong. The scales are tipped to the right."

Rose rubbed her eyes and looked again. "I think I am correct."

"Do you think he's created an optical illusion?"

"I have no idea! Either that or I have become completely cynical," she joked. "I'll have to come back and see this in the morning."

"This is so exciting. It could look completely different in daylight."

"I hope so," she said. "I would love to be wrong."

"I'm not sure of his entire meaning yet, but he definitely wants people to think about fairness. He has the top right and left panels to paint, so I wonder where he is headed or if he's done?"

Fairness. The word reverberated in her head. Rose wondered if she went forward and married Lyon, would she ultimately resent not having children with him? Shifting her attention back to Beatrice, she responded, "You'll have to ask Mike tonight and let me know tomorrow morning."

"Yes, I'll let you know. . . Is everything okay? You seem a bit out of sorts."

"Oh no. Everything is great. Couldn't be better," she said, turning away to hide her emotions. "I'm ready to have more insight into Michelangelo and Leonardo, whom I've avoided talking about all night so as not to tempt you."

"That's why you're such a good friend," said Beatrice warmly. "Be ready to dive into the past because it's endlessly interesting."

Rose smiled genuinely for the first time all night. "I'm ready to uncover another mystery."

"So am I," said Beatrice, staring at Mike. "He's an enigma."

"You have a tender spot for genius," said Rose with a wink.

"Am I crazy?" asked Beatrice with a helpless expression.

"Absolutely, but you have to ask yourself, is he worth it?"

Rose headed back to the hotel and checked her phone for messages. Lyon was gone.

Chapter 8

THE HOURS HAD MELTED AWAY, and after Mike finished painting, they had ended up at Beatrice's. She admired the golden light emanating from the fireplace in her apartment, amazed at how it transformed the space into a cozy oasis. Mike had expertly taken her meager supply of wood from the large dark wicker basket and added newspapers to create a roaring flame. She shifted comfortably on her leather sofa and sipped another cup of coffee. For once, she hadn't planned her meals for the week, gone over her work checklist, or watched a Sunday-night movie alone. Now, even though it was well past midnight, she didn't want to stop talking to the most fascinating man she had ever met.

"I enjoyed meeting your friend," said Mike, sipping his espresso to warm up. "What was her name again?"

"Yes, it's Rose, and she's wonderful. She bought an apartment in Florence last year. She wanted me to tell you how much she loved the mural. That you've created something special."

"Thank you," said Mike, averting his gaze. "I always feel a little embarrassed with compliments."

"It's high praise indeed because Rose is passionate about the life and works of Michelangelo. It was one of the reasons that she wanted to live in Italy."

"I share her passion for the great Michelangelo. His work has inspired generations of artists. Did you know that he never signed any of his work after he became enraged when someone attributed his masterpiece, the *Pietà*, to someone else? As I recall, Michelangelo put his signature across the sash on Mary's chest. He later regretted his actions and vowed never to sign any of his work again."

"Yes, that story is legendary. After that, the Great One put his own face in his work rather than signing it." Beatrice thought for a moment. "For example, I know in the Sistine Chapel, he put his face in the panel of the *Last Judgement*. St. Bartholomew is shown holding a piece of flayed skin and it appears to be a likeness to Michelangelo. He's also appeared in a crowd scene in a fresco with St. Peter. Why don't you consider doing something like that?"

"What?" Mike asked sharply.

The abrupt change in his mood was unnerving. "I thought," she said, swallowing hard, "that it might be an interesting way to take credit for your work."

"And become the laughingstock of all Italy? Why would I do that?"

Beatrice quickly added, "It was just an idea."

"A very ludicrous one." He stood. "It's getting late, and you have to work tomorrow."

"You don't need to go. Sorry I mentioned it. I didn't mean to upset you. I'm used to being alone with my thoughts. I've never connected with anyone this way."

He relented. "Beatrice, I'm not an easy man, nor will I ever be domesticated." He laughed at himself. "Is that even a word?"

His humor broke the sudden tension in the room.

"Will I see you again?"

"I don't know. I make decisions on a daily basis." They embraced, and he left her apartment, seemingly taking the air out of the room.

"I understand," she said sadly as she watched him go. His mood swings were a concern, but not enough to prevent her from wanting to see him again. *Why did I make such a ridiculous suggestion?*

Beatrice tossed and turned until the alarm woke her back up. Thinking that she would stifle it, she realized that Rose had come all the way to Rome to hear about her findings. The thrill of the meeting was tempered by her wondering if she would see Mike again. Pushing her melancholy aside, she took care in her appearance, putting on her best navy suit jacket and pants.

Today, her findings could shed light on a lost puzzle.

As Beatrice made her way to Vatican City, she observed two Swiss Guards in conversation. She was struck by their colorful uniforms, which reflected the colors of the ruling Medici family from five hundred years ago—red, dark blue, and yellow. The guards were there for the protection of the pope, and proudly wore insignia from the days of Michelangelo. Beatrice recalled a rumor that the great Michelangelo was responsible for the design of the uniform. She made a mental note to tell Rose about the myth.

The walk to the lab cleared her head as she made her way through a special underground corridor whose ceiling was decorated with frescoes in what they call the "grotesques" style. Beatrice recalled the story from the early fifteenth century when a young Roman fell into the crevice of the Colle Oppio and found himself in a grotto covered with painted scenes. It was emperor Nero's lavish palace known as the Golden House that he had built between 64 and 68 AD. Several young Renaissance artists soon rushed to the caves to see for themselves these new and amazing paintings. The great Michelangelo and Raphael were in that group. This type of décor became wildly fashionable as it appeared all over the walls of the Vatican as well as palaces and villas in the city of Rome.

The lab was quiet. Dropping her tote bag on a chair, she found the kitchen and poured herself a cup of smoky brew. This morning ritual awakened her, providing a sense of mundane. Her mind ticked through the appropriate points as she sifted through the information in her head. Back at her desk, she scribbled some final notes in the margins of her presentation. When Rose appeared in her office door, Beatrice thought her smile seemed strained, but she didn't comment.

"Good morning," she said warmly. "The cardinal will be down shortly."

"Wonderful," said Rose, taking a sip of coffee. "I must say that you've had me in suspense these last few days."

"For good reason."

The cardinal arrived, looking dignified in his scarlet robes; he was not a tall man, and yet his presence remained distinguished thanks to his regal bearing and thick white hair. He gave Rose a warm embrace. They headed to the conference room so Beatrice could use the video projector. It was a small and windowless room with a mahogany conference table surrounded by black leather chairs.

When they had taken their seats, the cardinal turned to Rose. "She's kept me in suspense as well."

"You know how I feel about Michelangelo, but it was surprising to hear that Leonardo could have a place in my find."

Beatrice stood at the front of the room so she could rely on her highlighter.

"Let me start at the beginning. In 1503, the great Leonardo da Vinci was at the pinnacle of his fame in Italy and around the world. He was commissioned to paint a large-scale and complex depiction of the Battle of Anghiari on one wall of the Salone dei Cinquecento in the Palazzo Vecchio. The actual Battle of Anghiari took place during the Wars of Lombardy in which the Florentines reigned victorious over the Milanese. It was supposed to be one of the finest battle scenes of all time and to honor the Florentine Republic. Leonardo worked to create a sprawling *cartoon*, the name for an ancient preliminary drawing, that shows swirling figures engaged in warfare."

Beatrice put up a slide that showed a circle of men on horseback, tense and ready for action. The revolving figures and glares were extraordinary in their intensity. "Some scholars have called this Leonardo cartoon the highest form of art for the world and believe it could be a tool to inspire other artists."

Rose asked, "I don't understand. How do you have a copy of this image if it has all been lost?"

"Given the genius of the original, there have been many duplicates made by artists, and this one is attributed to another artist and currently hangs in the Louvre in Paris."

"Is it possible to see it in person?"

"Absolutely," said Beatrice.

"Paris is always a good idea," said Rose, her face finally brightening. "Tell us more about what happened."

Beatrice explained how Leonardo tried a new way of mixing the paint, which proved difficult and frustrated his efforts. Expectations ran high for this painting, which was destined to be the next Renaissance masterpiece.

"At the same time, you have the great Michelangelo, who was also commissioned in direct competition with Leonardo to paint the Battle of Cascina. He was a younger prodigy, and his fame was on the rise as well, having created the *Pietà* and the *David*. Michelangelo also accepted a commission and worked furiously on a cartoon to out-achieve his older rival. According to historic records, his battle scenes were every bit as glorious as Leonardo's, though he never finished the project because he was called to Rome to work on the pope's tomb."

Beatrice paused for emphasis. "Fast-forward to Rose's discovery of three drawings in the wall of her apartment." She put up a slide of a young man dressed in nobleman's clothes and pointed to what looked like a dark stain on the far left. "This is what we first observed when you brought us the drawings. They were aged and dirty with paper that could crumble. Frankly, I didn't expect to find anything."

"Go on," said the cardinal. He leaned forward, and the gold embroidery on his white robes caught the light.

"I used a new solution to clean the area, which took weeks to painstakingly uncover what appears to be a flag with the words *Cerca Trova*. This phrase can be translated to mean 'those who seek shall find.'"

"What does that mean?"

"I think it's a clue. We assumed all the drawings that Rose originally found were sketched by Michelangelo. But we also know that Michelangelo hated Leonardo da Vinci. My theory is that the drawings in Rose's discovery were put in the wall by someone connected to both artists."

"How could we possibly figure out who that would be?"

"We've all accepted at this point that we may never know exactly what happened. My theory is that it was someone in the artistic circle of the late artist Giorgio Vasari, who was the most prominent historian of that time. He was the one who recorded the animosity between Leonardo and Michelangelo. His descriptions are the best-known insights we have into both men. Vasari was also a successful artist in his own right, sculptor *and* the man commissioned in the 1550s to paint over the Leonardo da Vinci. I believe that someone in his circle, perhaps a family member or close friend, knew these secrets and hid them."

"Fascinating," said Rose. "Why do you think this message is relevant to a lost Leonardo?"

"We have to be willing to accept that the drawings in Rose's original discovery may not have been all done by Michelangelo. There is a possibility that another artist could have been involved. Or I think the markings on the paper that I found were put there by someone who revered both artists and wanted to save a piece of history."

"So, you're saying that Vasari or one of his family members could have been the ones to hide the drawings Rose found," said the cardinal.

"Yes, it would make sense, and this new information follows my theory. Vasari was a historian, so it would lend credibility to the fact that this is, in fact, a clue." She put up another slide. "By way of background information, Giorgio Vasari was born in 1511 in a town called Arezzo in central Italy. He was apprenticed at an early age to Michelangelo in Florence. When he was young, he studied with members of the Medici family and established relationships with the ruling class of Florence.

"A noted architect, he designed the Uffizi Palace and was a major force in founding the Florentine Academy of Design, to name a few of his accomplishments. In the mid 1550s, Giorgio Vasari was commissioned to paint the *Sala Grande* in the Palazzo Vecchio. In short, this noted architect was asked to paint over the unfinished Leonardo. Rumors have said that he was so in awe of the great Leonardo da Vinci that he never would have torn down his painting nor painted over it. Instead, he put up another wall in front of it to hide Leonardo's battle scene, thus creating one of the greatest art mysteries of all time."

The cardinal pointed to the slide. "Given Vasari's architectural skills, the creation of a new wall makes complete sense to me."

"Me too," said Rose.

Beatrice exclaimed, "So, here's the linchpin. There is a scientist and scholar named Dr. Edwin Saunders. He's Harvard educated and a highly respected leader in the search for answers to this mystery."

"Excuse me?" said Rose. "Did you say Dr. Edwin Saunders?"

"Yes, he has led the charge to finding the lost Leonardo for the last thirty-plus years."

"You're not going to believe this, but I met him in the council hall," exclaimed Rose.

"That's rather fortuitous," Beatrice said. "Saunders has been on a quest to find what many believe would be the most groundbreaking art find of this century!"

"Let me get this straight," said Rose. "You believe my discovery gives us a clue to a hidden wall painted by Leonardo?"

"I think it's highly possible," agreed Beatrice. "In my mind, it confirms the message that's on the Vasari painting in the Palazzo Vecchio."

"That's thrilling," said Rose. "Beatrice, it was such a strange feeling being in the hall and wondering if there was a secret buried in the walls."

"You and hundreds of scholars and scientists have pondered this same question. So many theories exist, and there are a wide range of political and art opinions on this issue."

"It would seem everyone has an opinion," said the cardinal.

He clasped his hands. "Again, much of the evidence has been inconclusive."

"Until now," said Beatrice, moving to the next slide. "This find from five hundred years ago could substantiate the theory that there is a lost Leonardo behind the wall." She put up another visual and they all gasped.

"Look at this image of a flag that matches the one Dr. Saunders found at the top of the Vasari mural. This supports the theory that Vasari built a false wall in front of the Leonardo to save the work for future generations."

"When did Dr. Saunders do this research?" said Rose.

"In 2012, Dr. Saunders received permission to scan the wall with high-frequency radar. The scanning revealed a hidden space."

"It was all over the news," said the cardinal. "Both local and international."

"He planned to drill half-inch holes in the work approximately thirty to forty feet aboveground," said Beatrice.

The cardinal added, "When the story broke, art historians were outraged that a scientist would possibly ruin a magnificent and historic painting by Vasari."

"Then what happened?" asked Rose.

"The museum curators permitted him to drill in existing cracks and restored sections of the painting. That's when Saunders's team, in fact, found the hollow space giving credence to the mythical wall that had been whispered about for centuries."

This was all a conservator's dream. Momentarily overwhelmed, Beatrice paused to take a sip of her water. She was so in the present moment and continued. "They inserted an endoscopic camera into the void of rough masonry, and also observed grit in the space. Dr. Saunders's team found that the results suggested it contained traces of black pigment. The professor believed the pigments were similar to those found in the brown glazes used by Leonardo in his *Mona Lisa* and *St. John the Baptist*. In addition, the team also pulled red flakes from inside the wall, which was consistent with the theory that Leonardo had used that pigment to paint the battle scene."

The cardinal asked, "What happened next?"

"The professor's exploration was completely shut down for political and artistic reasons."

Rose's eyes grew wide. "If the flag in the drawing supports the professor's theory, could they possibly open the case back up again?"

"Yes, I would like to think so. Dr. Saunders has been trying for years to get permission to put his cameras back behind the wall."

"Beatrice, your hypothesis has merit, but this is all very circumstantial," said the cardinal. "And I'm certain that it could also cause a firestorm of controversy."

Beatrice cleared her throat. "But it could also lead to one of the greatest arts finds of the century."

The cardinal shook his head, taking it all in. "I find it fascinating that you met him this past week."

"He was very helpful to me. I actually got his card."

"We need to consider the impact of this information before we do anything," said the cardinal. "This is quite a unique situation. As a matter of fact, I worry that this information in the wrong hands could be disastrous."

"What do you mean?" asked Beatrice.

"We have to consider all of the possibilities," said the cardinal. "First of all, let's consider that this discovery supports Dr. Saunders's theory, and he gets permission to put his cameras behind the wall. If the lost Leonardo is there, how does this whole thing play out between the government, his team, and art history scholars? It's a huge conundrum!"

Rose pondered the issue. "How about assembling a team to respectfully remove the Vasari wall?"

"The wall is something like twenty feet high, so it would be a major operation to take out that wall to see what's behind it," offered Beatrice.

"My concern is that the person who benefits the most from our discovery would be Dr. Saunders, and that worries me."

"But it's a national treasure," argued Beatrice.

"I agree," said Rose. "It would be the biggest find in this century if this clue is correct."

"It's also a potential multimillion-dollar powder keg!" exclaimed the cardinal. "There would be so many competing groups to claim victory that it makes my head spin." He added, "That being said, it could also be a complete disaster if there is nothing there and a valuable Vasari painting was destroyed in the process. Let's not forget about the architecture of the Hall of the Five Hundred. It's complicated."

"I agree," said Rose, who stood. "It seems like we need more information on Saunders and his team." She added, "I would be happy to contact him and talk about his journey."

"But you must not reveal anything," warned the cardinal.

"You have my word," said Rose. She paused to consider all the information she had just learned and wondered if the find was a curse or a blessing.

"Excellent job as usual, Beatrice," said the cardinal. "Your research and analysis could not have been more clearly presented and explained."

"Thank you, Cardinal," said Beatrice, feeling relieved and proud that all the hours of seclusion and research paid off.

"Yes, Beatrice," said Rose. "You're so exceptional. I can't believe you went on that hunt based solely on your intuition! What a compelling piece of information."

"Thank you, Rose. You really did have quite the find! We need to unravel this story and decide how best to proceed. That's going to be up to the cardinal."

"There are pros and cons to getting this information out, as we learned in our last discovery. What do you think, Rose?"

She pondered his question for a moment. "I'd like to think that it was meant to be revealed, but this is a hard call."

"I think we all have a lot to process," said the cardinal. "Let's take a break for now and plan to meet again after Rose talks with Dr. Saunders."

Beatrice turned off the computer and gathered her presentation materials. Rose said, "That really was amazing. I'm not sure I need to race back to Florence just yet. Perhaps we could grab dinner sometime this week?"

"I'd love that," said Beatrice. She shook her head sadly. "Looks like I'll have nothing but free time on my hands. I'm not sure if I'll ever see Mike again." She went on to explain what happened and how she had inadvertently offended him by suggesting he put his face in his own work.

"You don't know if that's true," offered Rose. "I believe in fate."

"You and Lyon are a great example of that."

"Are we?" said Rose, trying not to betray her emotions.

"I've always thought that you're the perfect couple."

Rose smiled to acknowledge the compliment. "No relationship is perfect. I'd like to think that we're all on a journey to understand God's plan for us." Rose thought for a minute. "I didn't want to say anything, but Lyon and I are at odds right now."

"Do you want to talk about it?"

"I've got more thinking to do, so now is not the time, but thank you for asking," said Rose. "More importantly, we have another art mystery to solve. I'm going to contact Dr. Saunders and request a meeting. I'll keep you posted."

Beatrice smiled and waved goodbye. She called, "*Cerca Trova.*"

"*Cerca Trova,*" replied Rose. "Onward."

Chapter 9

ROSE MADE HER WAY back to the hotel, excited about Beatrice's theory and a possible new art discovery. A wave of sadness washed over her; she wanted to share the findings with Lyon. She wandered the streets to clear her head and ultimately decided that she loved him no matter what, although there was still so much to process. Taking out her cell phone, she dialed Lyon, and the sound of his voice immediately calmed her nerves.

"Hi. It's me. It's been a long twenty-four hours," said Rose.

"I wasn't sure when I'd hear from you."

"I'm not going to lie. It was a hard revelation, and I was really sad. Still am," said Rose, nervously looked down at her feet. "But I wanted to tell you about the meeting."

"Rose, we need to talk," said Lyon in a tone she hadn't heard before. "I want to hear about your meeting, but more importantly, we also need to talk about us."

"I called to tell you that I love you and I'm sorry for getting so upset. You caught me completely off guard."

"I know, but I don't want to spend my life feeling like I robbed you of a family."

"We shouldn't be having this conversation on the phone."

"I agree."

"What are your plans?"

"I'm going to head to my parents' place after work and talk about things."

"Don't you think we should be together?"

"No, I don't. As much as I love you, Rose, it's time I faced the reality of the accident with my family too."

"Can I do anything?" she asked.

"No. I think it's important you take time to consider our situation as well."

"That's fair . . . I love you, Lyon."

"I love you too, Rose, but I'm not sure about anything right now."

When she hung up, Rose felt physically ill. She wished she had someone she trusted completely to share her heartache. Her feelings were overwhelming, and she wandered around, trying to come up with a plan. She thought about phoning Zoey but discarded the idea.

Walking the busy streets, she was able to quiet the inner musings of her head. Not really paying attention to where she was going, she noticed a crowd forming around a building. Scanning the street sign, she saw Mike jump down from the scaffolding and survey the finished product. Rose was completely delighted to see it in daylight. The scales were in fact an optical illusion, and today they tipped to the right.

Mike had used bright blues on the upper right corner; the left side boasted a mix of blues and grays with what appeared to be a pastel rainbow. She thought the mural was absolutely breathtaking with the sun shining on it. Indeed, she was rather jaded since she had just admired Michelangelo's paintings in the Sistine Chapel, which was considered the greatest accomplishment in Western civilization. She made her way to the front of the crowd to get a closer look. Mike's talent captivated her in a different way, and the images lodged themselves into her heart. There was something rare and special about his work.

Her eyes locked with Mike's; he cocked his head in recognition, so she waved. When he came over to say hello, she reminded him that they'd met with Beatrice. His smile, albeit wistful, lit up his face, which made him far more attractive than she'd originally observed. Beatrice's fascination with him made more sense.

"This is amazing!" said Rose. "I'm delighted to see the work by day and note that the scales are tipped to the right."

"They can be interpreted more than one way," he offered. "Are you insinuating that I might be more of an optimist than I appear?"

"No, I wouldn't say that," said Rose dryly. "Hey, this is probably none of my business, but I feel compelled to ask you a favor. Would it be too much to say goodbye to Beatrice in person rather than storming out the door? She really felt a connection with you."

"I told her up front that I have no allegiance to anyone or anything."

"That's your choice, but a simple goodbye to let her know that you enjoyed her company would be the right thing to do."

He eyed her warily. "Rose, I'm not going to change but would appreciate you giving my contact information to Beatrice." Mike took out a pen and wrote it down on a scrap of paper. While his actions shouldn't have surprised her, they did. A business card must have been too much to ask.

"I will, but here is her card just in case you change your mind." She handed it to him and watched as he shoved it in his pocket.

"I make no promises to anyone. But who knows, maybe I'll reconsider for the enchanting Beatrice."

"Hopefully, she'll answer you. We both know she's a very special person."

"I realize that," he said gruffly.

Rose took his information and put it in her satchel, complimenting his work a final time. His mural emanated intensity, and she was sad it would not grace the building forever. There was a commotion in the crowd, so she looked up to see what was going on.

A tall, handsome Black man emerged, immaculately dressed in a suede jacket and jeans. He was wearing sunglasses, which added to his aura of mystery. Rose inadvertently stepped back as he strode up to Mike.

"Get out of here," said Mike, who seemed almost small and petulant next to the man.

He threw back his head and laughed heartily. "Hello," he said, removing his sunglasses to focus upon Rose. "I'm Vince. And you are?"

"Rose. Rose Maning," she added nervously.

"What do you want?" huffed Mike.

"To see the finished product of the great Mike from Milan." He stood back and folded his arms together, laughing at his own joke. "By the way, what's that blob on the lower left?"

Rose felt the hatred radiating from both men.

"You need to go, now!" said Mike, shoving him.

Vince pushed him back and sneered at him. "I've a good mind to create something extraordinary right beside this monstrosity."

"Careful, Vince, you're turning green. You match your ugly shirt."

"At least my shirt is clean. When was the last time you took a shower? You give street art a bad name."

"I don't think so. Look at this crowd. They love the mural."

"Do they?" Vince called to the crowd, "Listen up, everyone."

A hush fell over the crowd.

"How many of you want me to prove who's the better artist? We should have our work side by side." The crowd began cheering wildly. Their chorus of "Vince, Vince, Vince" echoed on the street corner. Mike looked ready to kill someone.

Rose was frozen by the exchange. Their intensity was surreal as the two men glared at each other.

***

The cardinal was still in a meeting when Rose arrived at his office. Usually, she would have admired the paintings by Raphael on the walls, but she wasn't in the mood. She left him a note on his desk that she would return later. Her fight with Lyon was weighing on her, and she needed an objective opinion. Had she been wrong to admonish him for not telling her sooner? Could she accept a life with him that didn't include children? Was she willing to adopt? Would she have to find a sperm doner? Most importantly, could she trust him to always tell her the truth?

Questions swirled, so she made her way to the Sistine Chapel to sit quietly amid its ethereal beauty. The lure of Michelangelo's work took her breath away as she walked around the closed sanctuary. The panels showed the story of *Creation* to *Noah* to the *Great Flood*. In essence, the master painted the creation of humanity, its fall from grace and ultimate redemption. Michelangelo's ceiling effused integrity. Every time she looked at the nine panels of the world's biblical history, something new would catch her eye. Today, she caught sight of Adam and Eve being expelled from the Garden of Eden; their feelings of isolation and fear radiated from above.

"Rose," said the cardinal, entering the sanctuary. His white robes gave him a stately air as he walked brusquely to reach her. "I'm so glad I found you. Beatrice said you were looking for me, and I thought you had left the building. Then I remembered how you love to visit the Sistine every time you're here. So, I thought I'd check to see if my hunch was correct."

"Cardinal, I can't tell you much I appreciate you finding me." They embraced and made their way to a vacant side pew.

"You seem troubled, my dear," he observed. "Does this have anything to do with the weight of your discovery?"

"I'm excited that the discovery has potentially shed light on another historical event. Beatrice did a first-class job explaining such a complex historical drama and all its unsolved moving pieces. But that's not why I'm here," she sighed. "It's my relationship with Lyon."

"Do you want to talk about it? Is everything alright?"

"Yes and no," said Rose carefully. "He just gave me some news yesterday that I'm having a hard time digesting."

The lines on the cardinal's face became etched with worry. Noting his strong jawline and intense stare, there was something about his expression that was eerily similar to her father's; his concern resonated with her, which made her miss her father all the more. She burst into tears and found herself in a moment of uncontrolled emotion. "I'm so sorry," she said. Getting ahold of herself, she dabbed at her eyes as she spoke, haltingly at first. "Lyon gave me some unpleasant news yesterday and I'm having trouble figuring out what I want to do with this new piece of information."

"Go on."

"Apparently, he had an accident when he was young, and there's a high probability that he can't father a child."

"I'm so sorry, my dear," he said. Another rush of tears flowed. He took her hand. "How can I help you?"

"Honestly, I'm hopeful that you can tell me what to do, because I'm so sad."

They sat in silence for a long while until Rose steadied her breathing.

"I could answer you as a member of the clergy and tell you to trust God's plan for you." He took a deep breath. "Or, I could point out that it's your life and have you look into your heart. What do you want to do, Rose?"

"I thought yesterday that I wanted to marry Lyon and have a family. I can't imagine my life without children."

"But can you imagine your life without Lyon?"

His words hung in the air.

"No," she replied. "But I still feel so confused and disappointed that he never told me."

"You do have options. I'm not a doctor, but you have the power to explore your choices and make one together that works."

Rose nodded. "I wish he had told me sooner and given me time to process a different future together."

"That's fair. You need to trust your love for each other."

"How do we do that?" asked Rose. "The wedding is only three months away. I just went over all of the details with his mother yesterday, and I don't want to disappoint anyone."

"I realize that the details of a wedding are important to a young bride, but marriage is a lifetime. It sounds as if you have some issues that first need mending."

His words reverberated in her head and heart. They had issues, but they could work through them. Rose felt a weight lift from her shoulders. "I agree. We need to figure this out together, and that's not what it feels like right now."

"Trust and communication are critical components for a relationship to work long term. Knowing Lyon, he was afraid to lose you, which is why he kept his medical history a secret. I'm not saying it was right, but I understand his motivation."

Rose nodded in agreement, feeling a bit calmer in the cardinal's presence.

"I recently decided that I do want a Catholic wedding ceremony," said Rose. "Lyon and I have discussed a religious ceremony as opposed to a civil one and how it would require extra time and preparation."

"Sounds like a good solution."

"Well," said Rose. "The perfect answer is to have you perform the ceremony next spring. This gives us time to work on things."

"My dear," he replied, taking both of her hands, "I'd be honored."

"Cardinal, as for the discovery, I'd like to talk to Dr. Saunders and hear his side of the search for the lost Leonardo. Maybe it would help us figure out what to do."

"I hope so, Rose."

"Do you think I'm correct in trying to understand all of the viewpoints?"

"Yes, but I fear we're opening the proverbial Pandora's box."

"Why?"

"The sheer magnitude of this potential art find is hard to grasp. As I said before, this art mystery is a major conundrum, and I'm not clear on what to do. I intend to pray about it."

Rose felt his fear. "I understand, but I feel the need to be practical and do more research. I want to think through the pros and cons of both sides of this issue."

"Absolutely," said the cardinal. "My dear, I will also pray for healing in your relationship with Lyon. I hope you find the answers you seek."

Chapter 10

BEATRICE DEBATED WHETHER a trip home to Switzerland would mend the gaping hole in her heart. Was love at first sight possible? She didn't know how else to explain the rush of emotions that had coursed through her when she first met Mike. Most people would think she was a dreamy teenager in the throes of a childhood crush on a rock star. It would certainly appear that way. Usually, she relied upon an internal calm that had served her well in her career. These tumultuous feelings were unsettling and yet invigorating.

She clicked on her computer and was surprised to see an unexpected email that Rose forwarded to her from Dr. Saunders. He wanted to share insights about his work to uncover the lost Leonardo. He was available to meet at his office in Florence on Friday. Rose wanted her to come along and talk with him too. She was worried about possibly missing a detail of his process given her own inexperience.

Delighted with the invitation, Beatrice agreed to attend the meeting and spend a few days in Florence. Coincidentally, the cardinal had asked her to continue her research privately while he consulted other members of the clergy for advice on how best to handle this delicate situation—a potential clue to an ancient mystery. Beatrice read the professor's email again, fascinated by his relentless quest. She had to admit that the clue she found haunted her. There was something surreal about being the keeper of a secret.

Was it a stretch to think there was a connection between Rose's find and the professor's research? At this point, it was just her hypothesis that supported his hunch. Clearly, the power of the clue was slanted toward the preexisting work of Dr. Saunders's group. It was these small details that had a way of lodging themselves in her head. When the story originally appeared in the news, she was a college student studying in the States. She had stumbled upon a BBC news report and had been fascinated by the idea of a masterpiece potentially hidden behind a wall. That moment when she uncovered the message in the lab a few weeks ago would always be unforgettable. Her heart raced at the memory.

It was painstaking work. She used a new solution and cleaned with a precision fiber-tipped tool that was slow and steady. As she cleaned Rose's second drawing, Beatrice gulped when she thought about the risk she had taken. This solution could have been too strong. Thanks to her persistence and uncountable hours wiping away each speck millimeter by millimeter, the results were extraordinary. There were several nights she worked until the early hours of the morning. She wasn't quite sure why she had felt this intensity, but it was almost as if she sensed that there was something there. The past called to her like one of the sirens in the *Odyssey*. Beatrice smiled, thinking she and Dr. Saunders would have a lot in common.

Yet, she wondered if they could trust him. Who funded his original discovery work and why? That was certainly something that could shed light on his motivation. Men killed for far less, and this would entangle many groups. A visit to the Palazzo Vecchio was going to be her first stop when they arrived in Florence. Perhaps if she stared at the wall long enough, an answer would emerge. The thought amused her.

Spying a familiar blond ponytail, she caught sight of Rose on the platform and quickly made her way there. Looking around, she saw a circle of young men in hoodies, smoking cigarettes and chatting on the platform. An elderly couple was falling asleep on a side bench while they waited for the train to arrive. A young woman sat on her duffle bag, which boasted an American flag. The billboards always entertained her, observing the profile of a cowboy smoking a Camel cigarette.

They hopped on the immaculately clean train to Florence. The plush seats and the oversized windows were a welcome distraction from her musings, and, of course, Rose was always good company. "I love riding the train here," said Rose. "It's so civilized compared to getting in and out of New York."

"I agree. That being said, my best friend Chelsea is relocating to the States to spice up her life, as she says."

"I love Italy and have no intention of going anywhere for a long while," exclaimed Rose as she hoisted her bag into the overhead compartment. Taking the aisle seat, Beatrice removed her jacket and got comfortable.

"I hope I'll get to catch up with Lyon. It's been a while."

Rose frowned. "I didn't want to burden you with our problems, but you need to know what's going on." She shared her concerns about Lyon, their relationship, children, and her conversation with the cardinal.

"I'm impressed with the way you're holding it together," she said. "I don't know what I would do in your situation. I know it's not what you planned."

"No, it's not. That being said, I love him and am definitely open to ideas," said Rose. "I must say that although I'm mentally drained, I feel that we can work it out."

"I'm sure you will."

"On a different note, I have some news," said Rose.

"What do you mean?"

"I ran into Mike and talked to him about you."

"You what?" said Beatrice, trying to stay calm.

"I did," said Rose. "I told him that you're special, and not to be a stranger."

"I'm not sure whether to laugh or cry," Beatrice said. She felt her heart accelerate.

"I have his email address."

"What? You do?" she exclaimed. "Don't you think he should contact me first?"

"Why does it matter?" said Rose. "The best part remains that you have a way to contact him privately."

"To be honest, I'm surprised he gave it to you. Maybe I should just reconcile that we made a connection and that's all it's ever going to be."

"Well," said Rose. "There's more to the story. While Mike and I were chatting about you, this artist named Vince came over. He was really handsome, but aggressive. He started to harass him and call his work amateurish."

"Oh my gosh!" said Beatrice. "That happened when I was there with my friend Chelsea."

"Really? I thought he was way out of line and quite rude to Mike. He told him he was wearing grungy clothes, which gave street artists a bad name."

"Sounds like our friends Michelangelo and Leonardo," said Beatrice. She had the strangest feeling about recent events. It was as if the past and the present were destined to collide.

"I've been trying to figure out why I found the drawings and how it relates to the research completed by Dr. Saunders and his team."

"I'd like to know what motivates him."

"Agree. I'd like to think that Dr. Saunders wants to uncover the past for the right reasons. The good news is that we'll find out tomorrow! I'm excited to meet him," Rose said.

"Me too. I think the more information we gather, the easier it is going to be to know what to do."

"I hope so!"

Beatrice looked out the window, scanning the green terrain spotted with a few bushes and a white house with a spice-colored roof. They passed a small body of water beside a lush field.

"Our modern-day street artists are fascinating," Rose said. "I forgot to mention that Vince issued a public challenge that he would put his work up against Mike's anytime or anywhere."

"That's really obnoxious, and I'm not sure I have a good feeling about it."

"Maybe it's not that bad?" offered Rose.

"Vince brings out the worst in Mike. Something bad could happen."

"Now I think you're being overly dramatic," said Rose.

"Mike already has a temper, and Vince knows just how to press his buttons. It's not a good combination."

"You're going to think I'm overzealous, but maybe the solution is a contest. It would certainly be exciting to see how they both interpret a given theme. Maybe it will put an end to the feud."

"Do you really believe that?" asked Beatrice.

"No, but it was worth a try."

Despite what Rose had shared about her relationship with Lyon, Beatrice thought it was odd that he didn't pick them up at the train station, but she said nothing. After all, it was really none of her business. Her job for the next few days was to immerse herself in Leonardo da Vinci and determine a strategy to deal with Dr. Saunders.

Soon after, they dropped their bags at Rose's apartment, and grabbed a slice of four-cheese pizza at the corner café. Beatrice practically inhaled the tasty lunch, proclaiming that the great Gabriele Bonci, otherwise known as Rome's Michelangelo of pizza, would approve.

They made their way to the Uffizi Museum through the Piazza della Signoria, marveling at Bandinelli's *Hercules and Cacus*, once a great symbol of the power of the Medici family during the Renaissance. The line didn't take too long. It had been a while since either of them had checked out the Leonardo Room, which housed some of the artist's earlier works.

"I think it's hall fifteen," said Rose, who had recently toured the room. "As I recall, a young Leonardo trained with the master Verrocchio. I think he was approximately twenty years old when he painted the *Baptism of Christ*."

Beatrice took in the painting as if breathing fresh air after being cooped up in a dark basement. It was absolutely breathtaking in its intensity, and she got the same chill of anticipation that she felt every time she came in contact with a historic painting. "This is the moment that St. John baptizes Christ, and his divine nature is revealed. We also see the Holy Spirit in the hands of God above."

"It's a magnificent painting," agreed Rose, loving having a friend who appreciated art as much as she. "I think it's interesting to think of the great Leonardo da Vinci as a student for another master."

"That was an extremely common practice at that time." Beatrice couldn't help not going into lecture mode. "It was also common for these artists to work on the same painting. So, you can imagine that Verrocchio gave young Leonardo an assignment to paint an angel one day. I would gather that Verrocchio did most of the work on this, but look at the young angel on the left and some of those figure outlines. This looks like the moment a young prodigy rose above his teacher."

"I love being with an expert! Forgive my ignorance, but please explain why," asked Rose.

"Look at the two angels who are placed side by side in this painting. The one on the right looks like a boy. It was typical of that time that artists used male models, and that is precisely what we have here."

"I agree," said Rose, moving closer to the painting.

"The round face looks very earthly. I would label Verrocchio's version of this angel as early Renaissance. Now look at the angel on the left, drawn by Leonardo. It's in a different league. You see the ideal beauty of the angel through the flowing lines of the face and hair. You can almost feel those feathery brushstrokes. Leonardo's angel marks the beginning of the High Renaissance because it has no earthly anchor. The angel's beauty suggests the divine, and therein we have the genius of Leonardo."

"But also of Michelangelo!" exclaimed Rose. "His depiction of the *David* had no earthly model for his face."

"Precisely," said Beatrice. "I knew I liked you," she added with a grin. "In this case, Leonardo took the lessons of the fifteenth century and reworked them to create ethereal figures that appeared to have no earthly representative. In a sense, he defined the High Renaissance."

"Now you've lost me again. It's not so easy keeping up with you. How did he do that?"

"The best way to explain it is that in the thirteenth century, artists used symbols like the gold crown around the saints to represent divinity. Leonardo, through his own genius and technique, redefined that model, almost making the early depictions look two dimensional. He was able to use his understanding of anatomy to create three-dimensional ethereal figures with a sense of transcendence and divinity."

"Is it too much of a stretch to think about the Leonardo's *Battle of Anghiari* as a possible divine rendering of wartime?"

"Perhaps that's what the Florentine government wanted when they commissioned him. Anything painted by the great Leonardo da Vinci was incomparable. I mean, here we are five hundred years later, still admiring his work. That being said, the figures and horses Leonardo drew in the cartoon were unparalleled."

"Except for the ones drawn by Michelangelo," countered Rose.

"You are relentless," laughed Beatrice.

They looked at the painting opposite known as the *Annunciation* with an angel so lifelike that she seemed to be floating divinely in the canvas. Beatrice paused. "I've always thought the seascape landing was one of the most beautiful backgrounds ever painted."

"I'm completely transported," said Rose.

"Did you know that Leonardo studied the anatomy of birds in order to create such real-looking wings. He was a genius."

"Should we be worried that you are all about Leonardo, and I will never surrender my passion for Michelangelo!" joked Rose.

"If that were true, my friend, then I wouldn't have gotten involved—maybe that's too strong a word—with Mike." She grinned. "You know I'm kidding, right? I wouldn't begin to compare him to the great Michelangelo."

"Of course I know that! But your Mike is charismatic and wildly talented. I get it."

"You do? I'd begun to think I was too passionate even though I know he's not relationship material."

"Absolutely," said Rose. "But don't ask me because I have plenty of unsolved issues right now. Love, even at its best, is complicated."

"I agree," said Beatrice. "Let's take in a few more paintings, and we can talk about our questions for Dr. Saunders over dinner."

"Great idea! I need to check in with Lyon and let him know I'm back in Florence."

"You haven't talked? I thought it was strange he didn't meet us at the train station," said Beatrice. She saw the look of hurt cross Rose's face.

"He hasn't returned my calls these past few days," said Rose, looking away.

"Maybe he's really busy?"

Rose rolled her eyes but said nothing. They left the Uffizi and headed back to Rose's apartment. Beatrice thought the walk very pleasant as they turned left onto Via dè Coverelli. They had walked several hundred yards when Beatrice saw a group forming. Her heart raced, thinking it may be Mike. She said, "See that crowd down that street? Perhaps we should take a look."

Beatrice appreciated that Rose didn't chastise her for her childish notion that it could be Mike working on another mural. She simply wandered down the street as if it were on their way. She inched closer, then her heart plummeted at the sight before her. It was Vince working on a new installation. Beatrice remarked, "You can see he's got the legs of the table done."

"I wonder what his message will be."

"I'm dying to know who is going to be sitting at the table in Vince's drawing. Another thought-provoking statement, I would think."

"Or a challenge," remarked Beatrice.

Chapter 11

DR. EDWIN SAUNDERS was a tall, approachable man graying at the temples and full of vigor. His firm handshake and warm welcome made Beatrice feel comfortable as he guided them to his office. It took a moment for her senses to adjust to this environment, which was a stark contrast to the stately, half-lit rooms of the Vatican. The wide-open integrated space showed refracted light as it bounced off glass and steel. There were several elegant gold-framed paintings on the far wall, which Beatrice identified as copies of the masters.

In contrast, the modern office décor boasted a series of long white worktables, high-tech lighting, and comfortable white leather seating. A nearby table was lined with Apple equipment, including a video projector. On a side wall, Beatrice noted an image of a Renaissance-dressed woman with seven projections of that image in varying colors and forms behind it.

Noting her glance, he offered, "That is a subject being dissected through multispectral diagnostic imaging."

Beatrice nodded in appreciation, ready to hear more of his ideas and research. Once they sat, Saunders asked all the obligatory questions on her background, including her time in the States as a student. He turned to Rose to ask her about her years as an art history teacher. They exchanged pleasantries about Michelangelo. Soon after, he cleared his throat. Saunders looked directly at Beatrice. "How can I help you?"

"We are trying to authenticate some artwork owned by the Vatican that may or may not be attributed to a master like Leonardo da Vinci." Beatrice looked over at Rose, who nodded in approval.

"You see, Dr. Saunders, I found some drawings in my apartment last year which I sold to the Vatican. Beatrice has diligently worked to clean and preserve them. We would like to know everything we can about what I found."

"You've come to the right place. I'm passionate about the life and works of Leonardo and spent the better part of my life searching for the link between science and art. Even though I'm a scientist, I've always had a love for art history. When I was in college, my best friend's family had a fascination for the lost Leonardo, and they loved to talk about it. Are you familiar with the story?"

"As a matter of fact, we know all about your theory that Vasari built a wall in front of the Leonardo's *Battle of Anghiari*." Beatrice added, "I saw your Ted talk."

"I like that you did your homework."

"Please go on," Beatrice said.

Dr. Saunders continued, "After I received my undergraduate degree, my friend's father, Malcolm Deckert, contacted me about using science to solve this mystery. It was his passion, and it soon became mine. He had the resources to fund my research. For years, I worked tirelessly to conceive and develop equipment that could analyze the wall and help determine what was behind it. The bottom line was that it took years and years to develop the needed technology. My son, Julian, has been particularly helpful in this endeavor. He recently pioneered a new device that can sharpen an image one hundred and twenty times."

As if on cue, Julian appeared, a tall, lanky younger version of his father. He offered his apologies for the delay and took a seat.

"I am fascinated by your work, and so is Rose," Beatrice acknowledged while thinking he couldn't be long out of university.

"Thank you. As a bioengineer, I want applied science to authenticate works of art. That is why I do what I do. I believe the combination of science and technology will change the art market."

"What do you mean by that?" asked Beatrice.

"For example, I think many paintings up for sale in the major auction houses have been both overvalued and undervalued to some degree. With technology, we can determine the exact age of the work of art as well as scan the drawing underneath." He turned his computer screen to face them. "For example, look at this painting known as the *Lady with the Unicorn* by Raphael. Scholars have debated for years the origins of the painting and the meaning behind the unicorn. When we scanned the painting with infrared light, we found that there was a puppy dog painted underneath the unicorn. As a matter of fact, we learned that Raphael did not paint a puppy or a unicorn. In short, Raphael did not finish the painting or include any type of animal. Therefore, the painting was subsequently worth less money than anticipated."

"So, you're saying that a majority of the time, the results appear not to confirm an initial hypothesis," asked Rose.

"Perhaps as high as eighty percent of the time. We recently looked at a still-life painting by Otto Masseuse that hangs in the Uffizi. It was very good news. His signature was found on the far-left corner, and we were able to authenticate this work of art. It was a positive union of science and art history. Let me be clear; I'm not a fan of subjective evaluation."

Beatrice recoiled. "What's that supposed to mean?"

Dr. Saunders cleared his throat. "I think science should determine information about art. People who remove dirt and debris the old-fashioned way are just plain ignorant!"

Beatrice felt like she had been punched. She cleared her throat. "I'm sorry, but those are strong words. I find them especially offensive, since that is what I do for a living." Beatrice looked over at Rose, who sat up straighter in her chair.

"Forgive me, Beatrice. I'm not insinuating that your process is not a good one. I believe diagnostic imaging and analytical diagnostics are essential to the study of our cultural heritage. And I thought that is what you needed my laboratory to do for you."

"Absolutely, that's why we're here," Rose said.

"I have a hard time being told that my career as a conservator is 'less than' without your technology. What about education, training, and instinct?"

"Beatrice?" said Rose, placing a hand on her arm.

"With all due respect, you are the one coming to my firm with questions about Leonardo da Vinci."

"That's correct. I didn't expect the work I do to be denigrated."

"The old techniques are too subjective, and I believe we need to change the way we do things. Again, that's why we use science to authenticate works of art."

"It was my skill that found the clue," snapped Beatrice.

The room went silent.

"I'm sorry, but what did you just say?"

"Nothing," said Beatrice. She felt the hot flush of embarrassment on her cheeks.

"That's not what I heard," Dr. Saunders huffed. "I heard you say you uncovered a clue to a Leonardo painting."

"Then you heard me incorrectly," said Beatrice, her voice heated.

"How about we discuss how we can work together in a respectful manner?"

His comment allowed Beatrice to compose herself. She replied politely, "Thank you. I think we have everything we need to know about you and your firm to make a decision."

"Absolutely," said Dr. Saunders.

"I'll be in touch," offered Beatrice, motioning at Rose to head out.

Beatrice swallowed hard, reining in her anger. Grabbing her bag, she marched to the exit, barely conscious of Rose beside her. She had lived and breathed art conservation for more than ten years, working nights and weekends because she loved her job. *How dare some scientist tell me that my passion is going to be replaced by machines.* Her anger changed to embarrassment about revealing her recent discovery. That was wildly stupid. She wasn't accustomed to feeling like a teenager who had forgotten her homework. Beatrice sighed. "I blew it," she said in frustration.

"No, you didn't. I thought you recovered quite well." Rose opened the door and ushered her outside.

***

On the Via Pier Capponi, they stepped out into the street lined with classic stone buildings that appeared well maintained. Out of the corner of her eye, Beatrice saw a black patch of graffiti gracing the front of Dr. Saunders's office. There was perverse satisfaction in the ugly swirls, which mirrored her angry emotions. For the next few blocks, Beatrice calmed herself, knowing Rose understood.

"Hmmm," said Beatrice, feeling the fresh November air on her face. "I know one of us will have to dodge any further inquiries." Coming upon a street full of activity calmed her rattled senses. Rose grabbed her arm to halt them.

"I know you may not agree," exclaimed Rose, "but what if we gave Dr. Saunders the drawing and told him the truth about what we know? He seems trustworthy. I've made a few inquiries about him, and he is highly respected."

"Yes, but then we open up Pandora's box."

"He's an expert, and I don't see that we have any other viable solution."

"I don't care," said Beatrice, knowing she sounded like a petulant child. "I'm the one that found the connection based on my *ignorant* skills." She could barely say the word.

"Absolutely," said Rose. "That does not diminish your talent, Beatrice! Honestly, you're being way too hard on yourself. Dr. Saunders understands the issues from a different perspective, which is why his input is invaluable."

"I don't like him," said Beatrice. Perhaps he reminded her that she had no life outside of her job.

"Listen to me. You're a professional, and this is your passion. You can't let your personal feelings get in the way of your endeavors. If you want answers, you're going to have to figure out how to develop some sort of rapport with him."

"You're right, Rose," said Beatrice.

Just as they turned the corner, the musical notes of an accordion stopped them in their tracks. An old Italian man in a black beret was perched on the street edge, producing a soothing melody that made Beatrice smile. "Why do I feel like every time I come to Florence, I see something unexpected on the streets?"

"That's why I love this city!" said Rose.

Beatrice looked up to see an impeccably dressed Vince, who nearly collided with them. His leather jacket was tailored to perfection, and his sunglasses gave him an air of mystery.

"Well, this is a pleasant surprise," he said warmly.

Beatrice watched as he eyed Rose with appreciation and then turned his gaze to her.

"What brings you to Florence?"

"I could ask you the same question," she queried.

"I live here," offered Rose. "Beatrice is my guest for a few days."

"Well, it's my good fortune to see you both! I'm here to work on a new commission," said Vince, inching closer to Rose.

"What are you working on? Do tell," said Beatrice, her curiosity piqued. She was accustomed to the way men looked at Rose as if she were a precious object. And yet, Mike had made her feel beautiful, like she was the only woman in the world that he noticed. A pang of longing coursed through her, but she quickly banished it.

"I'm afraid not," he said politely. "You'll have to wait and see. Unless, of course, you lovely ladies agree to have a drink with me tonight."

Beatrice was about to say no thanks just as Rose answered, "Yes!"

Vince suggested the Café Medici around the corner, and they decided upon seven o'clock sharp. As they walked away, Beatrice asked, "What are you doing?"

"I'm beyond curious to know what he's working on."

"Me too, but I'm not sure I want to have a drink with him."

"Looks like we have different opinions," said Rose. "I'd like to talk with him."

"I'm not going," said Beatrice.

"Suit yourself," said Rose. "But you don't owe Mike anything."

Beatrice wanted to tell Rose that she was wrong, but in her heart, she worried that Mike would never talk with her again if he found out she socialized with his rival. Was he really gone forever? "You're right. I'll think about it."

"That's the spirit," said Rose. "I've got a few errands to run. I'll see you back at the apartment." She handed her a key.

Beatrice wanted to clear her head and process their meeting with Dr. Saunders. She was frustrated at her impulsive comment and wondered how best to proceed. *Can I trust him?* And she wasn't sure what she hoped to prove. *Well, that's an understatement.* Her ego was at work, she decided, realizing that the lost Leonardo had wrapped its tentacles around her. After all, who wouldn't want to be responsible for uncovering one of art's greatest mysteries? The possibility was thrilling, and it gave her renewed purpose to continue to search for more information.

She wandered around the streets, ending up staring at the Ponte Vecchio bridge, which was filled with shops. The segmented three arches reflected the afternoon light. Beatrice stilled, taking in the setting. Staring at the Arno, Beatrice sighed heavily as she regained her equilibrium. There was something about water that always calmed her nerves. She felt her phone vibrate and wondered who was trying to reach her. She saw it was a text from a number she didn't recognize.

It's Julian, I'd like to talk to you alone as soon as possible. Can we meet?

Yes. Where and when?

How about the Palazzo Vecchio tonight at 5. I want to show you something. This is just between us.

I'll be there.

Beatrice didn't know what to think of Julian's texts, but she decided not to overanalyze. She planned to head back to the Uffizi to study more of Leonardo's work, then head to the Palazzo Vecchio early to study the Vasari painting on the wall.

The line was too long at the Uffizi. After waiting a half hour, she realized her time was limited and left. She popped into a coffee shop with a black awning, ordered an espresso to go, and made her way to meet Julian.

Beatrice couldn't help but marvel at the Renaissance architecture of the Palazzo Vecchio. The building had a militaristic look thanks to high windows, prominent heraldry, and a projecting balcony. Behind this cold exterior, Beatrice knew a sophisticated former Renaissance palace existed. And most importantly, she planned to meet Julian in the most impressive architectural space in the interior, the Sala dei Cinquecento—Room of the Five Hundred. She recalled that the room was named for the number of citizens it could hold for government assemblies during the glory days of the Florentine Republic.

They both arrived at the same time and headed toward each other through the crowds. Beatrice studied his intelligent brown eyes, high forehead, and clean-shaven face. He was quite handsome, she concluded, feeling a blush stain her cheeks. And he was the polar opposite of Mike.

"Hi," she said as he came to stand beside her.

"Thanks for coming. I wanted to apologize for what happened in the meeting. My father can be overzealous bordering on offensive sometimes." He smiled warmly. "He did not mean to insult you."

"That's very kind of you to say so."

"Let me say in his defense that he's been battling art historians for his entire career. To him, it seems like a never-ending conflict."

"I do believe that they are both important," Beatrice said. "But I also trust the painstaking work I do each day to preserve the integrity of historical masterpieces."

"Perhaps I'll get to see some of your work someday," he said.

"Well, you'd have to come to my laboratory in Rome."

"That's not a problem," he said. They smiled at each other. "In the meantime, I wanted to show you something."

Beatrice was curious. She dodged a few tourists, and they went inside the great hall to stare at the monumental Vasari painting.

"My dad mapped this whole painting out, indicating how and where he thinks the Leonardo is hidden." He took her over to the far left. "I've just created a device to magnify my father's earlier pictures and sharpen their intensity."

"I assume you're a scientist as well."

"I went to MIT to get my degree," he offered. "Dad wasn't happy because he wanted me to go to Harvard like him. He has several degrees, you know."

"I assumed so. By the way, I'm proud of the fact that I studied at NYU to become a conservator," she replied easily. "I'm glad that I had the experience of living in the States, but I love my job and life in Rome."

"Then we have something in common. I feel the same way," said Julian.

Beatrice was both surprised and delighted by this meeting on so many levels. Julian was charming, plus far more charismatic than she expected. She appreciated his smooth intervention when she took offense at his father's strong opinions. While she felt a lifetime older than him, his boyish charm was appealing. Eyeing his khaki pants and plaid shirt, he appeared dressed for the classroom, which she found oddly endearing. She watched as he picked a particular spot on the floor and pointed upward. With a swift movement into the black bag he carried, Julian pulled out binoculars as if he were offering her a glass of water.

"Look up there," he said, moving for her to take his place.

Beatrice held the binoculars and pointed them to the northwest corner of the Vasari painting. The image was vibrantly clear, and she sighed without moving a muscle lest she give anything away.

"*Cerca Trova*," she said coyly. "What does that mean?"

"It means, 'Seek and you shall find.' We think it's the biggest clue on record that there is a Leonardo behind this wall. It was almost as if Vasari planted it there between 1500 and 1560. My father was the first to see it in the '70s, and that's what started him on his quest."

"That's amazing!" said Beatrice. "Thank you for sharing this information with me, and your custom binoculars."

He nodded. "I thought you more than anyone would appreciate seeing a clue in full view."

"You made my day." Beatrice smiled, wondering why he had been so bold as to show her this clue. *Does his father know he is here?* she wondered.

"No," he said. "You made mine when you walked into my father's office."

Beatrice swallowed hard at the compliment. He was so earnest. Studying the Vasari message on the wall confirmed her hypothesis. "What's next?"

"That's up to you," he answered easily, placing the binoculars in his jacket pocket.

She wanted to say, *I feel like the keeper of an ancient secret.* Instead, she replied, "I need to ponder what you've just shown me."

"My father and I believe that the truth will be revealed."

"I hope so," said Beatrice, wondering at fate. "Do you know whether Vasari ever hid any other masters' painting behind a wall?"

"Yes," replied Julian. "That's why we think it's here." He glanced over at the mammoth painting. "Will you help us find it?"

Beatrice pondered his request. *Should I reveal my clue and begin the hunt?*

Chapter 12

ROSE FILLED THE TEAPOT with hot water, looking forward to unwinding on her own for a few hours until Beatrice returned. On an impulse, she dialed Lyon's number and got his voicemail. Thinking it strange, she tried not to dwell on the fact that they hadn't spoken in a few days. It really wasn't like him to ignore her. Quelling her fears, she hoped that he had visited with his parents or become bogged down with work. After all, she had made it clear that they could work out this situation no matter what. The cardinal had made her feel much better about everything. Communication was paramount for them, and she felt confident in their ability to sort things out.

A pang of sadness resonated as she contemplated giving up her dreams of having Lyon's child. It certainly wasn't the life she imagined, and yet she couldn't bear the thought of losing him. Her years as a schoolteacher had taught her how much she adored children, even when they weren't her own. She had even received an email from one of her top students, Lori Evans, who planned to visit Florence with her family over the Christmas holiday. She had asked if it was possible to get together. Taking a sip of her black tea, Rose eagerly wrote Lori back, saying she was delighted with the invitation.

When Beatrice didn't return to the apartment by seven o'clock, Rose assumed that she wasn't interested in meeting Vince. A wave of panic struck, and she contemplated canceling. Taking a deep breath, Rose decided to go ahead and speak with him. His creative process intrigued her, along with his rivalry with Mike, which seemed overly dramatic. Rose sincerely hoped that Beatrice wasn't not joining her because of her connection with Mike. She really hoped that

Mike would disappear from her friend's life. Mike's behavior and comments to Beatrice raised so many red flags.

Grabbing her keys and coat, Rose headed out the door and down the street to meet Vince. He sat at the bar, tall and handsome in another gorgeous, black, tailored jacket and jeans. She eyed his black Gucci loafers and gold pinky ring; his taste was impeccable.

"You came," he said, greeting her warmly with a kiss on both cheeks.

"I wouldn't miss it," she replied, taking the seat that he pulled out for her.

The young, black-clad waiter with a skinny blue tie immediately took their order. He looked over at Vince and nearly dropped his writing pad.

"No way!" he exclaimed. "You're Vince and you're at my table!"

Vince seemed appropriately amused. "I'm glad to be back in Florence."

"You're a star. This is better than having Mick Jagger here."

Vince nodded politely, then turned to Rose.

"Red wine, *per favore*," she said.

"We'll have two glasses of your best Chianti," said Vince.

Rose liked his choice, not too ostentatious. When the waiter departed with a spring in his step, Rose offered, "You're quite the celebrity."

"I'm an artist. Nothing more. Nothing less," he said humbly.

"Well, you have quite a following." Rose liked his response.

"Indeed, but I didn't come to talk about myself. What about you, Rose? I saw your show at the Gallery Moderne."

Rose was shocked. "You did?" She couldn't help but feel flattered—and validated. "I'm new at all of this, but I would like to continue to learn and grow as a painter."

"That's admirable," replied Vince. The waiter arrived with the bottle, two glasses, and a crystal bowl filled with nuts. He seemed to have gotten ahold of himself, but Rose noticed that his hands shook a bit as he poured a small portion into Vince's glass to approve. Rose surmised that the manager probably told the young man to give Vince some privacy to relax.

The wine was light and very pleasing. They clinked glasses and Vince said, "To new beginnings."

"To new beginnings," she echoed, then asked, "So, are you going to keep me in suspense, or are you going to share some insights into your creative process. I must admit, I'm intrigued to learn what you are working on."

"Well," said Vince smoothly, "you know I branded the concept of a table to raise questions about our cultural mores. Every time I think about a new installation, I ask myself what the overall message will be and why. I don't necessarily want my artwork to be considered political or social. I suppose I want it to stand on its own and invite people to go deeper."

"In other words," said Rose, "it's an invitation, not a command."

"Absolutely," said Vince, leaning back in his chair to study her. "Are you married?" he blurted.

"Excuse me?" She gulped, feeling as if he had just dumped a bucket of cold water on her head. "Engaged," she replied, realizing that she was not wearing her engagement ring.

His wide smiled took her by surprise. "Aha! Good to know."

Rose was about to ask how Vince got his start when a huge flash went off in their faces. Vince jumped up and looked ready to hit someone, but the photographer quickly ran out the door.

"What was that?" said Rose, still startled.

"Nothing," muttered Vince. The manager came over to apologize for the intrusion and asked if they could move their table to the far back of the restaurant. Rose found the intrusion annoying. As they walked a few feet to a more secluded booth, a woman jumped out of her chair. "Vince!" she cried. "Can I have your autograph?" Vince reluctantly signed a postcard.

This is crazy! Rose thought, marveling at the group of people who wanted to talk with him. Fortunately, the manager intervened and ushered them briskly to a back booth.

"I'm sorry, Rose," he said humbly.

"No worries," she replied. "I'm thrilled that you wanted to chat with me."

"Once I saw your exhibit, I knew I wanted to meet you."

"Really?" she replied. "I'm so honored that an artist of your stature would feel that way."

"You can't mean you've no idea that you're extremely talented," he said, staring at her as if she were the only woman in the room. "I thought the idea of clasped hands as a nod to Michelangelo's *Creation of Adam* was unique and original. It made me ponder some of those age-old questions, like what is our purpose in life?"

Rose felt another wave of validation. "Thank you, Vince. You have no idea what a long week it's been and how much your compliment means to me."

"That's a good thing. Do you have time to stay and join me for dinner?"

Rose knew she should leave, but she was tired of calling Lyon and wondering where he was. Plus, she had to admit that Vince was a charming companion and took her mind off of everything. Her paradigm altered slightly. She felt normal again and full of possibility.

"You are fascinating. How can I possibly refuse?"

"I could say the same about you," he offered, signaling the waiter to bring them menus. Rose observed the gray leather back of the booth, brass nail heads, and the mahogany table shined to perfection. She looked over and saw a button on the left wall. "What is that?" she asked.

"I can call the manager from here."

"How lovely," she replied.

"You know, Rose, you have exquisite bone structure," he said. "I could model my version of Aphrodite after you."

Rose burst out laughing. "Honestly, Vince, don't be ridiculous."

"I don't joke about such things," he said quietly. "I study people for a living and think I am a good judge of the female form."

"Well, you've rendered me speechless," said Rose, reaching for her menu.

Vince looked at her and said, "I understand. May I suggest the Dover sole? It's outstanding. And I think I'll have the steak and fries."

Once they ordered, Rose asked, "So, who's at the table?"

"Wouldn't you like to know?" he joked. "My dear, as captivated as I am by you, I will not reveal my plan."

"Shoot!" cried Rose. "Can you give me a hint?"

"Let me say that I was inspired by the great Leonardo da Vinci. His *Last Supper*, showing Jesus at the table with his twelve apostles, begged the question, who gets invited to sit at the table and why? In a nutshell, this concept literally consumes me."

"Why can't we all sit at the table?" said Rose as she helped herself to a slice of warm bread.

"Therein lies the challenge!" Vince said.

"Indeed!"

They chatted and exchanged ideas easily as the evening wore on. Rose marveled over the moist sole marinated in a lemon and caper wine reduction. The garlic mashed potatoes and creamed spinach were the perfect complements to the decadent dish. She eyed the crispy french fries on Vince's plate, and, observing her interest, he took a scoop full of them and put them on her plate. "You're not at all what I expected," he said warmly.

"Neither are you," said Rose.

"We met under rather complicated circumstances," said Vince readily. "How well do you know Mike?"

"Not well at all. My friend, Beatrice connected with him. I understand that you are competitors."

Vince's expression darkened. "Rose, you and your friend seem like good people. Your friend needs to be very careful with him."

"I don't understand."

"It's not for me to say anymore. You know he's not a favorite of mine for many reasons."

"I'd say that's obvious."

"Be careful. He's a hothead and has a questionable past."

Rose nodded in accord but didn't say any more on the subject. They changed the topic, launching into a lively debate on the next exhibit at the Gallery Moderne, featuring the works of Andy Warhol. Vince was not a fan.

"Seriously," said Rose. "Warhol is iconic in America. Think of his Campbell soup cans or Marilyn Monroe."

"I know exactly who he is. My parents divorced when I was ten years old. My mother, brother, and I ended up spending a few years in a town outside of Savannah, Georgia. I took classes as a teenager at the Savannah School of Art and Design before returning to Europe at eighteen. Bottom line—I'm not a Warhol fan. An artist famous for his rendering of a banana or Mickey Mouse doesn't interest me!"

Rose was amused. "So, you won't be attending the show's opening-night exhibition."

"Absolutely not! Unless you're going to be there, and then I would consider it."

"You flatter me."

"I haven't enjoyed an evening this much in a long time," he said. "Your fiancé is a lucky man."

I'm not sure what he thinks right now, thought Rose, pretending to reach for something in her bag. She checked her phone and pushed aside her disappointment, giggling at Vince's analysis of Warhol's Elvis painting, claiming that the famous singer's hips were erroneously drawn.

It was after midnight when Rose returned to her apartment; she had no idea where the evening had gone. She padded lightly by the guest bedroom and peeked inside to see that Beatrice was sound asleep. Trying not to feel guilty that she had left for the night, she tiptoed quietly upstairs. Rose removed her jacket, and her cell phone fell on the floor. She looked down to see a text message from Lyon.

His words were clipped as he demanded that she call him back. Lyon wanted to know why she wasn't picking up her phone. A wave of anxiety passed through her, but she discarded it. She had called him numerous times over the past week and left messages.

Just as Rose was about to turn out the light, her phone buzzed. She heard Lyon inhale when she answered.

"You're home. Where have you been?"

"I've been trying to reach you all week and left tons of messages. I've been out with a friend. Where are you?"

"The hospital. My sister had food poisoning, then became dehydrated."

"Oh no, Lyon. I'm so sorry!"

"Everything is okay now, but she collapsed at her house two days ago. It's all kind of a blur."

"I wish you'd told me sooner. Where are you now?"

"I just got back to my apartment."

"I miss you. I really hated our fight in Rome, Lyon. I'm so sorry."

"I'm sorry too. I'm exhausted."

"Will you come over?"

Fifteen minutes later, Rose heard the lock jangle as Lyon let himself in. She welcomed the sound of his steady footsteps up to the loft. As she waited at the top of the stairs, she noticed the dark circles under his eyes and unshaven beard. Their eyes met and he quickened his pace. She rushed into his arms, and they clung to each other in a tight embrace. Tears welled as she felt his arms around her, breathing in the familiar scent of his musky cologne. He cupped her face with his hands, staring into her eyes as if he hadn't seen her in months. Raw emotion took hold as she sought his lips, wondering at fate. Passion took hold as he carried her to the bed. They landed with a soft thud on the mattress, oblivious to anything but the intense bond they shared. Rose felt as if her entire being was restored again.

There was still so much left unspoken between them, but she silenced the questions in her mind. Right now, all she craved was being in his arms. She told herself not to worry, to enjoy the intimacy. Lyon couldn't seem to get enough of her as he traced a line of kisses down her neck. Their joining was passionate yet tender, and Rose reveled in her love for him.

***

The sun rose over Florence as they gazed at each other after a sleepless night.

"I've got a busy day, so I'll get us some coffee." Lyon threw on a pair of jeans and a collared shirt, his chiseled profile and long eyelashes catching the light.

"You're the best," said Rose dreamily. She told herself that she would awaken in five more minutes.

What felt like seconds later, Lyon appeared and handed her a smoky, rich cup of coffee.

"I have so much to tell you, Lyon. I'm not sure where to start."

"Why is Beatrice here?" he asked.

"You're not going to believe this, but she found another clue in the original drawings that I found in my apartment last year. Beatrice thinks that her discovery relates to a centuries-old mystery about a lost Leonardo da Vinci painting. It's farfetched, I know, but her instincts have always been really incredible. And I'd like to support Beatrice in doing more research on this issue. There's a lot to consider."

"I admire your loyalty, but are you sure you want to take this on?"

Rose thought for a minute. "I plan to support Beatrice on this journey when and where it's appropriate. It's a lot bigger than us, so ultimately it will be up to the cardinal to decide what's best."

"Rose," said Lyon. "We need to talk about us."

"What about us?" said Rose nervously, not liking the sudden shift in topic. After all, she could talk about a lost Leonardo all day. She asked, "Did you get out to see your parents?

Lyon went silent. She sensed that she had hit a nerve, and it made her even more anxious. Glancing away at the vista of smoked orange rooftops through the balcony door, Rose gathered her courage and stared into his eyes for answers. The look on his face made her stomach flip-flop. His expression was closed and guarded—even culpable. "Lyon?"

"I was busy this week and never made it."

"That's strange. You seemed like you thought it was a good idea last time we spoke."

"I changed my mind," he said abruptly.

"What do you mean you changed your mind?" she asked, putting her feet on the floor. Rose grabbed for a robe, feeling awkward and uncomfortable being naked in his presence when there were still problems between them. "This is really important, and we're in the middle of planning a wedding. I spoke to the cardinal about our problems, and he seemed confident that we could work together to find a solution."

"I can't guarantee that I can give you a child, which is all you want, Rose. I don't want that responsibility of feeling like I robbed you of a family."

"You can't look at it that way!"

"I saw the look on your face when I told you. You didn't get how difficult it was for me to face the truth and share it with you. Your reaction was not what I expected."

"I'm sorry, Lyon. You caught me completely off guard, and I just reacted." She took a deep breath. "So, what was keeping you so busy this week?"

The look on his face told her something was very wrong. "Lyon? What's going on?" Rose's voice rose a notch and her hands began to tremble. She pulled the belt of her robe tightly around her body. Keeping her voice calm, she asked, "Last time you didn't level with me, you were with Dominique. Am I to assume you've seen her?" When he didn't answer, Rose knew exactly what he had been doing while they were apart, but she wanted him to admit it.

"Yes," he said quietly.

"I see," said Rose, feeling a sharp pain go through her. "Did you sleep with her?"

"Almost," he said softly. "I'm sorry, Rose," he said, looking away, unable to face her.

"I see," she said quietly. "That didn't take long, did it?" Her voice rose a notch. "How could you break us like that?"

Lyon became pale. "It's not what you think. It didn't mean anything!"

"Didn't mean anything? We're getting married in a few weeks! Didn't mean anything?" Rose started seeing black spots in front of her eyes and willed herself to be strong. "I can't believe you just came over last night as if nothing had changed."

"Rose, I was angry at your reaction."

"So, you decided to *almost* hop in bed with your ex? That bodes well for our future. So, anytime we have a fight or a disagreement, I know where you'll go."

"That's not fair and you know it."

They both stared at each other. Rose felt ill as her future blew up in front of her face. She took off her engagement ring and handed it back to him. "Here, I think this is yours." The ring burned her hand as she held it out to him.

"Please keep it." He looked upset when he stared at it. "I don't expect you to forgive me, but I do love you, Rose, more than anyone or anything."

"I find that hard to believe, Lyon. Love involves trust and responsibility, of which you have neither."

"It's true. I messed up, and I don't know what to say."

"Neither do I," said Rose, bursting into tears. "You've really hurt me, and I'm shocked that you failed to give our problems any kind of reasonable response. Instead, you just cheated on me to prove what?"

"I don't know," he exclaimed. "I wanted to shut everything out. I'm sorry, Rose. It was a terrible mistake. Say you'll forgive me," he pleaded.

"I'm going home," she announced suddenly.

"You are home," he said. "Here with me."

"I'm flying to Charlottesville as soon as possible." She knew that she was being rash, having just pledged her allegiance to supporting Beatrice in her quest, but the hurt was overwhelming. "I need to get away and think about things. You'll let your mother know that a December wedding isn't possible."

"Come on, Rose! I said I was sorry."

"Sure," she replied. "I can *almost* forgive you."

When Lyon left to get to an appointment, Rose did the unthinkable. She called Doris and poured her heart out. For once, her mother didn't offer judgment or recriminations. She simply said, "Come home, Rose. We love you."

Chapter 13

ROSE LOOKED AROUND her childhood room in Charlottesville, rubbing her eyes as if she were waking up from a dream. The once beige paint had been replaced with a blue floral wallpaper boasting a swirl pattern that jarred her senses. It was as if the design had a mind of its own, dancing wildly over the walls. Her princess-pink comforter was replaced with a textured blue-chevron design suitable for guests. A photograph of her parents in a silver frame graced the antique wood nightstand. They both grinned like Cheshire cats as if they personified the secret to happiness. Doris looked youthful with her blond hair pulled back in a low ponytail. Something about her expression suggested a side of her that Rose never witnessed. There was a softness that made her appear approachable. The angry, dramatic woman who raised her was a different person back then, and Rose wondered how the coming week would play out.

Thanks to a good night's sleep, she stretched and got out of bed, feeling the new plush blue rug on her bare feet. Indeed, she reminded herself that she hadn't stayed here in over five years, so her mother had every right to make improvements. On the far wall, her diploma, framed in silver, practically disappeared into the wallpaper. A pair of oversized birds dominated the left wall, and Rose wasn't sure what to think of the blue herons, which belonged in a hotel. Most definitely, they were something that her mother found in a home décor catalogue and ordered up for show.

Stop it, Rose commanded herself. She was not here to judge. Her mother was providing solace for the first time in a long time, and Rose reached out to greedily take it. It didn't mean that they were going to connect. A vision of Leonardo's *Battle of Anghiari* flashed through her mind with its snarling horses and lifelike warriors, making Rose practically laugh aloud. Perhaps, she told herself, she was being overly dramatic and could liken their relationship to the age-old cliché of oil and water.

Throwing on some black jeans and a camel-colored sweatshirt, she went to her black utilitarian suitcase to search for her favorite tan M. Gemi sneakers. Deliberately leaving the bag half unpacked provided her a measure of comfort; an escape was possible. Even though her idealistic heart wanted Doris to transform into a loving mother, Rose was too logical and pragmatic to expect the impossible.

Taking a deep breath, she checked her appearance, pleasantly surprised that she looked fairly pulled together after the long trip home. She craved her favorite Italian espresso but quickly banished the thought. She was not going to compare every aspect of this trip to her life in Italy. The timing was actually good, and the beautiful Virginia fall day welcomed her. She couldn't wait to see Zoey and Stan, and maybe even pay a visit to her old stomping ground at Bellfield Academy. After searching for her phone, she sent Zoey a cryptic text, saying she'd decided to come home after being away so long. Then she asked if they could get together after school. Zoey's response was an immediate *Yes!!!* Rose was elated and offered to stop by Bellfield that afternoon.

She wondered what Lyon was doing but quickly shifted her thoughts to the present. Her former fiancé had behaved horribly, and she was furious. Looking down at her hand, she wore the ring on her right hand as a compromise for now. The ring made her think of Faith, and how much she missed her and Joseph, who had been her surrogate parents. Their connection was special, but Rose realized that they knew the whole time about Lyon's accident. In fact, they were all complicit in Lyon's deception, and she was the only one blissfully ignorant.

After all, she wasn't a robot, and his news had hit hard that afternoon in Rome. It was so unexpected. What was she supposed to say? "Oh, it's all okay, sweetie. We'll just go forward and everything will be perfect. No problem!" *Damnit,* thought Rose, *I have a right to my feelings.* Rose walked into the kitchen to see Doris in a hot-pink track suit, cooking french toast, one of her childhood indulgences.

"Good morning," she said, going right for the coffeepot on the counter.

"Hi, darling," replied Doris with a wide grin. "I'm making your favorite. How did you sleep?"

"Very well," she replied, pouring the black coffee and adding a few raw sugars. "No jet lag! Can I help?"

"Nope, take a seat."

"Thanks," said Rose, pulling herself onto the counter stool to face her mother.

Studying her for a moment, Rose noticed that Doris looked very well indeed. Her porcelain skin was adorned by flawless makeup, and her hair was sprayed and styled. In fact, she looked camera ready. Rose asked, "Do you have plans today?"

"Well," she said, "as a matter of fact, I'm heading over to the club for a luncheon. What do you want to do today?"

The hot coffee tasted familiar and much more pleasing than she anticipated. "I'll probably take a jog around the neighborhood. I got in touch with Zoey, and I plan to head over to Bellfield after school today to see her."

"That's a wonderful plan, dear."

Is this really happening? Rose thought. She was in the kitchen with her mother, having a mundane conversation about the day's activities. No drama, yet.

Doris added, "I know you have a lot on your mind right now. I won't push you to talk until you're ready." She walked over and placed two perfect, lightly browned pieces of French toast on her plate. A bowl of freshly cut fruit was nearby, and Doris grabbed a small pitcher full of maple syrup.

"Thank you so much," said Rose, then choked on the word *Mom.*

It just wouldn't come out, and she felt embarrassed. *Appreciate this pocket of normal,* she told herself, staring at the beautiful breakfast in front of her. It wasn't like she would ever eat French toast any other time in her life, and certainly not on a Friday morning. Coffee and a croissant were as creative as she got—unless, of course, Lyon treated her to his pepper-fried eggs, which she loved. Annoyed that she was mulling over Lyon, Rose took another bite of the breakfast.

"I suppose you've heard the news?"

"What news?"

"Zoey is pregnant with her first child!"

For some reason, Rose had blocked that from her mind. Maybe it was self-preservation, but the realization jolted her heart. "I know, I know!" she said casually. "I'll go out and get her a gift this morning. I'm so happy for her."

"Well," said Doris, filling her coffee cup. "You know what that means."

"No idea," offered Rose.

"She's going to take maternity leave next spring, and they are looking for a temporary replacement at Bellfield."

"What does that have to do with me?"

"Rose, I can't think of a better way for you to"—Doris cleared her throat—"engage again with your family and friends here. You could take a temporary teaching position that not only helps your best friend but also gets you back where you belong, dear. You're a great teacher, and everyone loves you at Bellfield." Doris paused, assessing how hard to push. "Eric and I are so proud of you for following your dreams and buying an apartment abroad. Your art show was fabulous, but I think you need to use this time to really think about your future. After all, you're not getting any younger."

Zing. There it was. The first Doris maneuver to take control of her life. Yet, Rose was so confused that a temporary teaching position sounded like a lifeline. Zoey could map out her English lesson plans for Rose to follow. She could help her and regroup. Did she want to rent out her apartment in Italy for the spring? Where would she live? She absolutely couldn't stay here, but she was sure Zoey would have some ideas. Rose wondered if she was losing her mind for even considering such a plan!

Rose liked the idea of a temporary teaching position at Bellfield. She took another sip of her coffee, pondering the concept. Zoey was her best friend, and there was something very appealing about being here to welcome her first child. Rose was tired of so many things right now and furious with Lyon. The words tumbled out before she could think the idea through. She said, "You know what, I think you're right. I'll talk to Zoey about it today. Maybe I could fill in for her this winter while she gets ready for the baby."

Doris beamed, and her look of pure joy was almost as bright as her tracksuit. Had Rose ever told her mother, "You're right"? *A new direction*, Rose thought, feeling satiated by the delicious breakfast and having her mother take care of her. *Lyon,* she thought sadly, *you may not be the one for me.* Catching sight of her engagement ring on her right hand, Rose started to nervously twist the ring around her finger. She made herself stop and instead reached for her coffee to soothe her overwrought senses.

"Can I get you anything else?" Doris inquired sweetly.

"No," said Rose. "This was wonderful. I really appreciate you letting me sleep in and the lovely breakfast."

"I'm so happy you're home Rose. You belong here."

***

That afternoon, Rose wandered around Charlottesville's historic Downtown Mall area with its outdoor patios and pretty shops. Everything was familiar and comfortable without the language barrier, foreign customs, or ancient monuments. A black Labrador wandered up to have her pet him, and when she looked up, there was her ex, Ben, and his beautiful little girl, Emily. Her heart jumped into her throat at the sight of them, and Rose steeled herself for a degree of awkwardness. Emily came running up to give her a hug, and Rose tried not to come unglued by the moment. Of course, Ben looked as handsome as ever in his navy sweater and several-day-old beard, which suited him.

"Hi," he said. "This is a surprise! What are you doing here?"

"Hi," she replied. "I could ask you the same question." She tried to sound detached and willed herself to stay calm. They had parted on bad terms, and his friendliness was disarming.

"I'm looking for a present for my dad's seventieth birthday. We're having a small family gathering this weekend."

"Oh, give him my best. I'm looking for something for Zoey, who is expecting her first child. I'm excited for her."

Emily tugged on her jacket. "You should get her a fluffy bunny!"

Rose pondered Emily's idea. "What kind of bunny?"

"Like this," said the little girl, pulling it from Ben's tote bag. Emily showed her the little white bunny with half an ear missing. It was the stuffed animal Rose had selected for her and clearly looked loved. She had been so close to being Emily's stepmother. The concept was utterly poignant at this very moment.

"Now I understand," said Rose. "Thanks for the idea, sweetheart."

"How come you left?" Emily asked. "My dad says he misses you."

Rose and Ben stared at each other for a long moment. Ben looked down at her hand, noticing that she wore her engagement ring on her right hand. He cleared his throat and offered, "Emily, this is between Daddy and Rose. We can talk about it later." He looked up at her and said, "Sorry for that."

"No, absolutely. I assume your wife is back at the house."

He eyed her and said, "We aren't together anymore. It's complicated. Angie is in the Greek islands on another modeling assignment. This is my only girl," he said, pulling Emily close to him. "So, how long are you in town?"

"A few weeks," she replied without thinking.

"Good to know," said Ben. With a wily grin, he offered, "I'd really like to talk at some point. You owe me after that donation to

Feedmore. As a matter of fact, I just wrote them another check. You should know that I've thought a lot about my priorities. I deeply regret how we ended."

Of all things she had thought would happen on this visit, she had not considered interacting with Ben. Yet, she felt pulled. If Ben was anything, he was a good father and son.

Rose smiled warmly. "Let me think about it. I really hadn't planned on running into you."

"I understand," he said patiently. "Maybe it was fate."

"Maybe," said Rose, kneeling to look Emily in the eye. "I love seeing you, sweet girl."

"Bye, Rose," said Emily, as Ben nudged her to come with him.

"Bye," said Rose, wondering how on earth she had come face-to-face with Ben on a random September afternoon. She had worshipped Ben all her life, fallen crazy in love with him until he proved that money was his Achilles heel. Soon afterwards, her knight in shining armor, Lyon, appeared and they shared a dreamy Italian romance.

Rose pulled her wayward thoughts together and walked over to a small shop on the corner that carried baby things. Emily's rabbit idea and some books were a great start. As luck would have it, she found a pretty basket and filled it with books, a stuffed gray rabbit, a couple of patterned onesies, and some cute socks with little dog faces on the ankles.

***

The trees are a symphony of gold, red and orange, thought Rose, marveling at the Virginia landscape as she made her way to meet Zoey at Bellfield. Virginia was a beautiful state, with its rolling hills and horse farms. But Rose admonished herself not to compare Charlottesville to Tuscany. They represented two completely different lifestyles.

Rose observed Bellfield's stately red brick façade and felt a wave of nostalgia. There was something about this building that always took her breath away. She felt such a sense of joy at being back here. Seeing a group of girls talking in a circle, she chuckled softly to herself and relished her native tongue in a way she had never experienced before.

"Ms. Maning," called Lizzie with her blazing red hair. "You're here!" She ran to give her a hug.

"Ciao, Lizzie," said Rose. "It's great to see you, sweetheart. I've missed my girls."

Rose basked in their enthusiasm at seeing her again, realizing how great it was to be back at her alma mater. A series of hugs followed as she was peppered with questions about her life abroad.

"We heard you're famous now," offered Melody, causing everyone to stop talking at once. "You did that big art show in Florence last June, and we saw pictures of those giant wall-sized canvases."

"I'm hardly famous, but I'm proud of the work that I did."

Rose looked up to see Zoey emerge from the front door, clearly looking for her. A chic black-and-white tunic covered her baby bump in a professional manner. Rose broke free of the girls to greet her dear friend.

"Zoey, you look so gorgeous. You're practically glowing."

"Oh," she said, blushing as she put her hand on her belly. "You're too kind. I feel like I've got the beginnings of a basketball in there, and I think I've started to waddle just a tad bit too much."

"Stop!" exclaimed Rose. "You're being ridiculous."

They walked inside arm in arm, where Rose looked at a beautiful rendering of a horse in a meadow drawn by a student. The painting was well done, and Rose realized that she had been so caught up in her and Lyon's problems that she hadn't even thought about drawing or painting. That desire returned, and she thought she would head to the art store after their visit to purchase a few supplies while she was in town. They made their way to a new teacher's lounge, which boasted a fresh coat of gray paint, a small kitchen area, and new sofas.

"What is this spa-like space?" asked Rose. "What happened to that broom closet they had when I was here?"

"Isn't it fabulous?" said Zoey. "Look at the new Keurig. What can I get you?"

Rose watched and exclaimed, "Don't tell me that you're going to put foam on my latte? Seriously?"

Zoey chuckled and handed her a warm mug as they took a seat together underneath a sunny window overlooking the green where students milled about.

"It's so great to see you!" cried Rose. "I still can't believe I'm actually back in Virginia!"

"Let's not beat around the bush. Why aren't you in Florence planning your wedding?"

Rose froze, realizing that Zoey knew her better than anyone. "It's just that—"

"Spill it," demanded Zoey, who leaned in to hear her side of the story. "And don't you dare try to sugarcoat anything. It has to be serious if you flew all the way back here and are staying in the same house as Doris."

Rose burst out laughing, then the tears flowed. "I thought everything was great. I mean, I was busy all summer doing interviews and talking about the art show. Some dealers had contacted me about doing more work. Lyon was very supportive the whole time and then. . . " She paused. "And then he finally told me that he may not be able to have kids. He was in an accident when he was younger."

"And here I am sitting across from you, very pregnant indeed," said Zoey.

"You know I'm beyond happy for you," said Rose.

"I don't doubt that for a minute," said Zoey, pointing to the basket. "You went overboard as usual."

"Oh, did I mention that I went to the mall this morning and ran into Ben and Emily? He's no longer with Angie."

"The plot thickens," said Zoey, getting up to add some more milk to her herbal tea.

"Let me do that," insisted Rose, taking her mug. She doctored up both of their drinks, admiring the mahogany countertop with the pretty labeled ceramic jar filled with sugar packets and the matching white cup filled with wooden stirrers.

"What happened with Lyon, Rose?"

"He was embarrassed by the admission and didn't expect me to get so angry."

"Go on."

"I worked things through and spoke to the cardinal. It took a few days for me to calm down, but I did. While he was supposed to be contemplating our options as a couple, he almost had sex with his ex."

"No way! You guys are the perfect couple." Zoey asked. "Sorry, that's what I thought. I digress. So, you decided what before you left Florence?"

"I told him I wasn't sure about marrying him because that's how I feel. His solution to the problem was immature and just plain dishonest. I'm furious he decided to spring this on me three months before our wedding. I just can't think straight right now. I expected more from him."

"But he said *almost* not that he did. Clearly, he regretted his actions and stopped himself before the sex."

"Have you been taking law classes?" joked Rose.

"He didn't sleep with her, Rose," said Zoey. "And he admitted it to you. That has to count for something."

"I disagree. I'm still furious, but I want to talk about you and your baby, not my very melodramatic love life!"

"I feel great, but I do get tired by the end of the day. On a bright note, Stan eats mint chip ice cream with me every night. We are super excited and have been looking to buy a house before the baby is born."

"That's exciting! Any leads?"

"As a matter of fact, I'm planning on seeing some listings this Saturday. I could really use your help in finding our forever house. Stan has to work, but I thought we could go together, and all have dinner afterwards?"

"I can't think of anything better!"

"How long are you here for?" asked Zoey, taking another sip of tea.

"I was thinking of staying a few weeks."

"There's no way you're going to last more than a week with Doris!" exclaimed Zoey, stifling her laughter.

"I know, I know. I need a plan."

"Well, believe it or not, one of my students' parents has a carriage house that they rent. I just received a notice about it."

Rose bit her lip. "I'm not sure what I want to do. I need time to sort through everything. I'm so confused right now."

"Selfishly, I'm glad you're here. My baby needs her godmother."

"Ohhh," said Rose. "I'm so honored. And is that before or after you kill me for messing up your airline flights? I hope they're refundable."

"Nope."

Rose felt horrible, but an idea surfaced. "How about if you go and stay in my apartment as a romantic getaway?"

"So, you really think the wedding is off?"

"Oh, Zoey! Help!" Rose covered her face with her hands.

Chapter 14

NO WORD FROM LYON. Rose put down her phone, wondering why she thought he would get in touch with her in the first place. Hadn't they said everything? The pain of their separation was harsh on this grayish fall morning. Rose tossed and turned all night, trying to make sense of everything that had happened in the past few weeks. How in the world did she go from planning a wedding at Lyon's family villa in Tuscany to staying in her childhood room in Charlottesville so quickly? It was surreal. Her future unexpectedly splintered apart, and Rose felt a wave of melancholy so strong it made her want to hide under the covers all day.

Rose got out of bed, willing herself to live vicariously through Zoey's happiness. Giving herself a pep talk of the same ilk that helped her students for years, she thought about the positives in her life. She was lucky to have a supportive family and friends. Maybe her Italy experience was an adventure that needed to end. Thanks to her discovery, Rose had enough money to support herself, continue her art, and help others along the way. *Not a bad situation,* she thought. As for her love life, she decided that she was better off alone at this point. Love was just too complicated. *Lyon could live happily ever after with Dominque,* Rose lied to herself, twisting her ring from side to side, then removing it. Why hadn't things turned out differently?

Pushing her own sadness aside, Rose pulled herself together and thought of her best friend. Zoey was so helpful to her last year, and she wanted to return the favor. A strong cup of black coffee made Rose feel infinitely better. *It's the little things in life,* she told herself.

Grabbing her purse, she went to look at the first address Zoey gave her, which was about ten minutes away. She scribbled a note to Doris and headed out the door.

Based on the number of open houses they attended, Rose knew Zoey wanted a move-in-ready home that was low maintenance and close to Bellfield. Stan, however, wanted a farmhouse with a big backyard for their future kids to play. After a very short drive, Rose found the cul-de-sac and the townhouse. Hopping out of her car, she was greeted by a beguiling Asian woman who was professionally dressed in a dark pants suit. Rose was relieved that they had taken the plunge and decided to work with a realtor rather than trying to do it themselves.

"Hello," she said. "You must be Rose. Zoey told me you were coming. I'm Maya Li."

"Good morning, Maya. Thanks for letting me tag along." A vision of her first meeting with Lyon that June morning flashed through her mind. Her excitement had been palpable at the prospect of an international house hunt and then meeting a handsome realtor. *Stop it!* Rose willed herself.

"No problem!" said Maya. "What do you think?"

"It's a very well-maintained complex," offered Rose, waving to Zoey, who was just driving up in her used Volvo wagon—another new acquisition to suit their upcoming lifestyle shift. Rose looked over the manicured lawns and spied the tan clapboard unit with a nice front porch. The sun peeked out from behind a puffy cloud, kissing her face. *What a good sign,* she concluded, telling herself that today was all about Zoey and Stan. They were going to find their dream home. A wave of optimism coursed through her.

"Good morning," she said cheerfully.

"Hey, so sorry I'm running behind," said Zoey, looking adorable in a blue smock dress and cognac-colored boots. "I had to get some food in me, which was a bit of a challenge this morning. Anyway, enough about that. I see you two have met. Maya, Rose lived in Charlottesville for years before relocating to Florence."

"So, I should have said *ciao* when we met," said Maya. "I absolutely love Florence! I worked in a small jewelry shop on the Ponte Vecchio bridge one summer when I was in college, but that was a long time ago. How lucky you are to live abroad."

"Yes," said Rose. "It's been quite an adventure!"

They all laughed. Maya said, "Zoey, this is the corner unit townhouse, which is hard to find, I might add. As you saw, it's only about five miles from Bellfield. This home is a three-bedroom, three-bathroom unit that's completely renovated. It just came on the market yesterday, so you're going to have to act fast if you're interested."

"How many square feet?" asked Rose.

"It's just under two thousand. Perfect for a young family. It's what I like to call *turnkey*. Let's take a look inside."

Rose nodded at Zoey, who was looking around at the neighborhood. She spied a couple running with a baby jogger and gave Rose a thumbs-up sign. "I love that there are other families here."

"That's a plus," said Rose.

The first thing Maya pointed out were the fresh-looking hardwood floors and the open floor plan. "This is the formal dining room, but it would also make a great office."

"I like that idea," said Zoey. "I need to come up with a space for Stan to play his music."

"You could easily add a set of French doors, or better yet, you could find a cool vintage sliding barn door," Rose said.

"That's a great idea! A vintage door would add more character to the unit." Maya pointed out the crown molding and gas fireplace.

"I really do want an all-white kitchen," said Zoey.

They turned the corner and spied a dazzling, newly renovated white kitchen with white subway tiles and stainless-steel appliances. Rose thought of her tiny kitchen in Italy that had more charm than function. This setup seemed ideal for them to cook and entertain.

"You're in luck because you wouldn't have to do a thing to the kitchen," said Maya.

"I don't even cook very much, but I love this long prep-space counter." Zoey laughed. "Maybe I'll start."

"That's the spirit!" said Maya.

"I can even fit a small round table in that corner as well as a highchair for the baby."

Rose tamped down her jealously as she envisioned Zoey here, feeding her new child. She really wanted the best for Zoey and was glad her dreams of a family were coming true. She offered, "You could also add a small square table on the end here."

"That would work," said Zoey, taking out her phone to snap a few pictures.

"Hey, you're really good at this!" Maya said.

"My fiancé is a realtor in Florence. I guess I must have absorbed some of these ideas from him." Rose couldn't believe she'd just said that. Had she really called Lyon her fiancé? Hadn't they just broken up? She watched Maya look at her left hand, but she didn't comment.

Her eyes met Zoey's, and she suddenly felt completely awkward.

"Are we ready to see the main bedroom?" asked Maya, walking with them to a light, bright room with pale-gray carpet.

"This is a good-sized room which fits a king-sized bed," said Rose.

"Stan loves his California king," said Zoey as she opened a door to check out the size of the closets. "The closet space is a little small."

"Well, you're going to love the updated main bath with double sinks and a jacuzzi-style jet tub."

"Rose! Can't you see me getting into this at the end of the day? Life would be good!" Zoey said.

Rose admired the gray and white hexagon floor tiles and the white vanity units. "This is about three times the size of my bathroom in Florence. Remember there wasn't any kind of door on the shower? This is a spa, Zoey."

"Do you think I can convince Stan to give up his dream of a farmhouse on five acres for this?"

Maya showed them two more bedrooms connected by the Jack-and-Jill-style bathroom.

"So, where can Stan set up to play music?"

"I have two more things to show you," said Maya. They headed down a flight of stairs to a small basement area. Rose looked around her, observing the windows, which let in nice light.

"You could turn this into a great playroom."

"This seems a little devoid of any charm," remarked Zoey, walking around.

Rose jumped in. "I could paint it. Can't you see a few animals on this right wall, and how about a few ABCs over here?"

"Well, that's a nice friend."

"Godmother," corrected Zoey.

"Are you an artist?" asked Maya.

Rose was about to give some nonsensical comment on how she didn't have much formal training. Zoey answered, "Yes" for her.

"That was one of the main reasons I relocated to Florence," said Rose. "I wanted to pursue a career as an artist."

"She did an amazing opening at a major gallery in Florence last spring," interjected Zoey. She reached in her bag and grabbed a water to stay hydrated. "I feel like I'm always hungry and thirsty now."

Rose wished she could relate.

"I wish all of my clients had someone who could offer such great suggestions and also have the skill set to make it happen." Maya added, "But do you have the time?"

"I'm here for a few weeks," said Rose. "And this would be a perfect project." Rose paused. "That is, if Zoey and Stan decide on a townhouse."

Maya took them to the two-car garage, which she thought would be the perfect spot for Stan to play his music. "I like the idea of a door on your office space, and maybe there's a way to soundproof this space."

Rose watched Zoey take a short video of the garage and text it to Stan, who was on deadline for a work project at the insurance company where he had taken a full-time job.

"So, what should we call this one, Zoey?"

"The Move-in-Ready Palace!"

"With a future animal farm in the playroom," said Rose.

The next house was twenty minutes away, so Rose hopped in the car with Zoey for the drive. Zoey said, "I'm not going to lie. I absolutely love that fresh and modern townhouse."

"And it's in budget," said Rose.

"We sound like an episode of house hunters on HGTV! I've certainly watched enough episodes." She blushed. "It's my guilty pleasure."

"Gosh, it's funny how little television I've watched this past year. Anyway, this isn't about me. It's about you. I can certainly see the merits of such a pristine home, but do you think Stan wants more character?"

"We're off to a hundred-year-old farmhouse on five acres way outside of town."

"That's a very different concept."

"You think?" joked Zoey.

They chatted easily for the car ride, following behind Maya, who got on 64 West. Three turns later, after exiting, they drove up to a large red brick farmhouse with white columns in the front.

"This is big!" announced Rose, looking dubiously at the house.

"I know," said Zoey, peering at the expansive lawn. "It's beautiful out here."

Maya joined them, pointing out a large magnolia tree and a row of English boxwoods.

"Who's going to take care of all this property? Stan?"

Zoey bit her lip. "This seems like his dream house. Look at the front. It's really stately looking," Zoey said.

Maya found the lockbox and took them inside the enormous front hall with the high ceilings.

"Character," offered Maya. "This is a historic home built over a hundred years ago."

"Look at all of this wallpaper," said Rose running her hands over a dated, fading yellow flower print. She mouthed, *"This is really ugly."*

They went into the living room and observed a carved white mantel. Traditional dental molding adorned the top, and the homeowner had brass sconces on either side, contrasting with emerald-colored wallpaper. Rose didn't say anything as they proceeded to the red dining room, then blurted, "You could have Christmas all the time here."

The kitchen was old with peeling paint and ancient appliances.

"Look at this wonderful butler's pantry," said Maya, pointing to a small corridor.

"Does a butler come with the house?" asked Zoey.

Maya laughed dutifully. Rose whispered in her friend's ear, "Just remember you'd be the butler and the maid here!"

"I heard that!" exclaimed Maya. "Let's take a look at the first-floor principal bedroom which has a working fireplace."

"More wallpaper!" said Rose. "This would be quite a job removing all of it."

"You'd never get bored, and you could do it over time," said Maya.

Rose walked around the bedroom, noting the wide-plank hardwood floors and the four-poster bed. "That's a beautiful handmade four-poster bed, but I doubt Stan wants a queen-sized option." Rose studied the wall. "Will it fit a king?"

Maya whipped out some measure tape. "It would be very tight, but it's possible."

The primary bath needed major updating. "More yellow wallpaper!" said Rose.

"All I see are house projects," said Zoey nervously, looking around her. "This house needs a lot of work. Everything is old." She turned to Maya and asked, "Has anything been updated?"

"In a word, no," said Maya. "But you could do it all in stages."

"Honey, you're going to be peeling off wallpaper for years," said Rose.

They walked upstairs to see three nice bedrooms, and when they went into the old bathroom. Zoey exclaimed, "Wow. No wallpaper. Is this the only room in the house?"

"Maybe the unfinished basement," said Maya, who led them back downstairs to a rickety set of steps.

"Hold the handrail," ordered Rose, who didn't want her to trip. They got downstairs to an unfinished basement filled with cobwebs. "Character," said Rose.

"You need to see the outside," said Maya. "The land is incredible and would be a wonderful place for your children to grow up."

They walked out a screened door to massive rolling hills and beautiful old trees.

"This is amazing," exclaimed Zoey. "Stan would love this!"

"Agreed," said Rose. "No shortage of fresh air and green grass here."

Zoey looked around her and said, "It is really private."

They stood outside and looked at the rolling hills. The day had warmed up, and Rose considered this option. It would be a big undertaking. Maya explained that the house was almost three thousand square feet, and literally everything needed updating.

Rose could tell that Zoey was overwhelmed. Fortunately, Maya reached the same conclusion. "Why don't you head back into town and break for lunch? I've got a few calls to make, so I can meet you back to see the third house around one o'clock."

"I'm dying for a salad from Feast. I love that gourmet market."

"Great idea," said Zoey. "I'm a bit overwhelmed after seeing the Five-Acre Farmhouse."

"You mean the Wallpaper Wonder?" joked Rose.

"That's a good one," said Zoey. "How about something closer to town and in better condition?"

"I have the perfect third option," announced Maya. She gave them the address of the third house, promising to meet them there promptly at one o'clock. As she was walking away, she said, "You know, proximity to town carries a higher price tag."

"Of course," said Rose. "Everything is a tradeoff."

The concept echoed in her ears. She was attracted to Ben, but he had betrayed her. Ben had *accidentally* taken the centuries-old drawings she discovered on a trip back to the States. He was a businessman and felt they should be sold to the highest bidder at auction. Rose believed in her heart that she found the drawings to protect them.

After all that she went through with Ben, it seemed her prayers were answered when she fell for Lyon. Could she actually marry him without worrying that he wasn't going to fall back with Dominque, who adored him and pandered to his ego?

Zoey thanked her for coming about ten times on the ride back to downtown Charlottesville. "It's my pleasure," said Rose. "We're making progress."

"Maybe the third house is a compromise. Something in town with a bigger yard?"

"We'll find out soon enough. In the meantime, I can't wait to have my favorite margherita panini," said Rose. "Do they still have that on the menu?"

"Of course. I'm dying for their mac and cheese." She pursed her lips. "Maybe a salad too."

***

Feast was always Rose's favorite gourmet market. Watching the college students mill about, she ordered her sandwich and grabbed a table for them while Zoey went to the restroom.

"I feel like I know where every rest stop is located in downtown Charlottesville," said Zoey as she pulled out her chair.

"You look like the picture of health," said Rose. She sipped on a lemonade. "I'm so glad that I could share this experience with you today. You've got two great choices, though that last house is going to be a lot of work. Do you have enough time?"

"This is where Stan and I completely disagree. I don't want to be bogged down by the long commute to Bellfield. It would cost a fortune to remove all of that ugly wallpaper in the house too."

"The townhouse was gorgeous," said Rose. "And it was move-in ready. I would definitely paint the playroom for you!"

"I love that idea," said Zoey. "How long are you staying?"

"What if I told you I'm considering renting out my apartment next spring and staying here to take some time off from my melodramatic love life?"

"Have you told Lyon?"

A server called their name, and Rose popped up to grab their trays of sandwiches. She couldn't wait to taste the hot panini and promised herself she was not going to compare it to anything in Italy. Returning to the table, Rose handed Zoey her tray and sat.

"Thank you. This looks delicious. I could eat this table." She took a bite of some hot mac and cheese, then said, "Well, have you discussed this new plan with him?"

"No, I haven't," said Rose. "I'm still so angry with him, and I need to clear my head. What if this whole Italy thing was just temporary, and I'm supposed to be back here with my family and friends? I didn't realize how homesick I was."

"I'm so proud of you for chasing your dreams over there. It's not for me to tell you what to do. It all sounds very complicated."

"I'm so tired of complicated. I thought Lyon and I were the perfect couple until this latest curve ball."

"Do you still love him?"

"I'm too hurt to answer that question. By the way, did you ever check into that carriage house?"

"Yes. It's all good news. The house is owned by Ted and Regina

Perkins. Their daughter graduated last spring, and they want someone to keep an eye on their place when they travel. You could stay there on a month-to-month basis, which would work. They don't even want to charge any rent if you help dog-sit on weekends. You'd only have to cover your utilities."

"Did you tell them about me?"

"Of course," said Zoey. She looked Rose in the eye. "You need to talk to Lyon again before you decide not to return to Italy for six months."

"I'm not selling the apartment. I'm going to rent it and get my head together. And be the best godmother ever to your baby. That's a promise."

They hugged and made their way back to the car. They put the next address into Zoey's Google Maps and headed to a charming small neighborhood nearby.

"Just a ten-minute drive," said Rose. "Not bad."

"Not bad at all," said Zoey, peering at the houses in the neighborhood. "This is really charming. Look at the kids playing in that cul-de-sac over there."

They drove up to a white ranch house with a front porch, window boxes, and an exposed-wood door.

"This is adorable," said Zoey.

"This ranch house screams cute, young happy family," exclaimed Rose. "It's very well maintained, and I love the yellow pansies in the front beds."

Maya pulled in behind them and finished up a phone call to join them. "What do you think, Zoey? This is charming."

"I'm really pleasantly surprised," said Zoey. "It's super cute, and this is a great neighborhood close to downtown."

"This hasn't come up on the market yet, but it's a renovated ranch with about eighteen hundred square feet with a really nice backyard." Maya added, "I have a surprise for you, but I'll save it for later."

Rose watched Zoey's face light up as she walked up the front entrance, surprised by the white exterior, black shutters, and nice front porch. The inside did not disappoint. It was light and bright, and there were hardwood floors. As they wandered into the open floor plan, Rose noticed the built-in bookcases and room for a play area off the kitchen.

"This is really nice," exclaimed Zoey. "But the floors don't match. They are three different types of hardwood."

"Very few properties are as perfect as the townhouse I showed you earlier. You could redo all the floors to match, and I think that would make a huge difference."

"And there's nothing like fresh paint to change a room. I could definitely help pick the colors to freshen up these walls. I definitely think a rich blue with white high-gloss trim would look fantastic in here."

"You're hired," said Zoey.

"Now, that's a good friend," said Maya with a wink at Rose.

"Oh look," exclaimed Zoey. "It's an all-white kitchen."

Rose ran her hands over the new cabinets and farmhouse sink and nodded her approval. "There's nothing to do here except the floors."

Maya offered, "They redid this kitchen less than two years ago, and it's in good shape. There's plenty of storage, and check out the pantry, which is beautifully organized."

Rose was impressed. She remembered those specific spice drawers from one of the apartments she looked at in Italy. A wave of melancholy coursed through her, and she reminded herself that today was all about Zoey and Stan's happiness.

They toured the main bedroom with the updated shower, but there was no bathtub. The closets were big enough, and the room could hold a king-sized bed. After figuring out which room could work as a nursery and a potential office, Maya showed them the garage, which would work for Stan's music.

"I saved the best for last," said Maya. She led them out to a sizeable backyard that had a full deck and pool area. "And this pool actually has a retractable cover for safety reasons."

"This deck is perfect," said Zoey. "Stan's going to love the pool. I can just see him over there grillin' and chillin'." She got into a conversation with Maya about price, discovering that the property was at the top of their budget.

"These are three great properties," exclaimed Zoey. "Rose, help!"

Rose smiled. "I know which one I'd pick, but it's up to you and Stan, not me!"

"Which one do you like best?" asked Zoey.

Rose felt her phone buzz. She walked over to the corner and heard Lyon's voice when she answered. "How could you, Rose?"

"How could I what, Lyon? What are you talking about?"

He clicked off the line, making Rose's stomach feel queasy.

"Is everything okay?" asked Zoey. "You're as white as a sheet?"

A few minutes later, she started receiving dozens of texts. "Something's happened," said Rose. "And I've got no clue!"

Suddenly, she got a text from Beatrice. *You're not going to believe this, but you were photographed with Vince. You're on the cover of several tabloids because he is painting a likeness of you at the table.*

"What?" cried Rose. "He did what? Oh no!"

Chapter 15

BEATRICE STILL COULDN'T BELIEVE that Rose had left Italy. It was all so heartbreaking. The past two months felt like a lifetime. Loneliness gnawed at Beatrice, and she found herself increasingly calling on Julian. Despite Rose's absence, Beatrice hadn't given up; she was bound and determined to validate another clue.

After weeks of work, Beatrice concluded that there was a high probability that Rose's second drawing showed a likeness of the great Giorgio Vasari as a young man, and she was close to proving it. In the last few weeks, she uncovered the figure's high forehead, patrician nose, and slight beard. Now Beatrice believed that the nobleman in Rose's drawing bore a striking resemblance to Vasari's self-portrait hanging in the Uffizi Museum in Florence. She knew every inch of the drawing and wanted to compare the image with the oil painting.

She thought if she could establish a clear connection between the phrase *Cerca Trova* located on the wall in the Hall of the Five Hundred and in Rose's drawing, Vasari's self-portrait, and a possible link to Leonard da Vinci, then there would be enough evidence to prove to scholars that the case needed to be reopened. A wave of self-doubt washed over her, as she contemplated the enormity of what she was trying to do. Was it complete madness to think she could expose the truth?

In her meeting with the cardinal, she went over the likelihood of Giorgio Vasari's possible intervention in saving the Leonardo painting. Vasari had a reverence for his fellow artists as demonstrated in his sixteenth-century book, *Lives of the Artists*, which was the single most extensive compilation ever written on the masters. Many art historians believed that this reference book with its anecdotal stories forever changed how people viewed art history. Perhaps it was fair to conclude that Vasari was groundbreaking in elevating the status of the professional artist. To this day, his book provided helpful insights into the character and biographies of famous artists. The more Beatrice learned about Vasari, the more she admired his accomplishments. However, she'd be a fool not to consider that other art history scholars weren't as trusting of his accounts.

As much as she needed his help, Beatrice didn't want to provide Julian with too much information. It was a careful balancing act. While she liked him, she would never give up control of her own investigation nor reveal certain facts. Indeed, Beatrice would tell him enough to keep him interested without revealing the truth behind the lost Leonardo. Besides, she wasn't a big fan of Professor Saunders, so she was ready and willing to prove that human instinct could be superior to scientific analysis.

As if he knew she was thinking about him, Julian texted and asked her out to dinner.

Beatrice thought for a minute. Rather than extend the evening that long, Beatrice decided it would be easier to simply have a drink together. Her old friend Dante usually tended bar at a local dive called Mad Souls and Spirits, which specialized in craft cocktails. Mad Souls was the perfect place to take her mind off Giorgio Vasari and his work.

She walked inside the crowded bar, thinking she would grab a table before Julian arrived. With almost no attention to lighting or décor, Mad Souls still maintained a strong following with its quirky chalkboard, stickers on the walls, and casual atmosphere. Dante waved to Beatrice, motioning for her to take a seat at the bar area. Then, with lightning speed, he bounced over to take her order.

"Surprise me," said Beatrice, looking over at a couple chatting and playing cards nearby.

"Tonight's an airline theme. We've engineered a drink called 'flight insurance' made with rum, green tea, cinnamon, and lime. Very smooth," said Dante, wiping his hand on his white T-shirt.

"Sounds good," said Beatrice, giving him a thumbs-up. Her mind turned to Rose. Beatrice wondered where she was right now. She tried to envision Rose's mother's home or the private school she had attended and then later taught at for several years. Her students loved her, evident in the numerous emails and letters that she received.

"Anything else?" asked Dante.

Beatrice paused. "No thanks." She looked up and spied Lyon, who looked very unkempt with a new dark beard.

"Hey, Lyon, it's been a while. How's it going?" asked Dante.

"I've been better," said Lyon carefully. He added, "Really busy with work. How about you?

"Life is good. Things are busy."

"Any particular reason?" asked Lyon.

"This street artist came to town named Vince. He's supposedly some big deal. Women flock to see his latest mural and then come here for cocktails. My manager is happy, so that's a good thing."

"Never heard of him. Who is he?"

Beatrice leaned over so she could hear more of their conversation. There was still no sign of Julian.

"Vince paints murals on buildings about social issues and who gets to sit at the table. It's supposedly not political, but he has a huge following. I heard he came to Florence to do a mural for a big corporation. His messages are powerful. He's created a table scene with women of all nationalities. The dude is a genius. Everybody loves him, and he's got tons of women wrapped around his finger."

"Got it." Lyon nodded. "This is really good. You're not going to serve me airline food I hope?"

"You've got a few options," Dante announced. "Refill?"

"Who comes up with these clever names? I'm going to try the 'hand luggage' cocktail next."

"Good call. Vodka and grapefruit combination."

Intrigued, Beatrice jumped off her barstool. "Lyon!" she said in a loud voice. She could tell that he wasn't in any mood to talk to her.

"Hello, Beatrice," he said, staring at his drink. "Nice to see you. You're staying at Rose's apartment, I take it."

"Rose gave me a key, so I've been able to come and go. What a lifesaver. I'm having a wonderful time researching masters like Vasari, Michelangelo, and da Vinci, who are endlessly fascinating."

Lyon nodded, although he seemed completely disconnected from the conversation.

"I'm meeting my friend Julian, who has been helping me sort through all of the information. Have you talked to Rose?"

"About what?" snapped Lyon.

"Please forgive me for intruding." Beatrice cleared her throat. "I saw the picture in the paper and the tabloid gossip. You shouldn't believe any of it," said Beatrice, trying to get through to him.

"It doesn't matter," said Lyon. "We're not getting married next month."

"What a shame." Beatrice leaned closer. "You and Rose belong together. This is all just unreal. I've never seen two people more in love. She needs to come home."

"I'm not counting on that happening anytime soon."

"I hope not, for all of us. Besides, I need her help. I've found some interesting information."

"Really?" said Lyon.

"I just returned from Paris where I've looked at a copy of Leonardo's *Battle of Anghiari* done by Peter Paul Rubens in 1603. It hangs in the Louvre." She added, "It's absolutely stunning." Beatrice noted his glazed look. "I'm heading back to Rome early next week. Maybe we could have a cup of coffee before I go?"

"I'm pretty busy," said Lyon, turning away from her. He flashed her an agitated look. "Why would Vince paint Rose?"

"It's not what you think," replied Beatrice. "Sorry to ramble on. Good to see you. Maybe another time." She immediately texted Rose to let her know the situation at hand.

Beatrice looked up and spied Julian at the door. Making her

way through the crowd, she greeted him warmly, thankful to have a distraction from the impending drama.

"Hi there," she said as he embraced her, kissing both cheeks.

"You look amazing as always. Nice blouse," he offered gallantly.

Beatrice found his compliments endearing. "You're too kind. Thanks."

His navy cabled sweater and pants looked new. Soon after, they parked themselves at a corner table, ordered drinks, and talked nonstop for hours. Julian was a charming companion. Not ready to depart, Beatrice decided to look at a dinner menu. She studied the night's specials and practically laughed out loud at the PB&J finger sandwiches that were their only option.

"Beatrice," said Julian, clearing his throat. "I want you to know how grateful I am that we met. My life changed when you walked in the door of my father's office."

His declaration caught her completely off guard, especially in this crowded and chaotic space. "Um, that's such a lovely thing to say." She took another sip of her drink. In her mind, Julian qualified for the friend category, but he was awfully sweet. She was just plain confused.

"What I mean is that I'd like to take you out on a real date to an upscale restaurant where we can connect more"—he cleared his throat—"intimately."

Beatrice wanted to say that she thought they were connecting just fine. The words *How old are you?* were on the tip of her tongue, which she promptly bit. Where was Rose when she needed some advice? Julian was a cute and friendly young man, but she wanted information—not romance. Would he think that she led him on?

"That's not necessary," she replied quickly. "Do you have any idea how much I love peanut butter and jelly sandwiches? They're my absolute favorite."

"Alright then," he said with a puppy-dog smile. "You're so

easygoing and down to earth. Not to mention, beautiful and smart. I can't believe I found someone like you."

"Thank you," replied Beatrice. She gulped, then checked to see if her message to Rose made it to the States.

Chapter 16

WHAT MORE CAN I DO? Beatrice wondered after seeing Lyon. He looked terrible and so sad. Gone was the confident man that she knew through Rose. She didn't regret what she said to him because she really believed that he and Rose were made for each other. Hopefully, Rose would grow weary of her hometown and return to Florence.

Although she wished for Rose's return, Beatrice was feeling rather comfortable in her friend's beautiful apartment with the divine balcony view of the city. Rose had told her to stay if she liked, and the days kept melting away as she indulged her passion for art history. The cardinal had been extremely accommodating, telling her not to rush back. It was clear he didn't want to face any kind of decision on how to handle the lost Leonardo discovery. Fortunately, Beatrice had settled into a routine, happily using her time to explore and research the great da Vinci.

She opened her journal and began reviewing copious notes on one of the greatest artists of all time. Da Vinci was born in 1452 near Vinci, the Italian region of Tuscany. His father was a notary and landlord named Messer Piero Frusino Di Antonio da Vinci, while his mother, Caterina, was known as a peasant. They never married, which made Leonardo an illegitimate son. As a young man, he lived with his mother until he was five years old, then moved in with his father, who married another woman. He and his father maintained a good relationship throughout their lives.

Beatrice skipped a few pages and then noted that da Vinci never received any kind of formal education. He was taught such core subjects as reading, mathematics, and writing at home. When he was a teenager, he was sent to Florence to train under the great Andrea del Verrocchio. As a student, he exceeded his master rather quickly, Beatrice recalled, when he painted that angel in *The Baptism of Christ*. The work was so extraordinary that there were rumors that the great Verrocchio vowed never to paint again.

Leonardo did have problems finishing what he started. Many works remained in this gray zone, which provided for endless speculation among art historians. His *St. Jerome in the Wilderness* was all too familiar, and *The Adoration of the Magi* still hung in the Uffizi as a tribute to his genius. Both famous paintings were never finished.

She rubbed her temples and paced the living room. Her phone vibrated, indicating an incoming message from Julian, who wanted to have dinner together, again. His recent declaration made her anxious. He was a lovely young man who evoked none of the firestorm of emotion that she felt with Mike. It was strange how much she missed him after such brief encounters and a questionable connection. Beatrice was pragmatic, if anything, and tried not to think about seeing Mike again. *It's not right*, she thought, but her longing still felt legitimate.

An idea occurred to her. If Vince was in town working on his mural, was there a chance that Mike would try to do something that competed with him? She smiled at the thought. Their rivalry was well known, and it was a possibility. *Rose would have a few good ideas*, she thought, trying to channel her positive energy. That Vince had found her gorgeous came as no surprise. But it was rather aggressive to paint her likeness on the wall. Rose got a seat at the table, Beatrice mused, but at what price? Lyon was clearly hurt and angry, and the mural ultimately caused more harm than good. She wondered if they were ever going to reconcile and heal their broken relationship.

Julian texted her again, indicating that he had something new to share. Intrigued, Beatrice asked for more information, to which he replied, "Information comes with dinner."

She appreciated his charming overtures and readily agreed. *This better be good*, she texted back, adding several laughing smiley-face emojis. She returned to her notebook, writing the words, *Perhaps another clue in the mystery will be uncovered tonight!*

She had run out of clean clothes, which was probably a sign that it was time for her to return to Rome. Just as she was about to dust off her black pants, her phone buzzed, indicating a text from Rose.

Hi, Beatrice: How are you? I'm reeling from a call from Lyon yesterday. What did Vince paint? This is madness.

I'm planning to have dinner with Julian tonight, and I thought we would go take a look! I ran into Lyon the other night at Mad Souls and told him not to believe anything he reads.

Oh, you are a dear! Lyon and I are not in a good place . . . Anyway, I'm dying to know what the mural looks like. Can you take a picture?

Yes! Julian won't mind.

Another date? Please feel free to raid my closet! Help yourself to whatever you like.

Really?

Absolutely. Sounds like your research is going well and so is your friendship with Julian!

He's been lovely to me, showing me Florence, as we uncover clues.

Hmmmm. Clues or a connection?

Definitely clues.

Be well, sweet friend.

Did she have a connection with Julian? She had enjoyed working with him more than she was willing to admit to herself. Beatrice thought Rose's text couldn't have arrived at a better time. She'd been wearing the same two pairs of black pants for the past two weeks. Her outfits were pragmatic and utilitarian. Taking a deep breath, Beatrice felt out of her league wearing something that belonged to beautiful Rose, but her desire to look feminine won out. She opened Rose's closet to reveal a tasteful selection of lovely dresses. Pulling out a blue wrap dress, she held it up to herself on the hanger, pondering whether it would be flattering. *What's wrong with dressing up for a change?* she told herself. Beatrice felt a little like Cinderella getting dressed for the ball as she headed to the shower, determined to tame her wild hair for the evening.

Beatrice poured herself a glass of red wine as she peered out the window to the balcony, delighting in the twinkling lights of Florence. Opening the door, she breathed in the cold, crisp air, which titillated her senses. She pictured Lyon and Rose on this balcony and hoped that Lyon would listen to her.

When Julian came to pick her up, the tension in the air was electric, as if there were a secret between them. He wore a dark jacket and collared shirt rather than his usual jeans. She had to admit that she enjoyed the attention he gave her. They were on the same wavelength, having shed their daily casual attire for a change.

"You look absolutely stunning tonight in that blue dress," said Julian, who appeared genuinely surprised by her transformation.

"Thanks," said Beatrice, feeling sublime in Rose's pretty dress. "Nice to shake it up a bit! Tired of looking like a black widow," she joked, trying to ease the tension between them.

"Does this mean you're off duty?"

"Absolutely not!" she exclaimed. "I'm dying to hear your latest clue."

"Aha!" he replied. "You're just using me for information." He shut the door behind them and took her hand. His words hung in the air. Beatrice pressed on, suppressing any guilt that surfaced.

"Of course," she said easily. After all, she really did like exchanging ideas with Julian and hadn't thought about Mike all day.

***

Dinner was a welcome treat in an upscale restaurant with bubble-shaped floating chandeliers and oak paneling. Gold-patterned cushions warmed up their private booth where she happily perused the decor. Colorful modern abstract paintings highlighted the walls, which Beatrice admired not so much for their beauty but for their symmetry. The painting directly across from her was supposed to be a map of some sort, but it all looked like a set of amorphous shapes. Beatrice was wedded in her love of the old masters, and few artists impressed her with their skills. Rather a myopic viewpoint, but she held fast to it, thinking she was entitled after so many years of study.

They ordered the same thing, a couple of fresh artichoke salads and rare steaks with fries. Beatrice leaned back and studied Julian, noticing the tiny mole on his right cheek and how his face completely changed when he laughed. Gone was the uptight scholar, replaced by a jovial, kind young man. She liked what she saw and must have been staring at him because he stopped talking and cleared his throat.

"Are you ready?" he asked, raising one eyebrow. "Drumroll, please!"

Beatrice took a deep breath. "Yes!"

"We are certain that the great architect Vasari built a wall to protect another work of art, which lends credibility to the claim that he did the same thing with Leonardo da Vinci's *Battle of Anghiari*."

"Really?" exclaimed Beatrice, thrilled. "Go on. That's so interesting. Tell me more about what you know of Vasari."

"I think most people think of Vasari as the first real art historian. His encyclopedia of the art and artists of his time is called *Lives of the Most Excellent Sculptors, Painters and Architects*. It's like the bible of art history writing. Many people credit him with coining the term *Renaissance*."

"Yes!" said Beatrice, hiding her annoyance that he was giving her readily accessible information. "That book is such a detailed encyclopedia of the great masters, including Raphael, Michelangelo, and Leonardo da Vinci. But I think of him every time I walk along the Vasari Corridor, which connects Palazzo Vecchio to the Uffizi Gallery."

They paused while a waiter placed two savory salads in front of them.

"Yes, the Vasari Corridor is a well-known tourist destination these days. Needless to say, he was a gifted architect, and that's why Leonardo's war painting could very well exist, mainly because Vasari built a wall to protect another great artist's work."

"So, you're thinking this discovery sets the framework for my clue—*Cerca Trova?*"

"I think so. Wouldn't that be fantastic?" said Julian. "Let me start from the beginning. There was an early Italian Renaissance artist named Masaccio who created a painting of the Holy Trinity with the Virgin, St. John, and donors. It's located in the Dominican church of Santa Maria Novella. Masaccio probably did this work between 1425 and 1427."

"I don't know this painting, but go on."

"The *Holy Trinity* was his main masterpiece. Most scholars believe that it was a traditional rendering of Jesus on the cross, which was intended for personal prayer and devotions. Not much is known about the commission and which family or families may have paid for this artwork. The donors' faces are pictured, and they look like wealthy Florentines from either the Lenzi or the Berti families. But what's important to us is what happened when Cosimo I, ruler of Florence, brought in Vasari a hundred years later around 1568, to replace this mural in the church. For political reasons, Cosimo wanted him to do extensive renovations, including reconfiguring and redecorating the chapel. It was the same area where Masaccio's fresco was located."

"Vasari was a busy man," offered Beatrice. "As an artist himself and the author of an art history encyclopedia, he recognized the value of his fellow artists' work and didn't want them destroyed. Makes sense. So, what happened?"

"Around 1860, the church was being renovated, after three hundred years," said Julian with a laugh. "That's when art historians figured out that the *Holy Trinity* fresco was left intact and a new alter was constructed by Vasari to clearly save this work. You see, this event sets a very important precedent for your discovery."

"I see."

"Anyway, the short story is that a restoration was done to the top part with the crucifixion scene at that time. But it wasn't until the 1950s that the lower half of the artwork was uncovered. The entire mural was restored over a four-year period, from 1950 to 1954."

"I just got a chill up my spine," said Beatrice. "I can see why your father had every reason to believe that Vasari did the same thing with Leonardo."

"If only we had more evidence." His words trailed off.

Beatrice knew this was a pivotal moment in her search. She was either going to trust him, as Rose had told her to, or not. She swallowed hard, and just as she was about to tell him, the waiter appeared, carrying two sizzling steaks. Time seemed to stand still as the waiter took their plates and another woman appeared to bring them another bottle of water.

"I have another clue," said Beatrice, praying she wasn't making the biggest mistake of her life.

"I thought as much," answered Julian. "Or you wouldn't have sought out my father in the first place."

She nodded. "Rose found a set of drawings in the wall of her apartment last year that we think are part of work undertaken by Michelangelo. It was a drawing of the *Creation of Adam* in the Sistine Chapel, and the hands were clasped instead of the fingers touching."

"I can't believe it." Julian paused to take in what she told him. "That's brilliant!"

"Rose did an entire modern art exhibition on this concept, but she found, in fact, three separate drawings. After trying various approaches, I uncovered a clue and the words *Cerca Trova* on the second canvas, a drawing of a wealthy Florentine nobleman."

"So, you have no idea of who's in the portrait?" asked Julian. "Where is it now?"

"At the Vatican in Rome."

He nodded. "What if it's a young Vasari?"

Beatrice lied. "I hadn't thought of that. Why would that matter?"

"Maybe the drawing you found was his clue to uncovering these masterpieces. Was there anything else in the picture that symbolized Leonardo?"

Beatrice thought for a minute, going over the parchment in her mind. "The area around his hands needs work. Now I have an idea of what could be there."

"Absolutely. It's worth a try."

"I was planning on heading back to Rome in a few days anyway. You've just inspired me to take a new direction."

"I'm glad. This is exciting!" said Julian.

"I think so too," replied Beatrice. "I need to get back to the lab."

"I'm going to be blunt. I really don't want you to leave."

Beatrice smiled. "Really?"

"Not at all."

***

After dinner, they tried to go see Vince's wall mural of the table, but it was too crowded for Beatrice to get close. A movement caught her eye and sent her heart pounding. Across the crowd, she saw a man wearing a green skullcap. *Mike!* She knew he was going to do something to show Vince that he was a master. Beatrice gulped. How was she ever going to leave Florence now?

Once back in Rose's serene guest bedroom, Beatrice tossed and turned all night with her mind racing. What Julian had imparted set a precedent, making it plausible for Leonardo's *Battle of Anghiari* painting to still be hidden behind a fake wall. Could Rose's drawings lead her to one of the greatest art discoveries in the last five hundred years? It was a heady thought, and Beatrice wanted to hurry up and get back to the lab at the Vatican. There was a new technique she thought she could try on the hands of the figure in the drawing. And what about her theory supported by Julian that the figure could be a young Vasari as the keeper of knowledge? Another very interesting idea to evaluate.

She finally dozed and awoke when dawn came as a tiny sliver

of early-morning light. Anxiously hopping out of bed, Beatrice got dressed quickly so she could get to Vince's mural and photograph it for Rose. Last night, it was too dark and crowded for her to see the woman who favored Rose. Street art intrigued her with its transient messages and cult-like followings. The evening's crowd proved that Vince was viewed as something of a visionary with his social messages. Clearly, his ideas resonated and achieved an important social dialogue in a way that she had not realized existed. It was all utterly fascinating, and she was eager to squeeze as much into her day as possible. A voice inside her head warned that she needed to get back home to Rome, but she ignored it.

She stood alone on the street as the sun slowly rose in the morning sky. Words couldn't describe the mural adequately as she studied its clean lines and the oak-colored table. The angles were clever, depicting several women with their backs to the audience. One blond woman stood with her arm extended and index finger pointing at a document on the table. Beatrice cocked her head at the woman, who seemed to be making a statement about woman's rights. *It does resemble Rose, but it's not actually her,* thought Beatrice— rather an American ideal of every woman perhaps. She nodded her head in approval, thinking that this was a clever statement about women's equality. While she didn't want to admit it, the work was eye-catching and inspiring.

"What are you doing here?"

Beatrice's heart slammed into her chest. "I could ask you the same question," she replied saucily.

Mike stared at her and then at the mural. "I think he's a showman, branding himself as a modern arbiter of women's rights. That's bullshit, and people know it."

"I do see the merit in the work," Beatrice retorted.

"What? How can you betray me like that?"

"Mike," said Beatrice nervously, "I'm not betraying you by liking this mural."

"I thought you were different and smart, and yet you played me for a fool."

"What are you talking about?"

"If you think this work has any merit, then you have no taste." He got closer to her face. "I mean that, no taste!"

Beatrice was stunned, and her heart started pounding as she realized that they were alone in the alley. Quelling her fears, she said, "I would never think Vince's work was better than yours. Never!"

He looked at her harshly, then relaxed into a lazy smile. "Just wait until you see what I have started on, bellissima!"

"Where is it?"

"You'll have to follow the crowd, but I will show everyone that I'm the true talent!"

"Your *Lady Justice* is magnificent."

"I have something better in mind that will attract national attention," said Mike, smiling broadly.

"How exciting!" said Beatrice. "Will you give me a hint?"

"Sing to me of the man, the Muse, the man of twists and turns..."

Beatrice thought for a moment, then recognized the phrase from the Greek version of Homer's *Iliad* and the *Odyssey*. "Something from Homer. Brilliant!" she cried, knowing exactly what he was thinking. Indeed, the Romans had embraced Greek mythology, essentially adopting all of their gods and goddesses while only changing their names.

Mike reached for her, and their lips met in a passionate kiss that took her breath away. And then he was gone. Beatrice touched her lips, wondering if she had imagined their whole interlude.

Chapter 17

"EVERYTHING OKAY?" asked Zoey. "You look like you just got some bad news."

"That was Lyon. He's furious that the tabloids printed a picture of me with an artist named Vince." Rose paused, dabbing her eyes. "I need a minute."

"It's going to be okay, Rose. Take all the time you need."

"Thank you," said Rose. She breathed in slowly, willing herself to composure.

"So, who's Vince? You never told me about him."

"There's nothing to tell. He's an artist I met when he came to Florence to do a mural funded by a large nonprofit corporation. We were photographed having dinner together, and now there's all this speculation about us. There was no *us*. It's absolutely ridiculous. I'm engaged, for God's sake!"

Raising one eyebrow, Zoey looked at her and said, "Are you engaged, Rose? You tried to tell me that it's over between the two of you."

"It's what I keep telling myself."

"How's that working for you?"

"Not so great." She shrugged. "Anyway, today isn't about me, sweet friend. I'm so sorry to let my drama interfere in your big day."

"No worries! I just hate seeing you look so sad."

"You have no idea how happy I am to be here with you right now," said Rose, welcoming Zoey's hug. "Honestly, I'm so honored to be helping pick out your first house with Stan. You've got some great options!"

Zoey jotted a few notes. "Aren't I the quintessential teacher, making bullet points of the pros and cons of each one."

"I love that about you!"

"Okay, so that move-in-ready townhouse was really pretty, close to work, and every single thing was done. I also liked that we could paint the basement and make it a kid-friendly space. But Stan wants our kids to grow up with an abundance of nature because he grew up in an apartment surrounded by concrete."

"I get it. And if that's the top priority, the Wallpaper Wonder has the most phenomenal green space by far. It also needs the most work by far. You'd be scraping off wallpaper for years!" joked Rose. "That being said, you could put your stamp on it over time. You'd never be bored. It's a beautiful traditional farmhouse."

"The backyard is the size of a football field, which would be an amazing place to let the kids run around someday. I agree that the bones of the house are really pretty." Zoey scratched her head in thought.

"It's a strong option. But you've also got to love the Rocking Ranch."

"That pool is a huge selling point, and I can totally see Stan out there grilling every night. It's a great space to entertain our friends, and it's close to work."

"Well, is there one you can eliminate?"

Zoey pondered the question. "I think the move-in-ready townhouse is great, but there's not a lot of green space, and it's a little too cookie cutter of a neighborhood for me. It does pain me to let that one go because you know how I love everything being brand new."

Rose agreed. "I think you can bring Stan back to see two great properties that both meet most of your criteria. In my opinion, the ranch has far less work. I mean, you can easily get those floors done to match before you move in. I bet it'll only take a week."

"I know, I know, but Stan has to weigh in. I have a funny feeling about which one he's going to pick."

"You do? I think it could go either way. Can you give me a hint?"

"Nope, I want to surprise you."

Rose headed back to her mother's house after a productive day house hunting. She texted Beatrice and asked her for a picture of the infamous mural. It was baffling to her that Vince would use her likeness. They had enjoyed one evening together, which was why she couldn't fathom how he could create a viable image of her. Sighing heavily, she had to admit that it was nice to be home, despite Doris's mild attempt to keep her in Virginia.

Rose walked into her room to find her bed filled with shopping bags, boxes, and a large hanging bag. Doris marched into the room with a triumphant smile. "Surprise!' she said excitedly. "I bought you a few things!"

"Oh my goodness," said Rose nervously, trying not to sound ungrateful.

"Look," said Doris, opening a bright-orange bag. She pulled out a royal-blue cheetah-printed top.

"Oh wow!" said Rose, gasping at what else was in the bags. She wondered if her mother really did have some sort of Pygmalion complex. Only, in her case, it was a burning desire for a country club daughter makeover. *Zoey's going to have a field day with this one tonight at dinner,* thought Rose. She looked at her watch. Only two hours before she planned to meet them at Bizou for a drink.

Surveying the stockpile of items, Rose thought that her mother was every saleswoman's dream. She must have spent a small fortune. There were dresses galore in varying patterns, heels and flats, as well as a few large necklaces. "Is this all for me?" she asked. "You went way overboard here."

"I just wanted to surprise you," said Doris as she eyed Rose's monochromatic top and cream-colored skinny pants.

"Yes, well, you really surprised me!" She wasn't sure what to say except, "Thank you!"

"We're having company tomorrow night and I thought you'd like to have something extra special to wear."

"How thoughtful," said Rose. "Who's coming?"

"A friend of ours," said Doris breezily, as she fussed over a pair of camel-colored booties that she held up to her feet.

"I can't keep all of this," said Rose. "It's way too much." She eyed the bell-bottomed jeans with the hot-pink fringed edges, thinking she would feel like a complete idiot in them.

"Oh, darling! Just have fun with it. You can try things on at your leisure."

A wave of gratitude swept through her. Fortunately, her mother didn't expect her to model each item for her review like she did when she was sixteen. This approach seemed more civilized. Rose was sure that she would return the majority of everything, but she had to find a few things that she liked and would wear.

"This is pretty," said Rose, pulling out a soft, blue-patterned maxi dress. In a state of disbelief, she really did like it.

"I thought it would look amazing on you. The salesgirl was darling. Her name's Poppy, and she said she would wear it with those tan suede booties in that box over there."

"Oh, great idea!" said Rose. "Sounds like Poppy was very helpful."

"We had the best time together. We're going for a drink next week."

"Really?"

"Oh yes, she couldn't believe what good taste I have."

Rose told herself not to think a single negative thing about Miss Poppy, who probably had her biggest commission day ever.

"That's great. Oh, I wanted to tell you that we found some great options for Zoey and Stan. One property is in Crozet. It's a gorgeous old farmhouse. The other is a few minutes from the mall and Bellfield."

"When is the baby due?"

It was an innocent question, Rose knew, but her breath caught in her throat. She replied, "Sometime around Valentine's Day."

"How lovely! Who's giving her a baby shower?"

"Actually, we haven't talked about it."

"Well, I would be happy to have the event if you'd like."

"That's so kind of you. I'll let Zoey know!"

"You know how I love babies. Jack's girls have stolen my heart."

"They are really cute. I plan on paying a visit soon. Anyway, it was a great first weekend home and really productive. I can't wait to see what they decide!"

"Do you think they would really move to Crozet?"

"I don't know. I must admit, I think I would choose the renovated ranch house in town. It would make things so much easier on Zoey, in many ways."

"Keep me posted," Doris said. "Oh no, I need to get going on dinner. I'm trying out the most marvelous shrimp and grits recipe."

"Sounds delicious," said Rose, longing for linguine in clam sauce with fresh prosciutto.

When her mother closed the door, Rose looked at all the bags and boxes, feeling like she was eighteen years old. Did her mother really have her best interest at heart with this new shopping expedition, or was she trying to wipe away any and all Italian influence?

She let herself focus on her exchange with Lyon. What happened to him? Where was the man she fell in love with and was ready to marry? A tear slid down her cheek as she realized that her wedding was supposed to be in a few short weeks, and she had never felt so confused in her life. A vision of the Tuscan hillside outside of Lyon's family home came to mind, which made her feel even more wretched. She threw all the new clothes on the floor and climbed into her bed. Pulling the covers over her head, Rose wondered if she could hide in her room forever.

***

As anticipated, on Sunday afternoon, Zoey called her with the big news.

"We made a decision and just put an offer in on our first house!"

"Don't leave me in suspense any longer. Which one did you choose?"

"Believe it or not, we're going with that beautiful old farmhouse with the football field backyard. We feel it's the best house long term for a family, and we would simply stay there forever."

"Oh, Zoey, I'm so excited for both of you. Yes, it's a gorgeous house, and the land is extraordinary. And I fully intend to be captain of the wallpaper removal team. I can't think of a better project right now."

"Actually, Stan and I were talking, and we would love for you to live with us while you're here. It would be great to have your help with everything. I'm a bit overwhelmed with a new house and a new baby on board, plus all of my responsibilities at Bellfield."

"Oh, Zoey, that's the best offer I've had all year. I'd love to help you. It will be fun to work with you to get your house just the way you want it!"

"And a lot of hard work. Are you sure?"

"I can't think of anything better for me mentally and physically right now. I really just need time to myself to think about things. Besides, you know how I love a good project."

"So, the house is vacant, and we can take possession within the next two weeks, which gives us time to get organized before Christmas."

"That's perfect. Will you have access to the house so I can get to work? I'd love to jump in."

"I'll ask our realtor. We've already been approved for the loan, and I don't think we have any competition. Too many people don't want to do the work, which is a bonus for us."

"I'm ready and willing," announced Rose.

"I hope Doris doesn't pitch a fit when you tell her you're leaving."

"We've actually been doing well," Rose said, "and I have a whole new wardrobe."

"What? Are you kidding?"

"Nope, Doris went shopping and brought home an entire carload of dresses, shoes, pants. If you're nice to me, I'll loan you my new 1970s jeans with the hot-pink fringe."

"Is there a matching top?"

"That depends," said Rose, "if hot-pink fringe goes with blue cheetah or maybe a black leather halter option. She worked with a saleswoman named Poppy who was very helpful. So helpful, in fact, that they're going for a drink next week."

"Wonders never cease," said Zoey, laughing. "You've got to send me pictures of the stuff. Anyway, stay tuned on the house purchase, and thank you for everything."

"I should be thanking you for the project. I needed something to tackle."

"Well, it's hard work, and you better promise me that you'll be honest about how much you're willing to do!"

"I promise. I'll let you know before my arm falls off from scraping."

"I fully intend to wear a mask and get stuff done."

"You shouldn't overdo it."

"I'll talk to my doctor about everything, including paint fumes. Don't worry."

"Okay, I know you'll be smart about how much you can take on."

"Same goes for you. Gotta run. Talk soon."

"Bye."

A short time later, Rose did the unthinkable. She reached into one of the shopping bags in search of the blue-patterned maxi dress that her mother had purchased for her. It was surprisingly pretty with its soft floral neckline and puffy long sleeves. The lines were clean, and it fit her perfectly. She even put on the tan suede boots that worked well with it.

Rose brushed her hair and let it fall in loose waves around her face. Reaching for her phone, she sent Lyon a simple message: *How did things go so wrong? I miss you.* She took a deep breath and was about to send it when her mother called her from downstairs.

"Rose, darling. Come on down."

Her shrill tone made Rose wonder what she wanted.

Nothing could have prepared her for their dinner guest.

There was Ben, looking casual and comfortable, standing in her mother's living room. He was clean shaven and dressed in corduroy pants reminiscent of an advertisement for Ralph Lauren. She thought of a hundred things she would say, but instead she abruptly turned to head upstairs.

"Rose. Wait!" said Ben.

"I need to check on the jambalaya," announced Doris, making a quick exit.

"What are you doing here?" she snapped, trying not to notice how incredibly handsome he was. "Did Doris plan this?"

"Don't blame your mother. I asked her to invite me."

"What? Why?"

"I want us to be friends. That's all. I know I blew it and we have absolutely no future together. But we've known each other since we were kids."

"You were horrible to me, Ben. I still have nightmares about our relationship."

"I'm sorry again, Rose. I made a lot of mistakes and I want you to forgive me."

"The last time I forgave you, we ended up engaged, and then, your art-dealer friend tried to maneuver me to sell the drawings I found. Oh, and let's not forget that I wasn't even out the door one hour before you hopped in bed with Angie."

"Not impressive," he said quietly. "You make me sound so horrible, and I'm not. I promise you, Rose, it was all circumstances that messed us up! And while we're on the subject, you shouldn't have stolen my computer. That was terrible."

"You deserved it. You needed to learn to think about others and not constantly feed your huge ego." Would Ben always be her Achilles heel? Totally embarrassing, but true.

"You are the only one who made me stop and rethink my life."

"What does that mean?"

"I hit the pause button on who I am and went on a few excursions—one to the deserts of Arizona to figure out my path. It was eye opening and humbling. My ego has been effectively vanquished!"

"I doubt that," Rose snickered. "I'm surprised you can still fit your head through that door."

"Ouch!" he winced. "Come on, Rose, lighten up. We can be on better terms when we're in Charlottesville. Jack and I are still close, you know that, and Emily still talks about you all the time."

Rose gulped. "She's a lovely little girl. You're a wonderful father."

Ben leaned in. "Did you actually just say something nice to me?"

"Stop it," said Rose. "I don't hate you, Ben. I was disappointed in you." The words sounded all too familiar as Rose wondered if she was destined to fail at all relationships.

"I told you that I'm very embarrassed by what happened between us. When you left, I got back together with Angie, thinking it was the right decision, but things turned sour very quickly. We didn't even make it a month afterwards."

"Look, I don't know what else to say," said Rose, looking down at the tips of her suede booties.

"Say you'll be on speaking terms with me."

Rose considered his request. She wanted to prove to herself that she had *evolved*. That word resonated in her brain. Rose was steady and calm. "Fine. We can be cordial."

Doris came vaulting in the room, carrying a tray of ham biscuits, a favorite of Ben's. He whispered, "If you want me to go, I'll leave now."

She rolled her eyes and said, "Stay for dinner. I promise not to hurl a fork at you."

"Good," he laughed. "And I promise to think of others more. "

"You always know just what to say, Ben. It's why you've been so successful."

"I mean it," said Ben. "You forced me to look at myself through a different lens, and I didn't like what I saw. I've changed."

"That all sounds good. Time will tell," said Rose, reaching for a biscuit. She had to hand it to Doris. It was clever inviting Ben over for dinner, and she wasn't going to give her the satisfaction of pitching a fit. His words were validating, and there was a small, glib part of her that was glad he didn't end up with Angie, who displayed little to no maternal instinct. *Poor Emily.*

Eric came in from playing golf and gave Ben a big hug, then asked him about his parents and how long he planned to be in town. The two men grabbed a beer, and Rose offered to help her mother in the kitchen. As she looked down at her ring-free hands, Rose was sure Ben would have noticed it. *No matter*, she decided. This was her life, and she needed to pull the pieces of it together again.

As she sat down to eat, Rose eyed Ben out of the corner of her eye, realizing that they would have been married a year ago if things had turned out differently. Perhaps there was something wrong with her and she couldn't have a loving and healthy relationship. The spicy stew stung her dry mouth, but the hot liquid did little to warm the coldness in her heart; she warned herself to stop overanalyzing everything.

"Isn't that right, Rose?" asked Doris.

"Excuse me?" she replied.

"Zoey and Stan's house. Ben thinks it's the Berkley's place. Remember they went off to Cedarfield Retirement community in Richmond."

"Oh, that explains why Zoey and Stan can take possession right away. And, well, I guess this is as good a time as any to let you know, I'll be moving in with them to help with the painting and renovations until the baby comes."

"You what?" said Doris. "That's absurd when you have a perfectly lovely place to stay here. I can't believe that a married couple would want a third wheel with them over the holidays."

Her words stung, as usual. Rose gulped down a biscuit to keep from snapping back.

Ben jumped in. "I don't know, Doris. I'd have no problem with free labor, especially an artist as talented as Rose. I'm sure you're going to make the place look fantastic."

His words had the desired effect. Doris retracted her fangs, Eric said nothing as usual, and Rose felt like crawling under the table. Some things would never change. The conversation moved to golf, and Eric and Ben talked about the nearby golf course at Keswick and the vicissitudes of hole number seven.

Rose excused herself and headed upstairs, feeling exhausted from living with Doris and Eric. Her empty apartment came to mind. *I miss my own space.* Checking her phone by her bedside, she saw a message from Lyon that had come in a half hour earlier.

You have no idea how much I miss you. I am so sorry. When are you coming home?

His words practically jumped off the screen as she sat to think about what she wanted to say next. He had called Florence her home, but was it?

I miss you too, Lyon, more than you know. I am really confused right now. To her surprise, he responded immediately. Checking her watch, she realized it was three in the morning abroad.

I have some news that I'd rather share in person.

What does that mean? And you can't expect me to just forget about the whole series of events. I have to be able to trust you.

I understand. I love you, Rose.

I love you too, Lyon. But is it enough to last a lifetime?

Rose burst into tears, frustrated and angry with everything. She looked down at her blue dress and felt so utterly horrible about herself and her relationships. Her mother calling her a third wheel with Stan and Zoey made her question that decision. The last thing she wanted to do was impose on her best friend's holiday or be any type of burden on their joyful preparation for a new baby.

She wondered what Lyon wanted to tell her in person. What if he went to the doctor and there was hope for a family together? Would that solve their problems? Rose really didn't like the way he'd handled their first big hurdle as a couple, and she felt she had been right to hit the pause button on their relationship. Lyon texted again:

Love is always patient and kind. It is never jealous. Love is never boastful or conceited. It is never rude or selfish. It does not take offense and is not resentful. Love takes no pleasure in other people's sins but delights in the truth. It is always ready to excuse, to trust, to hope and to endure whatever comes.

Rose looked at the passage from 1 Corinthians and smiled at Lyon's ingenuity. He had touched her heart from across the Atlantic.

Chapter 18

NO MATTER HOW MANY TIMES she went over the same spot on the drawing, Beatrice wasn't coming up with anything conclusive that led her to Leonardo da Vinci or *The Battle of Anghiari.* "Damnit," she muttered, immediately crossing herself for cursing in the sanctity of the Vatican. She got up from her desk, scratched her head, and began pacing the floor. There was a reason the author of this drawing put *Cerca Trova*—seek and you shall find—off to the side. It had to be a clue, and it had to lead to something. *But what?* Her mind screamed in frustration.

"Working late again?" said the cardinal's familiar voice.

"Yes," said Beatrice. "I keep looking at this drawing and feeling like I'm missing something. Like the clue is right in front of my face, but I'm not sure what to do next."

"Perhaps a break might be in order," said the cardinal, handing her a cup of hot tea.

"You are such a dear," said Beatrice, gratefully accepting the cup. "It's like you have a magic antennae in your office that detects steam coming from my head!" She rubbed her aching temples.

"Hardly," said the cardinal with a chuckle. "I know we've discussed this project more than once this past week, I'm still not convinced we have enough evidence to prove anything."

"I'm determined," she announced.

"I can see that," said the cardinal. "What happens if you find another clue?"

"I thought you were going to have the answer to that," said Beatrice. "Seriously, I would assume we could take this information to the government and various boards to open up the discussion again. I told you that Julian showed me the clue with an advanced binocular type of device when we were at the Palazzo Vecchio. It's ludicrous that those words are written in the hall and tourists look at them every day."

"So, you decided to trust Julian?"

"Yes," said Beatrice. "I trust him completely. We all want the same thing—answers to the mystery and perhaps the satisfaction of uncovering a masterpiece for the world to see."

"Have you not considered the risks in this undertaking?"

Beatrice looked him in the eye. "Yes, but that's not enough reason to stop looking. I feel like I'm going to find it."

The cardinal seemed to ponder her words. "Well, I wish you luck, my dear. That being said, I do have a lead on a new project that may intrigue you."

Beatrice paused, noting the sparkle in his eye. "Is this just a ploy to stop me from driving myself insane over the clue?"

"Maybe, or it's a chance to work on one of the greatest Renaissance masterpieces of all time."

Beatrice felt her heart pound and her senses spring to life. "Don't keep me in suspense."

He smiled gently. "We are going to do some conservation work on Raphael's *Transfiguration*. It should make its way to the lab in about two or three weeks."

Beatrice squealed in delight. "You know that I've always longed to work on that painting."

"I think you're ready. You'll work alongside Gregorio, who will lead the project."

"Thank you, Cardinal. I'm honored that you are giving me such a prestigious assignment."

"You're welcome. You've earned it," said the cardinal, setting down his teacup. "It's getting late. I'm going to arrange for a car to get you home."

Beatrice felt exhaustion creep into her bones. "That's so kind of you," she said, very pleased with the offer. "I'm not going to argue. I think I need to get some rest. Thank you for everything."

"It's the least we can do. Your hard work is noted and appreciated."

They said good night, and Beatrice leaned back in her chair pondering her next big project—Raphael's *Transfiguration*. The enormity of the assignment made her a bit nervous, but she quelled any self-doubt. *I'm confident and extremely competent*, she told herself, as she rubbed her tired temples. Working on a masterpiece like the *Transfiguration* represented all that she'd been striving for over the years. As she recalled, the true meaning of the *Transfiguration*, taken from the Bible's New Testament, depicted the moment when Jesus revealed his divinity, becoming radiant on a mountaintop. This painting was originally commissioned by Cardinal Giulio de Medici (Pope Clement VII) around 1517 and conceived as an altarpiece for the Narbonne Cathedral in France. It was the culmination of the great Raphael's entire career; historians believed that it hung over his catafalque for a week after he died until it was exhibited at the Vatican. From the sixteenth century to the twentieth century, this masterpiece was the most famous painting in the world.

Beatrice took a deep breath, excited to share her accomplishment with someone special. Noting the time, it was too late to call home and talk to her mother. She thought about ringing Rose, but quickly discarded the idea since she was so far away in Charlottesville. Suddenly, an idea took shape. It was bold, she knew, but she couldn't help herself. Grabbing her purse, she rummaged through it for Mike's information that Rose had given her weeks ago. She thought of his kiss in the dark alley. It still burned on her lips. Idly touching her mouth, she decided to be bold and send Mike a text. Taking a deep breath, she urged herself forward and wrote:

Hi, Mike: I've thought a lot about you lately. Hope you don't mind me texting you out of the blue like this. The last time I saw you, you were about to begin a new undertaking. How is your mural going? I've just been assigned a rather fantastic project and I may take a few days off before I get started. How long will you be in Florence?

Her hands shook as she stared at the phone, wondering at her impulsive move. Had she gone mad? Several minutes passed, so she put the phone down to organize her desk area. Staring at the drawing, she decided she would tackle it another day. *The clue is there,* she thought, but she probably desperately needed to give it a rest. She grabbed her purse and looked at her phone to see a text from her driver alerting her that he was waiting for her. A wave of gratitude engulfed her as she thought about the dear cardinal, who had so kindly arranged the ride home. She wished all men were like him. He was indeed special, and it was a privilege to work with him.

The city streets were dark and frigid. The strangest feeling of loneliness overtook her as the car weaved through the empty streets home. A vision of Raphael's coffin invaded her mind, making her feel vulnerable. As usual, she shook off the whispers of melancholy. Shutting her eyes and leaning her head against the back seat, her phone vibrated, indicating an incoming message.

Ciao! I was so glad to hear from you that I nearly burst with joy. Your beautiful face has invaded my senses and I've found it hard to concentrate on the mural. That vain bitch's work can't compare to what I have done! You must come and see. You need to tell me about your good news in person immediately! I fervently await your arrival back in Florence!

She responded, *I think I can finish up by Friday and will let you know when I arrive in Florence. Where is the mural?*

Follow the crowds, bellissima!

I'm delighted for you, but not at all surprised!

I eagerly await your arrival . . . Passionately yours, M

Beatrice didn't know how to respond to such a declaration. Her hands shook while her heart expanded. She knew it was crazy, and yet, she felt a surge of adrenaline run though her. Suddenly, she was excited to figure out how to get back to Florence. She arrived home to her pristine apartment with a renewed sense of optimism. A vision of Julian's kind face surfaced, but she quickly abandoned it; they were kindred spirits, but that wasn't what she wanted. Mike made her feel crazy, impulsive, and alive!

***

In the early hours of the morning, Beatrice awoke from a turbulent dream in which she was swimming against a strong current, gasping for air. She sprouted wings, trying to fly away, but a monster arose from the sea, nearly grabbing her. A knight with a gleaming, silver, red-crest-embossed shield came to save her. Taking deep breaths, sitting up, and wiping the delirium from her brow, Beatrice shook her head, wondering at the dream. *Did Leonardo da Vinci have a family crest or shield, and if so, what did it look like?* She was energized to get back to the lab to do more research.

On a whim, she decided to trudge across the front of St. Peter's Basilica, one of the most renowned works of Renaissance architecture, on her way to the lab. The domed church also boasted elements of Baroque and Mannerist influence. Looking over at St. Peter's Square, she observed several groups of religious pilgrims, who were an integral part of this holy place. It was so early, yet the sun glinted on the colonnades. Beatrice recalled that this structure took nearly one hundred twenty years to build. *Michelangelo designed the signature dome,* recalled Beatrice, as she paused to listen to the beautiful fountain in the square. The melodious sound of the cascading water reminded her that she was not alone in this vast universe. Water always calmed her nerves, albeit briefly.

Stop gawking. I need to get to my desk.

Her first order of business was a cup of coffee, which tasted so good after such a long night. Rose's drawing held the secret to the mystery, she concluded while contemplating the *Cerca Trova* reference and the resemblance of the nobleman to Giorgio Vasari. What she needed now was a symbol or inference that connected these ideas to the great Leonardo. Beatrice was convinced that the necessary clue was buried beneath hundreds of years of mold and dirt. She worked painstakingly on the drawings, millimeter by millimeter, then changed directions, shifting her focus back to the words *Cerca Trova* and selecting an area right beneath it. As she gently peeled away flecks of dirt, she saw the beginnings of an object. The lines were curled, and she continued to chip away at the paper, all the while being supremely careful not to poke a hole. Her senses homed in on one particular spot, and through the muck, a corner image appeared. As Beatrice stared at it, her nervous energy grew with anticipation.

"What are you doing?" asked Gregorio, who came up behind her to survey the paper.

"Nothing," she replied quickly. "Just putting the finishing touches on one of the cardinal's private drawings. Don't ask, it's a surprise for him."

"I'm sure he'll appreciate your due diligence."

"I hope so!"

He nodded in silent understanding and walked away.

As the days passed in a blur, Beatrice painstakingly cleaned the fragile spot using only the lightest touch with her custom fiber-tipped pen, removing particles as small as the eye of a needle with deft and steady strokes. One evening, as her hands were beginning to cramp, she looked up to survey the half-inch surface that was becoming clearer. It appeared to be two interlocked swords forming the letters *LV*. Beatrice felt like she was going to explode. *LV must stand for Leonardo da Vinci.* She gasped as she studied the words. Was this the clue that had been missing for centuries?

Beatrice grabbed the drawing and ran to find Cardinal Baglioni. Her heart hammering, she was one-hundred-percent sure that this was a message from an ancient scholar, folded up and hidden in the wall five hundred years ago for safekeeping. It was late, so the cardinal was not in his office; his secretary said she might find him in his personal apartment, preparing for a papal visit to Latin America.

She knocked aggressively on the door. "Cardinal," she exclaimed. "It's Beatrice. Are you there? I need to speak to you."

When he opened the door, Beatrice couldn't help but notice that he looked frail without his glasses. Cardinal Baglioni ushered her inside a beautiful sitting room adorned with a gold-framed picture of the Virgin Mary wearing a shimmering blue robe. If the matter hadn't been so urgent, she would have delighted in the stately room. Beatrice surveyed the antique furnishings, settling on a mahogany corner table. She turned on the blue-flowered ceramic lamp and motioned for him to come over.

"You've got to see this!" she exclaimed.

"Let me get my glasses," he said, peering at the side tables to find the black frames. He seemed a bit tired and confused, so she tried to help him in his search. This was certainly not the way she had expected this meeting to take place.

"Aha!" he said, placing them on his nose. "You look so pale, my dear."

"I've worked around the clock," she explained, "but I found it!"

"Let me see," he said, walking over to the drawing.

She pulled out a magnifying glass and showed him the swords shaped like an *LV*. "It has to be referring to the lost Leonardo. It's clear that he is telling us that it's hidden behind the wall."

The cardinal rubbed his temples. "Beatrice, this is excellent work, but I just don't know if these two letters are enough to open this case back up."

"What?" she practically shrieked. "Of course it is! We have an ancient drawing with the same words that are emblazoned on the Vasari painting, a drawing of Vasari himself, and now we have an *LV*, which clearly points to the Leonardo masterpiece behind it. This drawing acts as the map to the hidden treasure! What more do we need to get the government to reopen this case?"

"I do think this is compelling information, especially given the age of the drawing." He scratched his head, pondering her discovery.

"Cardinal?"

"It is evidence," he said. "It should not be ignored."

Beatrice breathed a sigh of relief. "I agree. I'd say that it seems pretty compelling."

He said, "These elements combined with the LV on this ancient document is more than clear. You're right, and I stand corrected. It is most definitely a clue. Let me get to work on it!"

"Excellent," she replied, grateful he agreed.

"My dear, you need to go home and get some sleep. You look exhausted."

"Actually, I was thinking I might take a few days off. I want to be fresh to start work on Raphael's *Transfiguration*."

"Absolutely," he replied. "I think a few personal days are in order after all of this work. I insist on it. In the meantime, I'll make inquiries on how best to proceed. Congratulations, Beatrice. I am proud of you."

Beatrice couldn't help but feel like she had done something extraordinary that gave her work new meaning. Her heart swelled with pride. They embraced, and Beatrice felt a wave of relief. The cardinal was going to get her discovery to the right people.

When she left, she contemplated calling Julian but refrained. She didn't want to alert him that she was coming to town to view Mike's mural and connect with the artist. Instead, she sent a text to Rose, telling her she had more information on the drawings and asking if she could stay in her apartment for the weekend.

You can absolutely use my apartment. Make yourself at home! It's so helpful for me to have you there to check on things, Rose responded. When asked about Lyon, she added, *I really have no idea!*

Maybe if you see each other in person, you'll know. Miss you, Rose. Xo

Beatrice couldn't believe that Rose had no plans to return to Florence in the coming months. It all seemed so wrong. She and Lyon belonged together, and if they failed, Beatrice thought, it would be such a waste. *And then what hope does somebody like me have of finding true love?*

***

Armed with a good night's sleep, Beatrice arrived at Rose's apartment full of anticipation and nerves. She had pursued Mike, who seemed to want to see her as much as she wanted to see him. *Is there anything there?* The question ran through her mind as Beatrice freshened up in Rose's bathroom. She trembled a bit, wondering how and when to contact Mike.

I'm here! Can't wait to see you when convenient, she texted.

No response.

An hour passed, and then another, and still no response. Her heart raced, and sweat formed on her brow. The last time she was this anxious was when she'd discovered the clue. Pushing aside her fears, she checked her appearance one more time and decided to follow the crowds as she went outside to figure out where his mural could possibly be. On the street, she wandered for a few blocks and headed over the Ponte Vecchio Bridge, peering at the beautiful jewelry stands and leather goods. It had been a long time since she had indulged in shopping, so she took her time. Beatrice peered inside a pretty little shop selling handmade jewelry. As she stopped to look at some modern rings, she casually put one on her right hand. The gold chunky setting was stunning, and it had a beautiful blue stone that reminded her of the endless ocean.

"*Ciao,*" the salesperson said. "You have good taste." The dark-haired woman came to stand beside her. "The ring is twenty-four karat gold with a blue topaz."

"It's absolutely beautiful. How much is it?" asked Beatrice.

The price took her breath away. It was more than she made in a month, so she quickly removed it from her finger and handed it back to the woman. "Maybe someday," she said lightly, gazing at it one more time. This moment, like too many moments in her life, seemed rooted in her feelings of inadequacy. She didn't feel good enough to own such a stunning object. Pretty women like Rose received this kind of ring from a man, and this would never be her fate. She couldn't shake the sadness.

"We could work with you on the price. Maybe a little bit off, say fifteen percent."

Beatrice shook her head. "Thank you. I'll think about it." She asked, "I've heard there's an artist named Mike who's done an extraordinary mural on one of the walls around here. Have you heard of it?"

"How could I not?" she replied. "Go to the end of the bridge, then head down two streets and follow the crowd."

"Thank you," said Beatrice.

The woman turned to her. "I hope to see you again. It's a beautiful ring, and you deserve it."

Okay, Beatrice decided, *she is indeed a good salesperson.* The seed was planted. Why did she have to wait for someone to give her a pretty bauble? She was a successful professional woman who could make her own rules! She added up the numbers in her head, thinking about her savings account and various other financial obligations. If they took fifteen percent off the price, then maybe there was a chance that she could afford it as a gift to herself.

Beatrice smiled at the idea.

It didn't take long to make her way into the throng of tourists and follow them down an unmarked side street. Beatrice stood in the back, shocked by the size and scale of Mike's mural. *Wow*, she thought, *this is simply amazing!* He has put a modern twist on the gods and goddesses of the past. In a nod to the Greek version of Homer's *Odyssey*, he recreated the ancient Greek and Roman gods by making them all different races. In the center of the mural was a large, Black Neptune with a trident in his right hand, rising out of blue water. The light hit his glistening skin, making him look ethereal. Beatrice recognized Demeter portrayed as a beautiful Asian woman, holding fruits and vegetables from the earth. Her daughter,

Proserpina, had long flowing hair as she stared down at the waters. *Mike,* Beatrice thought, *is a genius.*

A tear formed as Beatrice marveled at the beauty and intensity of the mural. Of course this mural would receive international attention. It was a magnificent idea. As she recalled her mythology, Beatrice eyed Proserpina, the goddess of the earth, who was so incredibly beautiful that Pluto, the god of the underworld, wanted to make her his wife, so he rose up and snatched her from a meadow. Ceres, her mother, was so distraught by the loss of her daughter that she wandered the countryside, killing all crops and vegetation. The land became barren due to her mother's grief. A deal was struck by the gods to return Proserpina to her mother for six months a year, which signaled the beginning of spring. Every year, this goddess came home, and the earth welcomed her with warmer temperatures and flowering trees, plants, and an abundance of crops.

A wry smile crossed Beatrice's lips as she pushed through the crowds to see more.

By the time she reached the front of the group, Beatrice saw Mike on scaffolding, working feverishly on a woman's ancient robe. *No wonder he hasn't responded.* By the looks of things, he had been there for hours, intensely focused on the lower left side of this amazing creation. She watched him for a while, marveling at his steady hands and fierce profile. The skull cap had disappeared, and his hair was in a low ponytail, which suited him. A tattoo was exposed on his forearm, but she couldn't make out what it was.

Finally, he stopped to take a break and stood to gaze at the wall. "Hey, Mike," a voice called from the crowd. "This is so cool!" "Yes!' cried another voice.

He nodded and grinned, and then looked into the crowd and saw her. Their eyes met, and Beatrice felt her heart pound. He stared at her with such intensity it practically took her breath away. *The connection's real,* she told herself, and his wide smile made her want to sing with joy and anticipation. It didn't matter how long she had to stand there. She would wait all night just to spend some time with him.

Several hours passed, and her hands and feet grew numb in the cold. It was late, and she hadn't eaten all day. Realizing that she couldn't gaze at Mike and his mural much longer, Beatrice decided to back away from the group, promising herself that she would return in an hour or so to find him.

"Hey, bellissima! Where are you going?"

Mike was yelling for her, and she waved back at him.

Mike quickly jumped down and turned to his assistant, looking like he was giving him instructions. He wiped his hands on his pants, put on his green skullcap, and came after her. The crowd parted as he came forward to take her hand. "I'm glad you made it!" Then he kissed her soundly in front of everyone. Cheers cascaded, making Beatrice think she was dreaming this moment.

They walked hand in hand several blocks and found a café with a green awning and a mahogany wood door. At that point, Beatrice could not have cared less where they went; she was chilled and desperately needed something in her stomach, which was growling in discontent.

Fortunately, a bottle of Chianti was served quickly by a waiter awestruck by Mike.

"I've been eating here all week," Mike said with a wink. "I guess that makes me a regular."

"Your work is absolutely fantastic, Mike," exclaimed Beatrice. "I don't know how you can work out there for hours at a time and not have it affect you. I must say, I'm still a bit chilled."

Mike lit a cigarette and offered one to Beatrice, who had never smoked in her life. She shook her head. "You're right," he said. "Nasty habit."

"I don't mind," she offered, allowing the wine to take the cold from her insides.

A piping-hot pizza with sausage and peppers arrived shortly

thereafter, and Beatrice greedily grabbed a slice, tasting the savory warm cheese that dripped from the crust.

She exclaimed, "I think this is the best pizza I've ever had."

"I aim to please," he joked, taking a slice. "We may need to order another one. I can't remember the last time I ate either. I'm famished."

"How is that possible?" she asked.

"I get lost in my work," said Mike, wiping his hands with a napkin. "It's all about sending a message, and when I do it right, the crowds come. Knowing they are listening to my voice always ignites a flame in me."

"Your idea is so beautifully conceived and executed. Congratulations on your success."

He blushed, which Beatrice found completely endearing. They clinked glasses, and Beatrice wanted to pinch herself that she was actually sitting in this cozy café with a man who fascinated her.

"So, enough about me. You said you have news?"

"Oh," replied Beatrice. "It was just a work thing I became excited about. Nothing important."

"Come on, it was important enough for you to come to Florence to tell me the news."

"I'll be working on Raphael's *Transfiguration* in two weeks. It is such an honor to help preserve a masterpiece of this caliber."

"That's excellent news!" said Mike. "We must celebrate this moment in your career."

He stood and offered her his hand.

"What are you doing?"

"We must dance."

Beatrice looked around the crowded room and felt extremely self-conscious. She looked at Mike, took his hand, and decided, *Who cares?* Life was about celebrating every precious moment.

Chapter 19

BEATRICE FELT AS IF THE LAST FEW DAYS were a dream. She watched Mike work by day, adoring his intensity and commitment to reimagining the past in his work. The mural adorned the side of a building with its array of lifelike gods and goddesses. His imaginary ancient community moved, swirled, and swished in thrilling motion as a Slavic Hercules slayed his enemies and brought the treasures to a radiant Jupiter. Beatrice loved how they fought, danced in glory, and reminded people of civilizations long gone.

She tried to stay in the back of the crowd so as not to disturb Mike. The visitors escalated each day as his vision came to life. He looked exhausted, so Beatrice decided that a home-cooked meal would help Mike relax. With newfound inspiration, she headed to the market in search of fresh ingredients, including the spices she recalled as the secret to her grandmother's recipe. She texted her mother and got a reminder to let the sauce simmer before adding the final bit of basil. Meal preparation helped soothe her troubled senses.

The clock's ticking, Beatrice thought, as she stirred some fresh linguini on the stove. The pungent smell of sauce permeated the apartment with its spicy aroma. She was delighted to have something fresh prepared for Mike tonight rather than her usual takeout cuisine. She refused to think about tomorrow, deciding that she must live in the present. The *LV* on the drawing invaded her consciousness, and she grappled with the notion of telling Julian, who might have some insights into the clue. On the one hand, she really didn't want him to know about Mike, which was no one's business. Also, she wasn't sure if it was smart to trust him or anyone besides Rose and the cardinal.

A quick text from Rose diverted her attention.

How's it going?

Making linguine and clam sauce for dinner.

For one?

Not really. Mike promised to finish up early and come over.

Are you happy?

Deliriously so. May meet with Julian about new finding. Cardinal is working on it.

Are you sure you can trust him?

Absolutely.

I can't wait to see what you've uncovered in person.

Come back home!!!

I'm starting to miss my life in Italy . . .

And Lyon?

Yes, I feel like part of me is missing.

It's about time, Rose. Come home!

I'm thinking about it.

Good. Talk soon. Xo

Beatrice imagined the holidays, picturing herself alone in her apartment; she shuddered at the premonition. Her time with Mike was limited, but she refused to indulge in any regrets. She had dared to do something crazy, yet in the back of her mind she realized the relationship would end and she would be heartbroken. Her mind shifted to her work and Raphael's *Transfiguration*, which would sustain her.

On impulse, she texted Julian, indicating that she had some new information for him. His response was immediate, wanting to know where she was and what was going on. Beatrice agreed to meet him the next morning at a café around the corner. Perhaps he could shed some light on her find. Cardinal Baglioni had promised to make inquiries, and Beatrice was tempted to pick up the phone and see if there was any news. Checking her watch, she realized the cardinal was probably deep in evening prayer.

A short time later, Mike arrived early, much to her surprise.

"I'm nearing the end," he exclaimed, taking off his skullcap.

A lump formed in her throat, but she banished her own sadness. "That's fantastic. I've heard from Rose and urged her to come home. I can't believe she would want to be away from this place for so long."

"I have news," he said, kissing her soundly. Next, he walked into the kitchen and exclaimed, "How did you know?"

"Know what?"

"This is my favorite dish. My grandmother used to make it for me."

"So, you're saying clam linguine is the key to your heart?"

"Absolutely!"

"Tell me, what's your news?"

"Not yet. We must first enjoy this beautiful meal you've prepared. It smells like onions and garlic in here. How can I resist such an odor?"

Beatrice raised one eyebrow at him.

"Bellissima, I'm joking with you."

She laughed.

Mike pulled out a bottle of Chianti that he had picked up on the way. The scene was so positively homey that Beatrice wanted to cry. It was a glimpse into what would never be. Mike was not a domestic animal; it would kill him and his creativity. The excitement would dim, transforming them into an ordinary, boring couple. She reminded herself to remain calm and be present, feeling the need to imprint these moments on her memory.

Being in his presence ignited so many emotions in her. She never knew what he was going to say or do, keeping her guessing, which enthralled her, given the predictably of her everyday life. The intensity was electric, and she couldn't help herself. As if in a dream, they had a glass of red wine and then talked about their hopes, their dreams, and their work. Mike was committed to sending messages of peace and unity throughout the world; Beatrice wanted to preserve the work of the masters, who sent powerful messages about God and Jesus.

"My work is transient. No one will remember me, but I think it's important, and the cardinal is a joy to work for."

"So is my work, but that could change," Mike announced, sitting up in his seat.

"What's going on?"

"I've been given a crazy good offer."

"A job?" she cried. "Where?"

"New York."

"Oh," she said, gulping to mitigate her anxiety. "What are you going to do?"

"They want me to do a permanent installation in the Whitney Museum. It's a two-year sponsorship, and I can create whatever I want."

"New York? Are you considering it?"

"Perhaps, but I have a lot to think about."

Beatrice dared to hope. "Such as?"

"I told you I have no allegiance to anyone or anything but my art. I'm not sure whether I would like it there or not."

His words slammed into her ears, and she knew that she was an absolute fool to have allowed herself to get involved with him. "That's wonderful news. I'm sure you'll make the right decision."

"That's a pretty bland answer."

"What do you want me to say?" snapped Beatrice. "Where does that leave me?"

"I've never lied to you about who I am and what I want. I've been up front from the start!"

"You're right. So now, please go."

He stepped forward, but she backed away. "Go," she said. "This was just stupid of me," she muttered.

"What did you just say?" he yelled.

"I said, go! Your world of gods and goddesses awaits. Maybe you'll settle on Mount Olympus someday."

Her jab ticked him off. He reached for her again, she wasn't sure whether in passion or anger. The space between them throbbed with emotion. He grabbed his cap, turned away, then slammed the door.

Refusing to indulge in useless emotion, she quickly cleared their plates and headed upstairs. She felt too numb to cry. *I'm such an idiot,* she told herself. Of course she knew this was how things were going to end, but it didn't make it any easier. Beatrice tossed and turned before falling into a dreamless sleep.

***

It was a crisp, late-fall morning, and the cool air was refreshening. Beatrice locked the door to Rose's apartment. Her suitcase was packed, and she planned to see Julian and head home on the afternoon train; she hadn't decided whether to pay one last visit to see Mike's mural. She arrived at the café a few minutes late to find an expectant Julian, who seemed delighted to see her again. His enthusiasm was a balm to her numb senses. Beatrice hoped he didn't notice the shadows under her eyes. They embraced, ordered dual cappuccinos, and took a seat at a corner table. Beatrice noticed a young couple with their son in a high chair across the patio. *Domestic bliss,* she thought, as she reined in her emotions.

A sip of the bold brew gave Beatrice the signal to wake up and focus on how best to handle this art mystery. Julian was ready and willing to do whatever she thought best, and Beatrice decided to tell the truth.

"You're not going to believe this, but I found another clue a couple of days ago that I think you should know about."

"No small talk here today!" he joked, eyeing her, and then taking a sip of his coffee. "Seriously, what's going on?"

"Well," she exhaled, "Rose's drawing with the words *Cerca Trova* has another notation on the document. I practically used the eye of a needle to uncover all of the mold and dirt, but it's there."

"What?"

"The letters *LV.* They add another layer of evidence that Vasari hid the Leonardo behind that wall."

"Who knows about this?"

"Only the cardinal. I haven't even told Rose the whole story."

"So where is the drawing now?"

"In my office, stored in a locked cabinet," she revealed, taking another sip of coffee as her eyes met Julian's gaze.

"Excellent! You're not going to believe this, but I have something to show you too! I literally think that my evidence and yours are about to unlock a centuries-old secret. We'll be famous."

"I'm not sure I have any interest in being famous," said Beatrice. "Actually, none at all. Is that why you're doing this?"

He sheepishly replied, "I shouldn't have said that. I'm sorry, I'm afraid I've embarrassed myself." His look of contrition was nothing short of endearing. "Let's head back to the office so I can show you. You'll be amazed."

Beatrice checked her watch, wondering whether to tell him that she was catching an early train back to Rome. Her bags were packed, so she figured she had an hour to see what he was so enthusiastic about.

"Can you give me a hint?"

"Nope!" he said with a wide grin. "I want to see the look on your face when I show you."

Beatrice's heart started pounding. The world could soon have access to another major masterpiece, which could influence a new generation of artists. Julian's comment about being famous bothered her, but she felt this slip could be forgiven.

"I must admit, I don't have much time. I've got a train to catch to Rome."

"I'll drive you," he offered gallantly.

"Thanks! Are you sure?" asked Beatrice. "I don't want to take you out of your way."

"No problem," said Julian. "It would be my pleasure to have you all to myself."

"Okay, great." She drained her coffee. "My bag is at Rose's place."

He nodded. "I can be ready shortly. Believe it or not, I have a full tank of gas, so it should be pretty easy to get us to Rome."

Beatrice needed to grab her bag, and he said he would pick her up in fifteen minutes.

A short time later, they were on the road. The time ticked by as Beatrice wondered if she should have left Mike a note. She felt out of sorts yet tried to focus on Julian's conversation about a new infrared scanning device that showed the artist's original drawings before he or she put oil to canvas.

Beatrice studied Julian's handsome profile, wondering why she considered him nothing more than a friend. He was certainly attractive enough and kind, she decided, but there was something about the way he interacted with her that seemed, well, almost calculated. Like he wanted the two of them to be perfectly in sync.

"Hey, how about we swing by your office?" he asked casually.

"Oh, I almost forgot, you were going to show me your clue."

"Don't you think it's a little late for that at this point?" he joked with a wink.

Beatrice realized that she had been so consumed with her thoughts about Mike that she really hadn't pushed him too hard on his findings.

"You could give me a hint on what you're so excited about."

"There's a widening crack in the wall, indicating a whole new opening," said Julian. "We may be able to get a scanning tool through to study the interior."

"Where in the wall?"

"I've got pictures in my bag."

Beatrice nodded, thinking his clue seemed a bit arbitrary. Hers was far more conclusive, she decided, as she directed him to her parking space. He grabbed a backpack and flung it over his shoulder as she collected her purse and stretched. The place was empty, and she wondered if the cardinal had returned from his trip.

There was no guard at the door, so it was a fairly simple process to access the building with Julian. Her thoughts wandered to Julian's finding, and she wanted to see the pictures he had in his bag. Pushing aside any analysis of his discovery, she moved into the office and went straight for the locked cabinet. Fortunately, the cardinal had the other two prints safely secured in his private rooms.

"Here it is," she said, putting on latex gloves before gingerly grabbing the delicate paper. Julian stepped forward, reaching for the ancient document. "Don't touch it!" she cried anxiously.

He eyed her warily with a strange look.

Holding the precious document, Beatrice carefully placed it on her drafting table and turned on the light.

"Is this the drawing Rose found in her apartment?"

"Yes, it is currently owned by the Vatican."

He studied the drawing for a moment, a nerve twitching in his cheek. "It appears that you've got everything you want. How convenient!" He added, "I've helped you every step of the way, and you're going to get all of the credit for this find."

"That's not true," said Beatrice.

"You put the pieces together based on all of our groundwork. How could you use me like that?" His eyes darkened with anger.

Beatrice looked at his twisted expression.

With a quick lunge, his hand dug into her shoulder, trapping her next to him.

"Oh my God!" she cried, desperately pushing away from him. "What are you doing?"

He lashed out, punching her in the face. "You've been using me all along. How could you be so cruel? All you ever wanted from me was information. I fell in love with you!"

"I thought we were work partners, Julian," she said, her squealing voice foreign to her own ears. "I never said that it was going to turn romantic."

His face turned red. "I saw you with that street artist. I saw the way you looked at each other."

"My personal life is none of your business."

"You shouldn't have led me on."

"I didn't, and if you come near me again, I'll call the police! Don't make me file assault charges against you. It'll ruin your career."

He came toward her with rage. Backing away from him, Beatrice accidentally stumbled as she received another punishing blow to her face. She fainted from the trauma, blacking out. The marble floor had no mercy on her head.

Chapter 20

"HEY," SAID ZOEY, peeking her head around the arched doorway to the farmhouse living room. "There's a really cool art opening on the mall tonight. Do you want to go?"

"Absolutely!" said Rose, wiping her brow. She put down her paint brush.

"You need a break after all you've done to our new house. This is definitely my treat."

Rose was about to protest but quickly decided that she did deserve a night out. She raised both hands and joked, "Do you think I can get this paint off my hands?"

"You'll fit right in," said Zoey. A white midi dress accentuated her flawless coffee-colored skin. Her big brown eyes twinkled with mischief. "Seriously, we're going to have some fun girl time, and I've made all of the arrangements. We're getting manicures and having our hair done too."

"What?" said Rose. "Do I look that bad?"

"Honey, it's not you . . . it's me. I feel like a giant raisin with skinny arms and legs. Will you look at this belly! I could play Santa Claus in the school's holiday show."

"Stop it! You're gorgeous," said Rose, plopping down on a covered club chair. "Who's featured at the opening?"

"I think it's cocktail party slash meet-and-greet type of evening for some professional artists who received fellowships from UVA."

"You know I would love that!"

"You need to get inspired again. You're an artist, Rose! You've done an incredible job painting the walls of this house, but enough is enough. I haven't seen you even try to come up with new ideas or work on *your* next gallery opening."

"You're right." Rose paused for a minute. "Life goes on, I suppose."

"Let's go have some fun today!"

"Amen, sister." Rose stretched her aching muscles, thinking that a hot shower and paint-free clothes would be heavenly.

That night, Rose felt like a new person in a chic black dress and heels as she and Zoey made their way into the crowded room. Zoey's burgundy flowered tunic and high ponytail made her look effervescent. They asked a friendly college student how the event flowed; the enthusiastic young woman with blue bangs explained that each artist had their own room to display artwork, mixed-media paintings, jewelry, or sculptures.

"I hope I can squeeze through this crowd," whispered Zoey, lovingly patting her stomach.

"You look radiant," replied Rose, taking her arm. She looked over as guests parted to let them through. "See," she said. "Nothing to worry about."

"Well, at least you don't feel like a Mac truck."

"Will you stop. You know I would give anything to be in your shoes."

Zoey swallowed hard. "I didn't mean to—"

"I know you didn't," said Rose. "Let's take it all in. That colorful painting over on the right wall looks like an ode to the Virginia Cavaliers basketball team."

"Look at that sculpture over there," said Zoey, pointing to the face of a woman with peroxide-blond hair and bright-red lips. "Do you think it's Gwen Stefani?"

"Maybe."

"Let's make our way to the back of the room and then work forward. I just overheard someone raving about an artist named Yoshi and her self-portrait."

Rose felt as if it were Christmas morning—the excitement of an opening, the creative paintings and sculpture. She paused at a table to look at an amazing topaz necklace that caught her eye. She said hello to the artist and tried it on.

A male voice startled her.

"It looks gorgeous on you," said Ben, standing beside her.

Rose blushed. "What are you doing here?"

He pointed to an attractive brunette. "Jeanie wanted to come, but I would have gladly brought you instead."

"Ben," said Rose firmly, "we're friends. Nothing more."

"Friends," he said with a smile. He perused her elegant form. "How about friends with benefits?"

Rose laughed. "Get out of here," she said.

"Think about it," said Ben as he sauntered away. "You know where to find me."

"Oh please. I thought you divorced your ego."

"Every now and then it makes a guest appearance," he joked, glancing at her left hand. "I see you're wearing his ring again. He's a lucky man, Rose." Ben ran his hand through his hair. "I have so many regrets."

Rose peered down at her engagement ring, back where it belonged. "Thank you." They stared at each other in a moment of understanding. "Hey, I need to find Zoey. Have fun tonight."

As Rose made her way through the crowds, she saw Ben reclaim his date. She went on her way, weaving in and out of people to find the infamous Yoshi.

A painting of green space caught her eye, and she remembered exploring, capturing the beauty of public parks in Florence before her life imploded. A wave of sadness took hold as she realized how much she missed her life in Florence. Looking for Zoey in the crowd, Rose went and got them both a couple of sparkling waters with lime.

"Are you inspired yet?" asked Zoey, grateful for the drink.

"Mission accomplished. Actually, this evening has been more than wonderful, but I'm starting to really miss Florence and my studio." She added, "Ben is here. Nothing like having good hair when you run into your ex," she joked. "Seriously, he hasn't changed."

"Hey," said Zoey. "I noticed you're wearing your engagement ring again."

"Yes," said Rose.

Later that night, back at the farmhouse, the night chill permeated as Rose gripped the covers tighter around her. *Zoey and Stan's place sure is authentic,* she thought, as she contemplated putting on a pair of socks to warm her up. Her cell phone rang.

"Hello," she said, wondering why he was calling so late.

"Rose," said Lyon urgently. "So sorry to wake you."

Rose rubbed her sleepy eyes, telling herself to wake up. She stared at the farmhouse wall with its tilted sunflower oil painting illuminated by the bathroom nightlight.

"Lyon? Is everything alright?"

"There's been an accident."

"What?" she cried, sitting straight up in bed. "What happened?"

"It's Beatrice. She's in the hospital."

"Oh no!" she exclaimed. Rose tightened her grip on the phone. "How is she?"

"I don't know," he said softly. "It's not good. Something happened at the lab. The doctors think that she nearly succumbed to smoke inhalation and barely made it out of there alive. The cardinal tried to contact you, and when he couldn't find you, he phoned my office. He wanted you to know."

"I'm so glad you called. Let me get this straight: there was a fire at the Vatican?"

"Yes, it was in the central laboratory where Beatrice worked. The alarm went off and so did the automatic sprinkler systems, which saved her life." He paused.

"There's more, isn't there," insisted Rose.

"They said, given her bruises, that she was hit by someone prior to the fire."

"What? Who would have done this to her? Do they have security footage?"

"Whoever it was also figured out how to erase the video surveillance so there's no trace. Beatrice is the only one who may know, and they've put her into a medically induced coma to heal the trauma to her head."

"This is awful. Why would anyone want to harm Beatrice?" She knew the moment that she mouthed those words that she was lying to herself and Lyon. Beatrice had found a clue that could lead to one of the greatest art discoveries of all time. "I'm coming back. I'll get the first flight out of here and be there as soon as I can."

"I can pick you up at the airport," offered Lyon. "I know this isn't the best time to talk about us, but I've missed you, Rose. I want us to be together. You know how much I love you."

"That means a lot to me. I've done a lot of thinking too, and I want to make it work. I love you too, Lyon," she said, exhaling. "But we have to think about Beatrice right now. I'll text you the flight information as soon as I figure out what I'm doing." Rose added, "Where is the cardinal now?"

"He's been in the hospital waiting room the whole time. He's been comforting her parents, which is helpful."

"This all sounds so surreal. You don't think we could lose her, do you?" asked Rose. Her voice trailed away as tears streamed down her cheeks. The thought of Beatrice not waking up from the coma was too frightening to bear.

"I don't know. We're all praying for her recovery."

"I'll get to Italy as soon as I can."

"I know you will," said Lyon. "Think about what I said."

"I can't wait to see you, Lyon," she said softly.

***

At dawn, Rose entered the kitchen to get a cup of coffee from the Keurig. Thanks to a sleepless night, she was already packed and organized, and it wouldn't take long to get her paint rollers, brushes, blue tape, and protective sheets and buckets into the basement. She didn't want to leave a mess for Zoey and Stan.

Zoey came into the kitchen, rubbing her eyes.

"Hey, what are you doing up so early?" asked Rose, looking at Zoey's adorable pink tunic that hugged her rounded belly. She added, "You're the only one I know that can look this good, this early in the morning."

"Ahhh, thanks," said Zoey. "I'll take all the compliments I can get because I feel like a giant watermelon in this top. You're up early too," she replied, taking a seat at the antique pine breakfast table that they'd recently found at an estate sale with the six cane chairs in varying states of repair.

"Let me get you a cup of coffee first," offered Rose, pulling a white mug from the cabinet. Zoey took her coffee black, while Rose added more milk and sugar to her steaming cup.

"I've got to get to Rome as soon as possible," said Rose, trying to hide her dismay. "A friend of mine is in the hospital, and I need to check on her." She handed Zoey the mug, then sat across from her.

"Who is it?"

"Remember Beatrice, the conservator for the Vatican? It feels like a lifetime ago that I found those drawings and connected with her. She's so special. I'll never forget how she was so helpful after the Ben breakup. I stayed with her for weeks while I put my head back together."

"Oh no! Tell me what happened." Zoey took a sip of her coffee, then grabbed an orange from the blue ceramic bowl at the center of the table.

"There was a fire at the lab where she worked. They said she barely made it out alive. I'm so upset."

"That's awful. I assume they have state-of-the-art equipment to protect everything."

"Apparently, the sprinkler systems kicked in and alerted the fire department." Rose thought for a moment. "They took longer than they should have. It was after hours, so it wasn't easy for them to gain access to the lab."

"I'm so sorry to hear about Beatrice. I'll send positive vibes into the universe, asking for a complete recovery," Zoey offered, leaning forward in her chair. "Rose, as much as I hate the circumstances, I think it's great you're going back to Italy. I was going to talk to you about it anyway."

"You were?" said Rose.

"Stan and I were starting to feel uncomfortable having you do so much work on the house for us. You've been absolutely incredible. It's crazy how much you've accomplished. Our house looks like a home thanks to you! I must say, you've been a force of nature taking down all that ugly wallpaper."

"Are you kidding me?" cried Rose. "The endless scraping was better than therapy."

"Not funny," said Zoey. "Seriously, sweet friend, you've been so amazing, but I think it's time you and Lyon communicate in person. The fact that you put your engagement ring back on your left hand last night says it all. Am I right?"

Rose looked down at the beautiful emerald ring, sparkling in the morning light. She smiled about being engaged for the first time in weeks. "I decided that Lyon and I need to work things out. I'm absolutely miserable without him."

"You could have fooled me," joked Zoey. "Unless, of course, you've been preparing to open your own decorating business here in Charlottesville."

"The hard work sustained me," Rose offered, noticing how bad her hands looked from all the sanding and painting. Tiny white specs were still imprinted on her fingers.

"Thank you, Rose, for everything, but you've done enough! Stan and I can take it from here," Zoey said. "You know that I'm really going to miss you. This period of time has been a real gift. So, dare I ask, what time is your flight?"

"I'm leaving here at four, and the flight to Rome leaves New York around seven tonight. Lyon is going to pick me up at the airport."

"That's perfect," said Zoey. "I'm not going to lie. I'm so relieved to hear that you're going to give your relationship another chance."

"And then there's Doris," said Rose. "She's never going to be happy with my life choices, so I may as well let it go."

"Your mother loves you, and frankly, look at the bright side. You did better this visit than in years past."

"True, but she hasn't accepted Lyon or my life in Italy."

"She'll come around someday. You have to do what's right for you."

"I know." Rose pondered Zoey's comments and blurted, "And what if we can't have a child together?"

"And what if you can't? You still have choices. You'll study your options and come up with a plan. Rose, you're so smart and resourceful. I'm no medical expert, but I've heard about procedures like in vitro fertilization. You could also hire a surrogate like the celebrities do, or you may want to adopt. The bottom line is that there are options, and that's what the two of you need to figure out together. I'm your best friend, so I can say this to you: you don't always have to be blood to love someone like family."

Rose felt the moisture in her eyes. Zoey was right. She could figure something out. After a huge exhale, she said, "Thanks for all the support these past few months. If I could pick a sister, it would be you."

Their eyes met as they acknowledged the strength of their sisterhood.

"I'm so incredibly happy for you and Stan. You're creating such a beautiful life here. This house looks fantastic if I do say so myself!"

"Well, we'll need a whole lot of insulation to get through the winter."

"That too!" she said. "Glad this place has so many fireplaces."

"I'm going to miss you. I've cherished our time together."

"Me too."

They tried to hug, and Zoey's belly got in the way, making them both laugh.

"Yup," said Zoey, backing away. "I feel like I have a linebacker in there today. The baby is packing quite a kick this week."

"What if it's a girl?"

"She's going to be the next Serena Williams. I like strong and confident women," said Zoey. She walked over to the refrigerator. "Speaking of which, you're too thin, girl."

"I think Italian food will fix the problem!" Rose laughed.

***

The weeks in Virginia melted away as Rose listened to the melodic sound of Italian cascading through the cabin. *Home,* she thought as she looked out the plane's small window at the airport, feeling a surge of adrenaline at the thought of seeing Lyon again. Strange how her time in Charlottesville ended abruptly, and despite the situation, she felt such joy in returning to the country that had captured her heart. The deplaning felt endless, as Rose got stuck behind what appeared to be a tourist group.

Once inside, she jogged to the baggage claim, searching for Lyon. Suddenly, her eyes fixated on his familiar form, waiting for her just as he promised. From a distance, Rose took in his beloved face, the high cheekbones and muscular appearance. As soon as he noticed her, Rose raced to him, wondering how she stayed away so long. Their kiss held the promise of more, and for a moment the rest of the world ceased to exist.

They made their way to the baggage carousel. When her large bag appeared on the conveyer belt, Lyon raised one eyebrow at her. He joked, "Looks like you might stay awhile."

"Of course," Rose explained primly. "I'm glad to be back home."

"I'm not sure what you missed more, Italy or me," said Lyon with a wink. "Don't answer that." As he rolled her large bag out to the car, he remarked, "Nice ring."

Rose looked down at the engagement ring on her finger, retorting, "This guy gave it to me. Tall, dark, and ruggedly handsome. He's promised to make me my favorite pesto herbed chicken, or shall I say, *pollo Genovese*, for all eternity."

"Rugged, huh? I like it. Looks like we've got a good plan," he offered, putting his arm around her, kissing her forehead.

Lyon had secured a room at a boutique hotel by the Spanish Steps on Via Gregoriana, where she was able to drop her bags and take a hot shower before they headed to the hospital. Two shots of espresso helped with the jet lag. Rose felt like she was riding an emotional roller coaster—the joy of being back in Italy with Lyon combined with the pain of wondering whether Beatrice would recover fully. Seeing Beatrice's exhausted-looking parents and Cardinal Baglioni in the waiting room set her tears flowing again. After she hugged everyone, the cardinal asked to have a word with her in private. Rose left Lyon chatting with Elsa, who looked ashen and frightened.

The corner meeting room with its simple chairs and table was austere. As Rose took a seat, a poster of black-and-white photographs depicting sculptures of Roman emperors caught her eye.

"I'm so glad you're back, my dear. I know it means a lot to Beatrice and her family."

"Of course," said Rose. "I've been praying for her, but I think you're more likely to have better results."

A hint of a smile appeared on the cardinal's mouth.

"Shall I be blunt?"

"Yes," said Rose.

"The second drawing you found is missing. I had the other two in a safe in my apartment."

Rose suspected as much. "I can't say I'm shocked. I've felt all along that this had to do with the clue Beatrice found. She wouldn't tell me over the phone."

The cardinal stood and began pacing the room. "This is a very complicated situation. This person harmed Beatrice, who I care about deeply. She's always been like a daughter to me."

"I understand," said Rose solemnly.

"We're the only people that really know about the drawings, and I trust you and Lyon explicitly."

"Thank you. That means a lot to me," said Rose as she grappled with the magnitude of the situation. If he wanted to be blunt, she thought she needed to do the same. "Might I ask about the clue?"

The cardinal sighed, rubbing his hands over his tired eyes and returned the glasses to his face. "I worry about your safety if I tell you. Right now, Beatrice and I are the only people that know."

"You must tell me, Cardinal. I promise not to involve Lyon, and it won't go past this room."

He nodded. The cardinal, subconsciously touching his white collar, explained, "After weeks of painstaking work, she found the letters *LV* located next to the words *Cerca Trova* on the ancient document. Needless to say, it was an awe-inspiring effort."

They were both silent for several moments as Rose pondered what Beatrice accomplished. It was no easy feat, given the delicacy of the paper. The level of patience and competence was unparalleled.

"Wow! I am very surprised again," said Rose. She pondered the efficacy of those two simple letters—*LV*. Rose realized that it could only be the great Leonardo da Vinci. It was a viable clue that his *Battle of Anghiari* was hidden behind the wall. The cardinal interrupted the swirling thoughts inside her head as she tried to piece together what happened.

"Who would benefit the most from this find?"

"Dr. Saunders and Julian," said Rose immediately, looking up at him. "But I can't imagine that Dr. Saunders would ever harm Beatrice in any way. He's so mild mannered."

"Greed and jealousy do strange things to people."

"There's another possibility. I know that she went to Florence to stay in my apartment so she could see a street artist named Mike. She was fascinated by him."

"That doesn't sound like Beatrice at all," exclaimed the cardinal in a fatherly tone.

"I know, but she thought Mike was a genius. Just so you know, these street artists are like celebrities. Mike has a huge following, and so does his rival, Vince. In short, they're committed to making social and political statements through their work, which pops up in cities all over the world. Anyway, Mike was painting a huge mural in Florence, and Beatrice went there to see him. You can figure out the rest. On some level, she knew it was crazy, but I suspect that they connected on a very deep level. Except, of course—"

"Of course, what?"

"Mike insisted that he has no allegiance to anyone or anything."

"What about God?" said the cardinal, affronted by the inference.

Rose shook her head. "I can't answer that."

"Are you insinuating that this artist might be responsible?"

"I don't think Beatrice would bring Mike to the lab to show him the clue. She was very careful. I still think Julian or his dad are the only logical explanations, unless the intruder was random."

"You know, Rose," said the cardinal, "I've been wondering how to handle Beatrice's find, and I've had a premonition that something like this could happen. It's almost too monumental for any of us."

"What are you saying?" said Rose standing.

"I'm saying there's a new faction of scholars that believe that Leonardo da Vinci never painted the *Battle of Anghiari*. A friend told me that there was a roundtable discussion at the Uffizi gallery last month. Dozens of scholars attended. This panel of experts claims that the painting was prepared with a technique using a layer of gesso and oil, a technique that made it impossible for Leonardo to create the final work. In short, the paint would not stick to the wall. Therefore, Leonardo's work has only ever existed as a preliminary drawing or cartoon, never as an actual fresco on the wall."

"What? But we have an ancient document to prove it! In my opinion, Beatrice uncovered a treasure map that I believe substantiates the claim that Giorgio Vasari or a member of his family hid the drawings that I found in the wall of their apartment. There are three important references in that drawing that Julian took. The words *Cerca Trova*, Vasari's own portrait, and an *LV* pointing to Leonardo da Vinci. In other words, the drawing provides a record to prove that he masterminded the building of a wall to protect Leonardo da Vinci's painting *The Battle of Anghiari*. Then, he and his considerable team of assistants and artists painted extensive new murals depicting six important Florentine battles, which is what is in the Palazzo Vecchio right now."

He looked sideways at her. "This group is powerful and made up of highly respected government officials, museum curators, and scholars. Who knows? They could be right, and this find is simply a red herring."

"But it's not. I was meant to find those drawings. I honestly believe that. And Beatrice was meant to find those three clues on that document."

The cardinal grew frustrated. "You're not listening to me. At what price does this discovery come? I don't want anything to happen to you, and look at Beatrice. I'm an old man, and my life is in its final phase."

"Don't say that!" cried Rose. "What are we supposed to do?"

"Nothing until Beatrice recovers."

"Does this mean that you're going to get behind this new group even though you know there's a legitimate clue out there somewhere?"

"I haven't decided," replied the cardinal

"You don't have to," said Rose. "But assuming it was Julian, he attacked her once. What's to stop him from doing it again?"

"That's what I'm trying to figure out," said the cardinal.

"She can't die," said Rose quietly, wiping tears from her eyes.

The cardinal opened his arms so Rose could take comfort in his embrace. "My child, I pray she wakes up soon."

"My heart is breaking," said Rose.

"So is mine, Rose."

Chapter 21

THE STEADY HUM of a machine woke her, and Beatrice slowly regained consciousness. Looking down at the tubes in her arms frightened her as she tried to recall the events that led her here. She remembered Rose's apartment and the moment when Mike walked out the door. The rest was a blur as she struggled to sit up.

"My dear, you gave us quite a scare," said the kindly white-haired nurse, who leaned over her.

"How long have I been here?"

"A week," she replied, checking her IV.

"What happened?"

"There was a fire at the lab in the Vatican. You were knocked unconscious and succumbed to smoke inhalation. Fortunately, the alarm sounded, and you were rescued."

Beatrice knew that an important piece of this story was missing but she failed to recall exactly what it was. "Do my parents know?"

"Your parents, Cardinal Baglioni, and your friends have been here around the clock, praying for your recovery."

Beatrice was touched by their concern. She moved her head from right to left and was thrilled to wiggle her legs and toes. *Definitely a good sign,* she thought, as she took in the white walls and curtainless windows.

A short time later, the doctor came in, telling her to take it easy and be very gentle with her movements when her family came to visit. When her parents and the cardinal entered into the room, Beatrice remained still even though she wanted to jump out of bed and hug everyone. Her mother grinned widely, but Beatrice couldn't help but notice the dark circles under her eyes. "It's a miracle," she declared, leaning down to hug her.

"I have friends in high places," joked Beatrice as the cardinal stepped forward to wish her well. When her father wiped a tear, Beatrice asked, "Was I that bad off?"

Everyone laughed nervously, breaking the tension.

Her mother explained, "We've had time to figure out a plan for your recovery, darling. I'll stay here in Rome with you for a few days while you regain your strength. After that, your father and I want you to come home to Switzerland for the holidays."

The cardinal cleared his throat. "We have delayed the restoration of the *Transfiguration* until early next year to give you plenty of time to rest up for the project."

"That's wonderful news," said Beatrice, relieved beyond measure. She balled her hands into fists, silently testing her manual dexterity. Her left hand was sore but seemed all right. Beatrice felt safe within the confines of her hospital room but wondered what it was going to be like to return to her normal routine.

The doctor asked everyone to wrap up to give her more time to rest, and Beatrice promptly fell asleep. That evening, the door opened, and Mike sauntered in, quickly removing his green cap. He seemed very nervous.

"Rose told me that I could find you here," he said, inching closer to her.

"She called you?" Beatrice couldn't believe her eyes.

"Yes, and I came straightaway."

"Thank you so much, but you don't need to worry about me. The last thing I want is to burden anyone. The doctors say that I'm going to be fine."

"My heart exploded when I heard the news. I wanted to be here."

"Really?"

"I've thought about you a lot, and I want to be by your side right now. What happened?"

Beatrice shrugged. "I can't remember anything, and I've still got a terrible headache."

"I'm so sorry," he cried, leaning over the bed to touch her cheek with his hand. "I would like to help out."

"My mother is here. She's going to stay for a few days after I get discharged."

"And after that?"

She thought for a moment. "Rose is back, and she can help," said Beatrice.

His tone turned gruff. "I won't take no for an answer, bellissima!"

"We'll figure it out."

"Goodbye for now, my love," he said as he backed away.

Beatrice couldn't believe that he had made the effort to travel to Rome to visit her. *Miracles do happen,* she concluded, before she fell back to sleep.

*** *

A week later, Beatrice was delighted with her progress. The headaches had abated, and she was slowly regaining her strength. *Having Mom stay with me was a blessing,* thought Beatrice, as she turned the pages of a book. Beatrice was determined to get her life back together as quickly as possible, too. As she dozed off on the living room sofa, her dream brought flashes of the document, Julian's menacing face, and the fire. Beatrice screamed herself awake. Fortunately, she was alone and could pull herself together before her mother returned from grocery shopping. Grabbing her phone, she called the cardinal and asked to speak to him in person the following morning.

"I remember," she said softly.

"I suspected as much," he replied. "I will see you in my private apartment in the morning. Your mother can wait in my office for you."

"You've thought of everything," she replied.

"I hope so," he said.

Her mother came bustling in the door with bags filled with fresh vegetables and spices.

"I'm cooking tonight," said Beatrice, taking a bag to the counter.

"And I won't take no for an answer. You've been so helpful, Mom. It's the least I can do."

Elsa acquiesced, volunteering to set the table. She insisted on linen napkins and real china. Viterbi white plates with a gold edge and her grandmother's silver utensils dressed up the table. There was a tiny Christmas tree boasting silver balls as a centerpiece, which Elsa had found at the market. A green magnolia wreath with a red velvet bow hung above the mantle.

"What are you making?" Elsa asked, placing the salt and pepper shakers on the table.

"Eggplant parmesan and salad because I know you love that dish." Beatrice added, "I can't thank you enough for all of your help. I love you so much." Her mother came over and wrapped her arms around her.

"I love you too. I'm so glad you're feeling so much better. You look wonderful."

"Thanks," said Beatrice. "The cardinal called. I thought I would go by and see him tomorrow morning. Maybe bring him a little Christmas present." Beatrice didn't feel entirely awful with the white lie. The last thing she ever wanted to do was involve her mother in any drama.

"That sounds lovely. Maybe we go tomorrow morning after breakfast."

"I feel like I can go myself."

"Nonsense!" exclaimed Elsa. "I found some homemade jams at the market for the cardinal. I'd like nothing better than to wish him a merry Christmas."

"Okay, but I have a few work details to discuss with him first. He said to meet him at his private apartments."

"That works. You know how I love to spend time in the Sistine Chapel. I can wait there until he's available." She added, "It was wonderful to see Rose again. She made quite an effort to be by your side."

"I really appreciated it. I'm glad she and Lyon are back together." *Good news,* Beatrice thought. Their reconciliation gave her hope for her own future. The bad news was the fact that Mike would always be unpredictable. *Will I grow tired of his mercurial personality?*

The next morning, Beatrice checked her appearance in the mirror. Surprisingly, the bruises were healing, and she delighted in the red Christmas scarf that her mother purchased for her.

After parting from her mother, she made her way to the cardinal's apartment with a basket of goodies. As soon as he opened the door, Beatrice ran into his arms, so grateful for all his love and support during her illness.

"My dear, it is wonderful to see you looking so very well."

"Thank you, Cardinal. Your prayers and good wishes were much appreciated."

"Come in and have a seat."

Beatrice sat in the gold damask-upholstered chair, trying to quell her nerves. Sitting up straight, she sensed that the cardinal had figured out what happened all on his own. The whole incident made her feel sick to her stomach. She stared at the needlepoint rug, then garnered her courage. She exclaimed, "It was Julian who stole the drawing."

"That was my conclusion," he replied. "Rose and I discussed the situation at length, and he was our prime suspect." He added, "I'd like to press charges against him."

"I feel so conflicted. On one hand, I hate the idea of having to relive what happened. I want it all to just go away. But, in truth, I'm furious that he took the document."

"Let's not forget that it's a stolen document, which prohibits him from opening the case with government officials. I've given this issue a great deal of contemplation and analysis." He crossed his legs. "I want you to know how seriously I take your discovery. That being said, you should know that there's a new revelation that came to light while you were ill."

"What is it?"

He cleared his throat. "A new faction of experts thinks Leonardo's *Battle of Anghiari* never really made it to the wall. That it only exists as a preliminary drawing. I've just heard about it. Apparently, there was a meeting at the Uffizi recently to discuss the technical aspect of this theory. Their evidence is strong and has made the news lately."

"Really? I think my evidence is compelling too," replied Beatrice. "I worked on a five-hundred-year-old document that Rose found in the wall of her apartment."

"A stolen document at this point."

"I let Julian into a private art lab. We can prove he's guilty!"

"It's not that easy, Beatrice. I believe we can have Julian brought to justice." The cardinal leaned forward. "Your find is controversial even in the best of circumstances. Please listen to me. I've met with dozens of scholars in the past few weeks. I have taken your discovery very seriously. These experts wrote a detailed book with compelling technical evidence that the painting never happened. They say beyond a shadow of a doubt that the paint would not hold. The painting only ever existed as a preliminary drawing, just like Michelangelo's version of the Battle of Cascina."

"What about the black pigments they found? Surely, that must mean something?"

"Their analysis concludes that those pigments were used widely at the time and may not point to anything specific."

"What does that mean?"

"Scholars say those black pigments could have also come from the wall. This argument presents a great deal of merit and precise technical evidence to prove it."

Beatrice grew frustrated. "What if we challenge their findings?"

"At what price?" The cardinal stood and began pacing back and forth. "Beatrice, need I remind you that you almost died a few weeks ago? I can't let that happen again, my child. You're like a daughter to me. Rose is vulnerable too. How can I support anything that puts both of your lives in danger?"

Beatrice sighed. "Thank you for your concern, Cardinal. I'm not sure what we should do next."

"After we call the police and have Julian arrested, our first order of business is to get the drawing back."

"I concur with that plan and will gladly help in bringing him to justice. And then?"

"We celebrate Christmas. I'm not willing to commit right now to opening up the lost Leonardo mystery."

Beatrice felt the beginnings of a headache forming at her temples. Had she been so blinded by the potential of her find that she had failed to analyze the evidence properly? It was all so complicated. Cardinal Baglioni was clearly worried about their safety, which she appreciated, but she wasn't sure that she wanted to give up. Perhaps some time off might produce a new perspective.

"You're right. I suppose I could use a break. I head to Switzerland in a few days for a nice reunion with my family."

"Absolutely, my dear."

A short time later, Elsa arrived to embrace the cardinal, thanking him for being so helpful to her daughter. "She's lucky to have you as her friend and mentor," Elsa exclaimed, "and to do meaningful work in such a glorious setting. I'm so impressed that Beatrice will help restore a masterpiece like the *Transfiguration!*"

"It's truly an honor, Cardinal," said Beatrice earnestly.

"You have earned the privilege."

"Now on to more important things," said Elsa, uncovering the gift basket.

The cardinal was delighted with the jam and goodies tucked inside. His eyes lit up when he pulled out a chocolate confection.

"You realize that we live in Switzerland, Cardinal. There's no better chocolate on earth."

"I might be willing to challenge that statement." He said with a gleam in his eye. "Perhaps we can have a chocolate taste test in the new year."

They all laughed together. Beatrice recalled a certain chocolate shop in Switzerland and envisioned trying to get one of their oversized bars through security. The image evoked a smile.

***

The rest of the day was a flurry of activity. There were so many errands to run and a few special gifts to stuff in her already full suitcase. Holiday decorations made the streets look joyous as Beatrice eyed the red ribbon wrapped around a light pole. A newfound appreciation for all of life's important things—namely her health, her family, and God's grace—put a spring in her step. When a cranky shopper cut in front of her at the checkout line, she reminded herself that life's petty incidents weren't worth worrying about. She thought about her Christmas shopping list, noting that a new pair of lined leather gloves would make a wonderful present for her father. Her doting mother was sure to love a beautiful Italian cashmere sweater. Now was the time to celebrate life and her family.

A call from Rose interrupted her shopping excursion.

"Hi," she said. "When do you leave?"

"Thursday evening. I'm getting excited to be with my family."

"You're not going to believe this, but your image is gracing the side of a building."

"What are you talking about?"

"It looks like Mike has painted your likeness as some Grecian goddess, white flowing robe and all."

Beatrice had to sit. "I don't know what to say."

"I do. I think he's sending you a message."

"I still can't believe he came to see me in the hospital."

"Uh, Beatrice, the goddess is standing on top of what appears to be the Empire State Building." Rose burst out laughing, and Lyon's voice was in the background. "Did you hear that?"

"You're both laughing so hard. I don't understand."

"There is a series of hearts all over the place. I'm going to take a picture and send it to you. The mural is gigantic. Everyone is talking about it here. They are saying it could symbolize a new trade relationship between Greece and America."

"That's ridiculous."

"If only they knew the real story," said Rose. "Seems pretty obvious that he cares for you."

"This is crazy! We can't communicate through murals."

"Why not?" said Rose. "I'm learning all about being flexible."

"Did you actually set a wedding date?"

"We're working on it!"

"I'm so glad you guys are together again."

"Me too," said Rose. "Have a wonderful Christmas with your family in Switzerland."

"Thanks!"

The knock at her apartment door was unexpected. Beatrice stopped packing and went to answer it. To her surprise, Mike stood in the doorway, awkwardly holding a present.

"I got you something," he said, looking down at his feet. Beatrice invited him inside and ushered him into the living room.

"I'm not very good at this."

"Let me make us some tea," she offered, trying to break the tension.

"That would be nice. Are you trying to domesticate me?"

"Never," said Beatrice. "You're perfect just the way you are."

Mike threw back his head and laughed. "You may be the only way that sees me that way!"

Beatrice poured water in the teapot and brought both porcelain cups on a lacquered tray to her coffee table. "What are you doing for the holidays?" she asked.

"I can't stand the suspense!" he announced, jumping back up. "You must open my gift!"

"Alright!" she cried, enjoying his exuberance. Beatrice was surprised by the box and wondered what in the world was inside. She removed wads of tissue paper to reveal a smaller box.

"What is this?" she asked as her hands shook.

"Open it!" he exclaimed with childlike excitement.

The sparkling blue topaz ring glinted in the light. The gift was a wonderful surprise, leaving Beatrice completely speechless. "It's beautiful." It looked almost like the one she found.

He came over to put it on her finger. "Your friend Rose helped me." He cleared his throat. "It shines bright just like you."

"Are you becoming a poet?" asked Beatrice.

"Hardly. I will say that life with me will never be predictable."

"That's for sure!" They laughed. "About that mural?"

"I love you, Beatrice," he announced breathlessly. "I never thought I could feel this way about anyone."

Beatrice was so shocked that she started crying. "Oh, Mike, I love you too. I can't believe this is happening."

"The mural was my way of asking if you'd come to New York with me."

Beatrice was overwhelmed. "I don't know what to say. This is all so sudden. You know how much I love my job."

"Are you sure?" He reached for her and began a trail of kisses down her neck.

She gently broke free of his embrace. "Oh, I got you something."

Mike was delighted with a new pair of gloves, a new gray skull cap, and a set of glow-in-the-dark paints that she'd found through much research.

"I'm so sad that I'm going to Switzerland tomorrow for the holidays." She looked sidelong at him. "But I could always come back early."

"You're just trying to stop me from creating another mural. I would like to paint more of your beautiful body," exclaimed Mike, taking her into his arms.

"Don't you dare!" warned Beatrice modestly.

"Why not, bellissima? Artists have been glorifying the human form since the beginning of time?!"

Beatrice rolled her eyes. There was nothing better than being crazy in love, but she prayed Mike wouldn't dare to paint her naked form on the side of some building.

Chapter 22

THE ELEGANCE OF IL PALAGIO was not lost on Rose. She felt like a teenager on her first date. Rose caught sight of their reflection as they passed by a mirrored lobby. She was pleased with her new comfortable, high-waisted, black velvet pants, a welcome back to Florence gift to herself. Her long blond hair flowed onto her shoulders. Lyon wore a dark jacket which complemented his olive skin. She thought she was the luckiest woman on the earth.

Lyon whispered, "You look beautiful, my love."

They were seated in a quiet corner with plush green seats. Lyon ordered champagne and cleared his throat. "Rose, you know how I feel about us—"

She cut him off. "I know what you're going to say, but I want you to know that I did a lot of thinking while I was back in the States. I'm sorry I reacted so strongly to things, and I take responsibility for my immature response."

"What?" said Lyon. "You did nothing wrong. It was me."

"Let me finish. One of the things that became really clear to me is the fact that you don't have to be blood to love someone fully and completely, including a baby." She paused. "Zoey is like a sister to me, and I would do anything in the world for her. She was my rock and my sounding board the whole time. I was able to realize so many things."

"There's absolutely no excuse for what happened with my ex."

"I trust you," said Rose, taking the hand he reached across the table. "We've both made mistakes. I made peace with Ben while I was home. We're on good terms, which I think was healing for me. You know, Doris hasn't given up, and please don't expect her to accept my living in Italy. Anyway, I want you to know that I thought a lot about what I wanted. I came to the conclusion that adopting a baby is our best option."

He coughed, surprised by her convictions, then smiled. "Rose, we may not have to worry about it."

"But I like the idea. Really."

"My mother had me see a doctor, who referred me to a specialist. I think we have a very good chance of having a baby on our own."

They stared at each in silence for a few minutes, both relieved and happy. Rose celebrated with an order of a seafood and champagne risotto; Lyon asked if she would share some of his Chateaubriand. The waiter thought a pinot noir would work well with both selections.

"Well," Lyon admitted, leaning forward in his chair. "I was planning on coming to Charlottesville for Christmas. Zoey and Stan invited me."

"What? You're kidding me," she said.

He smiled at her genuine surprise. "I have the plane tickets to prove it."

"She's such a good actress!" Rose said of Zoey.

"Actually, we've spoken quite a few times."

"Really? About what, Lyon?"

"I wondered if you might like to start planning a wedding again. I know Zoey's baby is due in February. Anyway, I talked with my mother this morning, and they're thrilled that we're back together. She'd like to see us both on Saturday morning to come up with a new plan. Oh, and my mom offered you her dress with no strings attached. She wanted me to mention it to you first, so you didn't feel any pressure."

"That was so lovely of her. I'll definitely give it serious consideration."

"Does that mean you're ready?"

"Yes! I've never been surer of anything in my life!"

"I feel the same way."

"If possible, I'd like to ask Cardinal Baglioni to perform the ceremony."

"You and *forever* pretty much covers it. On that note, I'll get the check," said Lyon with a wink.

***

On Saturday morning, Rose looked over as Lyon accelerated the Tesla along his parents' driveway, eager to be on time for breakfast with his mother. They looked at each other in complete adoration. Since her return, Rose felt as if everything had turned right in her world. A smile formed as she contemplated the conversation ahead.

Faith had placed a colorful Christmas wreath on the front door. Little details seemed to demand attention lately. The house was decorated with greens and some sort of red berries, adding to the air of holiday cheer. Faith cascaded down the stairs, her dark hair flowing to her shoulders, adding to her youthful appearance.

"Lyon, darling," said Faith in her melodious voice. "You're looking well." She embraced him warmly, surveying her son's appearance as she was wont to do.

"Thanks."

Faith turned to Rose. "You have no idea what joy it brings me to have you here." Rose's eyes welled with tears as she was enfolded in a warm embrace. "Having Rose back is the best Christmas gift ever," exclaimed Faith. She moved forward, waving her arm at the gigantic tree. "Your father went a bit wild this year. This tree is enormous."

"I love it," said Lyon, tapping into her enthusiasm.

"It's absolutely stunning."

"I'm eager to hear your news. Let's get some breakfast and talk more."

There was something comforting about sitting at the large, white, marble kitchen island while Faith cracked eggs and they chatted over coffee. The modern kitchen was the family's gathering space, and she appreciated all its amenities. Rose offered to help, but Faith insisted on cooking.

"At least let me pour some orange juice."

The scrambled eggs, bacon, and hot coffee made her appreciate Faith as her future mother-in-law even more, if that were possible. She knew beyond a shadow of a doubt how fortunate she was to have such a special relationship with Lyon's mother. They chatted easily about Rose's time in the States, the holidays, and the fact that Beatrice was on the mend.

"Do you have any news for me?" asked Faith. "I didn't want to ask over the phone."

Rose admired her direct nature and glanced knowingly at Lyon.

"I went to see a doctor after we spoke about my fertility last time," announced Lyon. "See, I listen to my mother," he joked.

"And?"

"There's hope. I've got to jump through a few more hoops, but he's more optimistic than I anticipated." He smiled and reached for Rose's hand. "I want to thank you for helping me to address the issue."

"I'm delighted," said Faith, clapping her hands. "We have much to celebrate!"

Faith smiled. "Speaking of which, have you picked a date yet?"

"We've settled on late spring," said Rose thoughtfully. "Zoey's baby is due in February."

"I need something more concrete if I'm going to call back the caterers and ask to be on their schedule. Wait! I've got an idea," announced Faith. "Give me a few minutes!"

Rose watched as Faith scurried from the room. She poured another cup of coffee, feeling so peaceful in this house. A short time later, Faith returned to the kitchen, holding a hat. Lyon's brother, Peter, followed.

"That's my favorite baseball cap, I'll have you know."

"Mother," asked Lyon. "What are you doing?"

"Let's leave it to fate. Pick one!"

Rose laughed at her game, wondering what Faith had in mind.

She gingerly reached into the baseball cap and pulled out a strip of white paper.

"March 6." Rose raised an eyebrow at Faith. "That one may be too soon for Zoey to get here."

"What's the significance?" asked Lyon.

"You should know this one if you're going to marry me," exclaimed Rose.

"No idea," said Lyon. He looked at his brother. "Do you have a clue?"

"Nope."

"March 6 is Michelangelo's birthday!" She turned to Faith. "Very clever, but I'm going to have to try again." She took a sip of her coffee. "Your turn, Lyon."

Lyon reached into the hat and pulled out another strip of white paper with the date on it.

"April 15." He shrugged. "Sounds good to me."

"Do you know why I picked that date?" said Faith.

"It's Leonardo da Vinci's birthday!" cried Rose. "This is too funny! How incredibly perfect."

"Finally, you have a date!" said Peter wryly. "It's about bloody time."

They all laughed.

Chapter 23

BEATRICE WAS STILL ELATED after a glorious holiday visit with her family in Switzerland's snowcapped Matterhorn mountains. Cozy family dinners and time together had helped her make a full recovery. She was starting the new year refreshed and eager to get back to the lab. Cardinal Baglioni phoned and said he needed to speak with her immediately. He had major news to share with her about recent events and was on the way to her apartment. Before she could digest his unexpected visit, an urgent knock sounded at the door.

"This is a surprise," said Beatrice wryly when the cardinal came bustling inside. "Is everything alright?"

"Yes. I mean, no. While you were gone, Dr. Saunders asked for clemency for Julian. Apparently, the young man was in love with you. He apologized for his actions, stating that his youth and immaturity led him to make such a huge mistake. He didn't want this incident to ruin his life."

"Julian almost killed me," said Beatrice sadly. "I was really lucky. I'm blessed that there's no long-term damage."

"Amen," said the cardinal. "You should know that Dr. Saunders plans to return the document immediately, but he made an intriguing proposal. He's found a way to test the document's veracity. There's no one else that has the technology that could make that happen."

Beatrice thought for a moment, weighing the pros and cons of the proposal.

"He thinks you're right and that you may have substantiated the last thirty years of his work."

"Well, that's good news, I guess. It upsets me that Julian was questioned by the police but they let him go thanks to his father's influence. But even if we press charges, I don't ever want to see Julian again. Is that clear?"

"I understand. Julian is very sorry. He's on a plane to focus on another study in South America. His father swears that he will never bother you again."

"And you believe him?"

"Yes. I have something else to discuss with you. I've taken the liberty of contacting a very prominent government official who is going to let Dr. Saunders run a test on one section of the wall. The professor is a highly respected scientist, so we believe he could handle this most delicate issue."

"What? That's great news!"

"There's a catch," said the cardinal, clearing his throat. "This is all a secret."

"What do you mean?"

"This official, who shall remain nameless, is going to give us access to the Hall of Five Hundred this evening. As a matter of fact, my driver is ready to get us to Florence right now so that we can meet him. In other words, we have access to the Palazzo Vecchio tonight only."

"What?" exclaimed Beatrice. "You mean, sneak into a government building?"

"My dear, we do have permission in a roundabout sort of way."

"How is this going to work?"

"I've discussed this process at length with Dr. Saunders. Basically, he knows a spot where a major crack already exists, so he will direct his efforts on a precise area. He plans to remove a two-by-four-foot section of the wall to look underneath. He has assured me that the crack is going to expand and break apart in time. Anyhow, he has the tools to take it out and put it back."

Beatrice still couldn't believe it. "But he'd be cutting into another Renaissance masterpiece! He would be harming a painting with enormous value." This went against everything she had been trained to do. It was her mission to preserve the past, not to poke holes in it. *I must be crazy to do this!*

"But it will give us a definitive answer," said the cardinal. "After five hundred years, it's time to know the truth. Can you pack a bag and come with me now?"

"Absolutely!" exclaimed Beatrice, pushing aside her misgivings. "What about Rose?"

"I've already spoken to her."

***

The cardinal's driver picked up Rose at her apartment and headed to a discreet location to park. Dr. Saunders was there to meet them with two black bags of equipment. A man wearing a dark surgical mask let them in a side door of the government-owned building. Dr. Saunders handed Rose, the cardinal, and Beatrice small head lanterns so their presence couldn't be detected from outside. He knew exactly where he was going, and they followed. The interior was dark, and Beatrice shivered in her black wool turtleneck.

"Can you believe this?" whispered Rose. "The last time I was here was for a concert. Now I feel like an intrepid explorer."

"I want to know the truth," announced Beatrice. "Either way."

"I believe we were meant to be on this quest," said Rose.

They positioned themselves in the gallery where orange cones and makeshift aluminum gates surrounded the painting. The professor announced, "There is a private company funding some conservation and restoration work on the wall, so our timing is impeccable."

"Hence, the urgency to get this done immediately," added the cardinal. His white collar looked ethereal next to Rose and Beatrice, who were both dressed in jeans and dark sweaters.

With precision born of experience, Dr. Saunders began his work, asking her for assistance with a drill and a few screws to take out the section of the Vasari painting. Beatrice had spent her career putting great works of art back together; it was certainly an anomaly to do the opposite.

Sensing her hesitation, Dr. Saunders said, "The cracks were already here, Beatrice, as part of the aging process. No one will know that we used this enhanced drill to cut through the stone so cleanly." He added, "I developed it myself, and it's state of the art."

Beatrice was impressed and said as much. She watched how he pointed an infrared beam on the section to indicate the precise spots that he had clearly studied ahead of time.

"Art and science," she said aloud as she watched him pick up various pieces of equipment, take a few readings, and continue the painstaking process of drilling a rectangular strip into the wall of Vasari's painting.

Beatrice and Rose stared at each other, realizing the importance of the moment. She watched as the professor carefully pulled a strip from the wall and handed it to the cardinal to lay on a makeshift table. He placed a light on the hole.

He gasped. "It's here! Beatrice, you need to see this!"

Beatrice felt butterflies in her stomach as she walked slowly to view the wall. She took a step up on the ladder and stared into the hole. "Oh my! I see part of a horse's face!" Reaching for her flashlight, she shined it on the three-inch gap. There was indeed another wall behind it. An almost iridescent glow surrounded the face of a soldier engaged in battle. When she illuminated the left side, the ochre and red in the fresco popped in the light. She could make out the soft flowing lines of the clash of horses and soldiers. Beatrice could have stayed in this position forever. This was a conservator's dream—a da Vinci masterpiece hidden behind a wall for the past five hundred years. The mural seemed in very good condition, but the darkness made it hard to come to a complete conclusion.

She turned back to Dr. Saunders. "It's in good condition, too. Rose, you must see this!"

"I never thought I'd see this day!"

The cardinal came over to see inside and gasped. He looked over and offered, "How does it feel to have your hypothesis proven right?"

Dr. Saunders exclaimed, "I feel powerful!"

Beatrice would never forget the look of sheer joy on his face. "We found it!" she cried. "I can't believe it!"

They all cheered.

The victory was bittersweet. No one would ever know.

"We can't tell anyone about this!" exclaimed Dr. Saunders. "We could face serious legal and financial consequences for tampering with a Renaissance masterpiece in a government building. It's a moral victory as they say, and not an actual one."

The secret bonded them in a way that nothing else would again. They all stepped forward to hold hands, acknowledging the weight of their discovery together. Cardinal Baglioni said a prayer of thanks while asking God that the truth only be revealed in His time for good.

Beatrice wished she could take her feelings of elation and wonder and bottle them up forever so that she could always remember the amazing result from mixing science and art history. After helping Dr. Saunders secure the stone back in place, Beatrice turned to him and asked, "What's going to motivate you now?"

"I believe that there are other mysteries out there. Maybe I'll write a novel."

"Are you kidding?" asked Rose.

"Why not? How else am I going to validate the last thirty years?" he shrugged, zipping up his bag. "Let's get out of here," he said abruptly. "I don't want to push my luck any more than I already have."

Beatrice understood his pithy remark. They had unveiled the truth to a centuries-old mystery which was controversial at best, and potentially catastrophic to their professional integrity. Beatrice gulped. She carved a hole in a Vasari masterpiece, which could ruin her career as a conservator. She understood the complexity of this mystery and how art historians might view this new revelation. Plenty of scholars would rejoice, yet there would always be backlash for anyone who tampered with these Vasari masterpieces, considered his best work. Too many warring factions were involved in revealing the truth, not to mention opening the door to criminal behavior in the Palazzo Vecchio. *I prefer to remain anonymous.*

As they headed to Rose's apartment to drop her off, Beatrice exclaimed, "What a night!"

"It was amazing," said Rose. "I still have goosebumps."

"I'm going to approach every conservation project with more confidence in my instincts and incorporate more scientific analysis into my decisions. What do you think, Cardinal?"

"I didn't expect to find anything, so I'm still in a state of shock. I'm not sure the professor did either."

"Does that change anything?"

"No," said the cardinal emphatically. "I think the Leonardo needs to remain behind that wall until someone else can prove its existence. In the meantime, we enjoy our moment of truth."

"What about you, Rose? What's next?"

"We have a wedding date! Believe it or not, we're getting married on Leonardo da Vinci's actual birthday. How ironic is that?"

"Seems absolutely brilliant to me," said Beatrice with a laugh.

The cardinal smiled. "What a perfect way to commemorate this quest."

"Wait a minute," said Rose. "It all started for me with Michelangelo."

"Maybe you can incorporate both masters into the decorations."

"How about a Michelangelo victory cake?" offered Beatrice with a twinkle in her eye.

"That's a great idea!" said Rose as she said her goodbyes.

A victory cake, she thought to herself, *seems very appropriate after this year. Let the wedding preparations begin!*

Epilogue

ROSE HURRIED TO THE CORNER café to grab a cappuccino before she planned to meet Faith for the final fitting of her stunning wedding gown. She noticed that the café wasn't crowded, so she decided to take time to collect her thoughts. It was simply amazing that she had only slightly altered Faith's gown, tailoring the sleeves to add a more modern touch. The silk was timeless and comfortable. They were planning on going over the final details from the flowers to the caterer to the lights in the tent. Surprisingly, everything was beautifully organized thanks to Lyon's parents, who made the planning easy.

As for Doris, she and Eric arrived a few days prior. Doris planned to wear shocking pink to the wedding, and her hair was a newly minted shade of peroxide blond. Rose prayed that she wouldn't make a speech. The thought of Doris reaching for a microphone made her cringe. She shrugged it off, taking another sip of her coffee. Well, after all, nothing was ever perfect.

Zoey had given birth to a beautiful baby boy, which made Rose's heart sing with joy. She and Stan were situated at their hotel room, taking a nap after the long trip to Florence for her wedding. With the big day in sight, Rose smiled and counted her blessings.

She caught a reflection in a shop window and turned around, only to have her jaw drop in surprise. The wall mural was enormous! It was a giant table with a blond woman on top, jumping for joy. Rose cocked her head in wonder. It wasn't her, was it? Rose burst out laughing.

She picked up the phone to call Beatrice. "Hey, you and Mike have got to see this."

"What?"

"There's a rather large mural near my favorite café with a blond-haired woman in the center of a table, waving her arms in joy. Vince has struck again."

"You can't be serious? That's too funny. You must have really inspired him."

"I'm humbled by the likeness, but it still feels strange. What do you think Mike will do when he sees the new mural?"

"He has plans for something bigger and better in New York."

"Does that mean you're moving?"

"Yes, and no. We're still trying to figure out our plans. The cardinal told me I could take a leave of absence after I finish work on the Raphael painting." She added, "Quit worrying about me. Your wedding is finally this weekend. We can't wait!"

Rose hung up, thinking she was going to get married in the nick of time. She looked down, placing her hand gently on her midsection. Faith was going to have her seamstress give her another inch on the waistline; Rose suspected Faith knew her secret, but neither of them uttered a word. Rose wanted to wait until the honeymoon to tell Lyon the news that she was expecting.

Our wedding is truly blessed, Rose thought, as she wiped a tear from her eye. A new chapter was about to begin, and she could hardly wait to start. They planned to settle into her apartment for the coming year, and Rose was sure there would be another house hunt in her future.

Her phone rang. It was Mike.

"You didn't tell me that Vince put a Joker in a green skull cap in the right corner of the mural."

Rose gulped. "I'm sorry, Mike. I'd hoped you wouldn't notice."

"You can't miss it. I'm going to blame the oversight on the wedding."

"Thanks," she replied, wondering if she'd ever get used to his mercurial personality.

"Just wait until you see what I've got planned for New York! Vince is going to regret this insult. Ciao, Rose."

"Ciao." Rose took a deep breath, feeling ever grateful for the gifts of love and laughter.

Acknowledgments

"Spread love everywhere you go. Let no one ever come to you without leaving happier."
Mother Teresa

MY BOOKS ARE A TRUE labor of love. My goal is to tell heartwarming stories that transport readers to beautiful locations like Italy. I'm also an art enthusiast who loves to share this passion with others. I will always choose a positive attitude in life and work.

A huge thank-you to my family and friends for their support and helpful advice along the way. Thank you, Ann Nicholson, for reading my first pages and making very helpful comments about Rome when I couldn't get there! Thank you to Sherrie Guyer for a fantastic edit on my first draft. And cheers to Dr. Heather McGuire, who always provides smart answers to my myriad questions.

It is such a pleasure to work with the team at Koehler Books, who do an excellent job. John, Joe, and Skyler—I appreciate all that you've done to support me and my work. It's a wonderful collaboration.

As always, much love to Bagley, Ellie, and Susanna. I love you to the moon and back.

Secrets in the Palazzo
Book Discussion Guide

1. Would you be willing to trade predictability for adventure and move abroad to Italy like Rose Maning?

2. Who do you think is the better artist: Michelangelo or Leonardo da Vinci? Why?

3. Rose and her mother, 'Doris,' find a certain level of understanding in the book. How well do you think they resolved their differences?

4. Street artist Mike did a mural of the mythological figure Lady Justice. He wanted to create a dialogue about equality in our society. Why do you think this could be a successful approach to generate important conversations? Why not?

5. Street artist Vince took a nod from Leonardo da Vinci's Last Supper to create murals that ask the question—'Who sits at the table and why?' Who would you like to sit at the table?

6. Can Rose really trust Lyon again? Was there a better way to handle their conflict?

7. Were Rose's expectations realistic or naïve?

8. Mike is a temperamental artist prone to angry outbursts. Do you think he and Beatrice will last?

9. Would you make the discovery public? Why or why not?

10. Could Leonardo's *Battle of Anghiari* have inspired a future generation of artists? Why is Leonardo da Vinci considered one of the greatest artists of all time? What do you think?

11. Compare Michelangelo's *David* with Leonardo da Vinci's *The Last Supper*. Do you believe that a painting or sculpture has the power to inspire you?

12. Can you think of a work of art that changed your perspective?